THE **MYSTERY**
OF THE
PORTUGUESE
HEARTS

THE **MYSTERY** OF THE **PORTUGUESE HEARTS**

MANJIRI PRABHU

JAICO PUBLISHING HOUSE

Ahmedabad Bangalore Chennai
Delhi Hyderabad Kolkata Mumbai

DISCLAIMER

This is a work of fiction. Names, characters, and incidents are either the product of the author's imagination or are used fictitiously. Any resemblance to actual persons, living or dead, or events, is entirely coincidental.

Published by Jaico Publishing House
A-2 Jash Chambers, 7-A Sir Phirozshah Mehta Road
Fort, Mumbai - 400 001
jaicopub@jaicobooks.com
www.jaicobooks.com

THE MYSTERY OF THE PORTUGUESE HEARTS
ISBN 978-81-19792-72-6

First Jaico Impression: 2024

Page design and layout by
Special Effects Graphics Design Company, Mumbai

Printed by
Trinity Academy For Corporate Training Limited, Mumbai

To my sisters Leena, Purnima, and Sonia, for their compassion, love, dynamism, and strength.

Prologue

Penafiel, Portugal, 1970

The atmosphere was charged with a primitive and fervent energy, and yet it throbbed with the promise of an exciting future.

"We can't let this happen!" the girl in the blue jeans whispered in a fierce tone, her eyes drilling into Ana's. She thrust a pamphlet in Ana's hand and muttered under her breath again, "We can't let this happen! Sofia will tell us why."

Ana followed the girl's progression through the crowd of women. She carried a heap of leaflets and moved from person to person, a determined expression on her face, repeating 'we can't let this happen'. It was like a mantra being bored into their brains.

Ana Ribeiro clutched the pamphlet and threw it a cursory glance. The illustrations and a book cover along with a list of civil rights printed on the cheap, wafer-thin sheet were alluring. She was tempted to quickly study the leaflet, but was conscious of her limited time.

It was a cold winter evening and the January sun was mellow through the trees in the Square. The wind played truant with the scarves and mufflers of the gathered women, of all age groups. Ana stood on the fringe of the group of protestors who were all warmly attired, wrapped in monotone sober jackets, as if unwilling to attract more attention than necessary. It spelled the tone of the protest.

Tall and athletic, with shoulder-length unruly curled hair overshadowing an intelligent forehead and intense brown eyes, Ana stood out in a mass of people. Something about her made people pause and take notice. Perhaps it was the lopsided head tilt when she listened, or her unflinching deep gaze which seemed to glean your innermost secrets in one swoop. Whatever it was, her presence *spoke* to people. She arrested their attention and their curiosity was piqued, but Ana was oblivious to it all. Her mind was focused on the task at hand, although momentarily distracted by the gathering of women.

Now, as Ana watched the scene before her, the buzz of impatience and frustration reached out to her. She experienced a strange thrill as another woman rose and climbed onto a wooden bench. The woman clapped her hands to get their attention. Instantly the murmurs turned into whispers and the crowd fell silent, as all ears strained to listen to the tall woman on the bench.

"I am Sofia and we are here today to peacefully protest against the wrongs meted out to us women. We are here because we have suffered enough. While the world has progressed, we have been forced to turn ourselves to stone— no free speech, no expressing our thoughts through the arts, no unions… and now when someone—one of us—has actually shown some self-respect and done us proud, what has happened? She has been prosecuted! That is why we women have to come together and show her our solidarity. Today she has been targeted because she voiced her thoughts through a book, tomorrow it could be one of us. If we don't stick together and voice our displeasure, we will be doomed. Do you agree with me?" Sofia asked, her voice forceful and loud.

A cheer of affirmation rang through the fifty-odd women and goose bumps rose on Ana's arms. Passersby shot them frowns and apprehensive glances, some barely disguising their scorn, while others displayed open concern. *Rightfully so*, Ana thought. She knew that it was dangerous to be a part of the protestors, out here in the open Square. *Estado Novo* was everywhere—in casual clothes, peeping from behind closed doors, in the balconies, in shops and saloons… they observed, they spied and they reported. They didn't like to be disobeyed. And if caught, they were merciless.

"'Men in the square and women at home', I am tired of this expression. How many of you agree with me?" the woman continued.

Hands went up instantly in a show of solidarity.

Ana was fascinated. This was what she believed in. It could be her up there, leading an uprising, voicing the innermost thoughts of women, encouraging them to stand up for their rights, *being* their voice… this was what she was meant to do… with fearless determination in her heart… She felt an instant connection with Sofia and her anger, with *all* the women suffering under the regime of the *Estado Novo*. Sisterhood for change… It was time to express their thoughts, especially now when censure was prompt and the consequences were dark and dangerous.

Ana longed to stay and listen to every inspiring word. But she was here for another reason. She touched the pocket of her jacket and felt the bottle of honey. She had a job to do. A seemingly harmless job. All she had to do was hand over the bottle to a man in a blue shirt with a cap. The April Captain. That's what they were called. The hidden voices of rebellion. The faces behind the curtain. The promise of the future… She didn't need to know more. All she was commanded to do was to deliver the bottle of honey and to vanish from the scene. And the April Captain was supposed to be here at sharp 5:00 PM. She glanced at her wrist watch. It was 4:55 PM.

Ana made her way unhurriedly through the crowd, keeping a sharp lookout even as Sofia continued her rousing speech, and the women listened to her with rapt attention.

"We aren't allowed to vote. We need equal wages; we need the right to create, write and publish books. If we don't voice our concern and protest now, we will be forever condemned!"

The crowd clapped in agreement and cheered. Ana spotted him then. At the far end of the mob. A tall figure, in casual blue shirt and black trousers, leaning against a street lamp, listening with keen attention. A cap was pulled low over his head, but the expression on his face revealed that he agreed with what Sofia was saying. Ana threaded her way through the crowd and approached him. She was barely a few steps away from him, when at that very moment, a siren wailed; two cars speeded straight towards the crowd and screeched to a halt. At least a dozen policemen emerged with sticks and angry expressions, shouting loud instructions. The peaceful demonstration instantly turned into a chaotic and frightened mob as the police began thrashing the women, cursing expressively. Panic drove the women helter-skelter, as they ran to protect themselves. Sofia continued to shout slogans at the top of her voice, encouraging the crowd not to disperse. Two of the policemen rushed towards her, their sticks raised in fury, and she jumped down agilely from the bench to face them without fear.

Ana barely had a chance to witness her valour. She hastened to the April Captain and thrust the bottle in his hand. Without awaiting a response, she whipped around and rapidly increased the distance between them, slipping into an alley.

"Hey you!" someone shouted behind her.

Ana didn't pause to consider who it was. Instead she broke into a sprint, heading deep into the alley, even as she heard footsteps and the sound of running behind her. Her breath came out in sharp gasps and she slipped into a side alley, ducking behind a pile of trash cans. Her heart was pounding as she saw women racing past, fear writ large on their faces. Two policemen chased them relentlessly, issuing ominous warnings in Portuguese. Ana shut her eyes. Screams ripped the air and she knew instinctively that the women were caught. God alone knew what their fate would now be...

She snuck back into her corner, afraid to breathe, sweat trickling down her forehead. The sound of sticks and shouts and screams seemed to be all around her, and she closed her eyes momentarily. Suddenly, she sensed a movement. A hand fluttered lightly over her shoulder and she almost screamed, but another hand clamped over her mouth.

"Shh…" it was a male voice.

Ana struggled to glance up and he immediately released the pressure of his hand on her mouth.

"You!" Her eyes widened in shock as the April Captain's face hovered next to hers.

"Shh… quiet."

He caught her by the arm, drew her through an open door and shut it softly behind him. Light streamed in through the glass windows at the end of a corridor, and Ana fleetingly wondered where they were.

"We shall be safe here," he whispered, his voice echoing slightly in the corridor.

"But… you aren't supposed to follow me. You are the April Captain. My job was to just give you the bottle and never to see you again," she hissed.

"I saw you being chased. It was my duty to ensure that you were safe," he responded.

"Thank you. But I managed."

"Of course, you did… I just pulled you to safety," he remarked.

He removed his blue cap to reveal a thick bush of straight hair, the tops standing out like a brush. He smiled at her. A beautiful smile that seemed to shine straight from his hazel eyes. They stared at each other, as seconds stretched into minutes. Something shifted in Ana's world, as if someone had jolted her awake… like someone had switched on a light so bright, that it blinded her…

"I am Ricardo and I'm just helping the April Captains to organize meetings, although there is so much more I want to do—what with the unrest. This regime is stifling and I want to do my bit."

Ana nodded, moving her gaze away from his.

"Me too… and I am Ana."

"That is why you were at the protest."

"Yes."

"Ana, I love your spirit but today you had a narrow escape. Anything could have happened; you do know that?"

"I am aware, but I can't sit back and see my friends and other women suffer. We need to take action, protest, show our indignation, hope for a change," Ana remarked, incensed.

"Change is coming, sooner than you think. It is in the air, there's talk of a rebellion. "

Ana's eyes widened in surprise.

"But keep this between us," Ricardo added hastily.

"My lips are sealed!" she promised, but excitement shone in her deep brown eyes.

"Democracy is our dream. The armed forces are restless with the regimental civic control and the oppression, the censorship of newspapers, books, the arts. And the secret police, who turn up on the sly—you witnessed what happened just now, at a peaceful gathering of people protesting, voicing their dissent… Not to mention the colonial war raging for years and the nationalist movements rebelling in African territories against Portuguese rule. It is time for things to change and they will… soon. The Armed Forces Movement is a reality."

Ana nodded. "I heard. What I am doing is nothing compared to what the others are doing. I want to do more, I just don't know how."

"You know what, would you like to attend one of the meetings of the April Captains? It is all very confidential, of course, but you are one of us, so that's fine. The meeting is this Saturday at the estate."

"Of course, I would!" Excitement radiated through her whole body. "Which estate?"

"Quinta de Monteiro."

"What? You are—" Ana almost stepped back.

"Ricardo Monteiro," he nodded. "But that doesn't mean anything. I have yet to prove that I am worthy of my father's estate."

"Oh, that sounds suspiciously modest." She smiled.

"No, I mean it. It's one thing to inherit a legacy, but quite another to *honour* that legacy. Luck can bring you the legacy, but it is hard work that will help you elevate it to new heights. I have yet to go down that path."

"Now, *that* sounds suspiciously mature."

Ricardo nodded. "I know. So, will you come this Saturday?"

"On one condition. You have to offer me a glass of your famous Vinho Verde."

"Ah… Our green wine is the best. So, you understand wine."

"Trying to. My dream is to have my own vineyards one day, with my very own special wine recipe. I already know what I plan to call it."

"Intriguing. Then you must taste ours. This Saturday then, nine o' clock in the evening."

"Deal."

Their eyes locked for long seconds and in that moment, Ana knew that her life had changed forever.

Penafiel, 25th April 1974

Ana Ribeiro paused at the crossroads to catch her breath and rest her aching legs. The physical pain was nothing compared to the deep ache of loss inside her. She had walked for miles, her only thought being to increase her distance from him. Almost as if distance could dilute the intensity of her loss— but was that even possible? Could anything ever weaken the incalculable degree of her bereavement? No, she knew that the anguish was a permanent entity inside her now.

Twilight had fallen quietly on the world but there was no silence in the air. Jubilations and celebrations resounded all over Portugal. The successful military coup in Lisbon had triggered the whole country into a triumphant frenzy. The autocracy was turned over. Democracy would be the new rule now. A new kind of history had been created. A new kind of coup and rebellion. It had been a peaceful revolution—no bloodshed, no gun shots. Soldiers everywhere were carrying carnations in their guns.

She heard the approach of a car—it was an open truck filled with people on their way to Lisbon. They waved and cheered even as they sang 'Grândola, Vila Morena', the song which had been banned all these years.

"Happy Freedom Day!" they shouted and showered carnations on her.

Ana couldn't help responding to the enthusiasm with a wide smile and a wave. She was a bag of mixed emotions at the moment. Her heart sang for Portugal, her beloved country. She had done her bit, taken part in the struggle for a better life, for equal rights, and helped the Armed Forces Movement as much as she dared. She had courted danger over the last four years and had barely escaped on multiple occasions, but her spirit had not been throttled. Instead, it had been ignited. And today she could enjoy the thought of freedom. The days of censorship were over. It was now time to celebrate freedom, love, family and equal opportunity. *Except that she couldn't!* Her heart felt as if it had been ripped from her forever.

She glanced back at the road she had travelled. It symbolised everything that she had to now leave behind. Ricardo, their life together, her family, her love—everything that she had wilfully manifested and encouraged despite the ring of uncertainty and instinctive censure. They had been the best four years of her life... and now that memory would have to last her for the rest of her life. She wasn't going to crumble or cry for what she had lost. Instead she was going to begin a new life with the rest of Portugal. A life of freedom, of possibilities, of love... yes, love too, because one day

Ricardo would realize that he could not live without her. Her absence would open his eyes to this ultimate truth. They had borne too much together. They were soulmates, meant to be together and nothing could keep them apart. Not people, not class, status, and certainly not distance… She would lead him to her, any which way she could… One day they would celebrate the joy of Carnation Day together… One day…

Chapter

1

Quinta de Monteiro, Penafiel, 2019 (45 years later)

Regret was the least of his emotions—the time for it had passed. He had had ample leisure over the years to think, act and regret. Anger was more the emotion he felt. Anger directed at how life had given him everything but had withheld his soul. Yet when he thought back, he didn't know what he could have done differently. But even as the familiar denial set in, Ricardo knew the answer. *He could have followed the path of love…*

Ricardo heaved a big sigh and leaned against his cushioned seat. A tall figure with his hair still surprisingly thick and shimmering silver, he looked the epitome of good health. Only he sensed a strange kind of hollowness in his chest. Like a deep well waiting to be filled, but which he knew was too dry now, no matter how much moisture was added. At eighty years, he wasn't at all surprised.

Ricardo stared out the box window at the stretches of vineyard, dappled in the pale rosy shades of the garden light. The scene never failed to fill him with pride. Quinta de Monteiro, their family estate and one of the oldest in Portugal, was not just a legacy—it was an heirloom. The land of his ancestors, the foundation of all their sacrifices, the springboard for all their ambitions and the foremost love of his family. And the special superior quality Vinho Verde—green wine made from the choicest grapes… He hoped that Filipa would carry the legacy forward with the same energy and dedication that he had. But then there was no doubt about that. Ricardo was proud of his granddaughter. She was bestowed with the essence of the Monteiro spirit. He and Juliet had raised her right. And she had no clue, but right now, she was on the cusp of setting the crown straight—at least marginally, and mostly for him.

He moved away from the window and headed to his writing desk. On an impulse, he sat down and extracted the letterhead with the embossed Monteiro logo. For ten minutes, he scribbled with the calm of a seasoned confessor. Finally, he sat back against his carved wooden chair, with the trademark Monteiro green and purple cushion. He delved into his coat pocket and took out a large iron key. For a few moments, he turned the key over in his palm, a little absently, then placed it in an envelope and carefully wrote the name 'Filipa' on it. He glanced at the letter again and reread it; then on a sudden impulse he tore it up into pieces and hastily dropped them in the dustbin. He would write a better note some other day with the right words and the right explanations, he told himself. She was the light of his life, and he couldn't risk alienating her with misunderstandings that arose out of awkwardly written hasty confessions—the way it had transpired with his daughter.

He opened the drawer and placed the envelope inside, locked it and slipped the drawer key into the pocket of his coat. Feeling a confused sense of accomplishment, he was uncertain why he felt the need to do this now. No conclusive answer popped into his head. Sometimes the heart instinctively knew things better than the head, and reason and logic played no role in it. He just knew that it was time to share his deepest secrets with Filipa and pray that she would understand why he'd acted as he had. If she didn't, it would break his heart all over again… and he wasn't sure he had the strength or the energy to face another loss. He glanced at the grandfather clock standing against the stone wall. It was time for his ritual morning walk across the estate.

The door opened and a girl in her late twenties walked in.

"Good morning, Grandpa. You are late for your walk," Filipa announced, planting a swift kiss on the old man's soft cheek.

"On my way. You are up bright and early." He glanced at her formal blue jacket and matching skirt.

Filipa was a beautiful curly-haired brunette, with distinct sharp features which sometimes turned soft. But most times, she was a composed, determined VP of Quinta de Monteiro and Penafiel county, with a no-nonsense attitude—someone who always knew her mind. He was proud that she was an elected mayor of the district.

"The big event is tomorrow and we still have tons to do. The gold symbol is arriving today and the committee would be meeting in the early afternoon to finalize details. It is going to be such a wonderfully special ceremony, Avô, and I am so excited. Joana's dream and brilliant idea will finally be realized tomorrow evening, on Carnation Revolution Day."

For a few seconds, Filipa's mind travelled to her days of mentoring with the passionate workaholic Joana de Cruz, ex-mayor, under whom she had trained. Those were days of intense but joyful learning, and she would never forget them. She experienced a momentary sadness… Joana was no more, but her dream of a unified world symbol of love would live on.

Ricardo placed a gentle hand on her arm. "You have staunchly supported her endeavours and principles. And although I never met her, I know that Joana would have been very grateful to you for realizing her dream."

Filipa smiled, her brown eyes moistening suddenly. "Thank you Avô, you have always appreciated everything I do… you are partial to me! But yes, Joana would have been delighted, because Basílica Santa Luzia will be shining tomorrow, like it never has before. We have received hundreds of emails of confirmation; all the five mayors are arriving this evening, and everything is set."

"Filipa, there's something I want to talk to you about," Ricardo cut in, gravely.

She instantly noticed the change in his tone. "What is it, Avô?"

Ricardo was staring at the garden light filtering through the window, forming a latticed shadow on the carpeted floor.

"Just a few words of wisdom, *caríssima*... Something I have always wanted to say to you but have been afraid you'd think I've become soft with age!" He laughed, awkwardly. "I am proud of what you have achieved—you are a true-blue heir of Quinta de Monteiro. It is good to be ambitious and it is great to do your duty, especially to the estate. But remember one thing my dear... never compromise on love. Follow your heart always, *caríssima*... in the end nothing else matters."

She glanced at him in surprise. "You've never said anything like this to me before. What's up, Avô? Should I be concerned?"

She expected him to laugh at her comment and crack a joke, but he pursed his lips and avoided eye contact.

The connecting door to the dining room opened just then, and a maid in a starched white uniform stepped in. "*Bom dia*, tea is served in the dining room."

Filipa nodded. "*Obrigada*."

"I have to go for my walk now. But we haven't finished talking... in fact there is lots I want to say to you... So please, meet me at the wedding lawn in half an hour." Ricardo rose hastily and gripped his walking stick.

Before Filipa could comment, he exited the room.

With quick strides, he stepped out of the front door and headed towards the garden. It was still quite dark, and the lights from the lampposts trellised the garden in geometric patches. But even without the illumination, Ricardo knew his way. He took the path into the dense garden with the towering trees huddling overhead, blocking the light. He trudged past the 200 year old Japanese cedar, the hundreds of varieties of camellias—his favourite flower—and the hydrangea bushes. The gardens and park were his pride. He had personally planted some of the varieties of camellias and delighted in their growth.

As he walked past the ancient Porter's House, fancy and funny with its conical thatched roof, he approached the goat tower and involuntarily his steps faltered. He had strolled down this route every morning, for more than half his life. And yet today felt different. Like he was seeing it all for the first time. The way the goats scurried to meet him and strained against the wired fence so that he could touch their fur, and then scampered up the little path to the tower. Even the lake, which glistened a dull green, had borrowed a strange hue.

The Ladies' Tea House on the edge of the man-made lake, where he and Juliet had often met to discuss and argue the future of the estate, had to be refurbished. He made a mental note about it even as he experienced an immense wave of gratitude to have been born in the Monteiro family—he was so proud of his legacy. He had done his best to keep the Monteiro flag flying. He had committed mistakes, of course, but nothing that couldn't be repaired. Except that one incident—the biggest mistake of his life... he sighed, regret and anger filling his heart again like a physical pain. For a few seconds, he clutched his chest, as uncharacteristic tears rose in his eyes. Wasted chances, wasted bonds... he brushed the drops away roughly. *Too late, too late...* he thought... *and yet...*

His feet crunched on the gravel as he finally halted at the rectangular lawn. The family wedding meadow—Ricardo's favourite spot on the estate. It was a large stretch of green land at the head of the fields, enclosed within dense tall trees. On one end, seven long moss-bordered steps led up to a tall carved wall with two pillars. Ricardo mounted the steps and stared at the high wall—a mossy concave stone cocooned a blue statue of Senhora Mary with baby Jesus in her arms. In the soft light of dawn, she looked peaceful and calm. Below the statue, in the centre of the wall, was a waterspout that emerged out of the carved face of a demon, the water flowing into a stone basin on the ground. As a child, Ricardo had always found that fascinating... the co-existence of the holy and the profane on the same wall.

He heaved another deep sigh and leaned on his stick, wondering how much longer Filipa would be. He couldn't wait to have a tête-à-tête with his granddaughter and finally reveal his heart to her—speak of everything in his life that was sacrosanct and especially that which he had carefully evaded mentioning, all these years. He wanted to describe the depths of agony that had engulfed him, and the journey out of it... he suddenly wanted to share every little detail of his life with his beloved Filipa... every single emotion, desire and the guilt that was weighing him down. With one sole yearning... he sought freedom, in the true sense of the word... to be free of a burden he had carried far too long, alone and in doomed isolation. He longed to end his lonely, crusty journey, to finally find closure... But would she understand? He didn't dare contemplate that question.

She had to understand! He prayed that she would… she was his last hope… to heal, to mend and to resurrect.

His shoulders drooped with an uncharacteristic fatigue, born more out of an anticipated moment of letting go. He was deep in thought when instinctively he sensed a shadow and a bodily presence right behind him.

"Filipa?"

He turned, but a second too late. Something hard struck him on the back of his head, and he lost his balance. Blinding pain seared through him as he collapsed, his frail body tumbling down the seven steps.

At the back of his mind he fought to stay conscious, even as blood trickled through his collar and seeped into his shirt. He heard shouts from afar and hasty footsteps approaching him. *Hurry…* he felt like shouting, but no words came up.

"Help… Someone help!" That was Filipa.

He raised a weak hand. "Filipa—" he croaked.

She caught his hand. "I am right here, Avô, don't worry, you are going to be fine." She gently caressed his head, tears flowing down her cheeks.

"Filipa—" His voice was hoarse.

"It's going to be ok. An ambulance will be here in a minute, hang in there, Avô. Who did this to you?" she asked, urgently.

"My pocket—" Ricardo's voice was hoarse.

"What?" she was confused.

"P…o…cket." His speech was slurred.

Understanding dawned. She leaned forward and fumbled though his coat pocket. Her fingers touched cold metal. A key. Surprised, she took it out.

"I found the key, Avô."

He seemed to rouse himself with all the strength left in his broken body.

"Promise me you will follow the trail of the *lenços*—" he whispered, his hand clutching hers in a sudden grip.

"I will, Avô," Filipa's voice choked.

"Good girl." His grip relaxed. "Ana… I loved Ana."

His whisper tapered and his sigh was long and shuddering as he slumped into the ground. Filipa stared at the still and lifeless body of her grandfather, a cold deathly hand squeezing her heart.

Freixo de Espada à Cinta (on the border of Portugal and Spain)

The truth was that he was hiding from the world. Love, such a simple word, but such a complex emotion. And above all, such vibrant, unbridled energy. Re had always known this, of course, but had fully experienced it for the first time, recently. No, falling in love was not a simple involuntary act. It was a journey into the abyss, and sometimes, just sometimes, you could return. Or not.

He stared way down at the Douro river as it wound between the range of emerald hills of two countries. The pink and saffron stains of the rising sun reflected on the undulating terraced vineyard landscape of the Penedo Durão, one of the major viewpoints of the Douro valley. The glittering olive-green water between the gentle hills of Spain and Portugal was calm on the eyes and soothing to the soul. The birds were tweeting from the pine branches. And yet Re sensed a now-familiar yearning resurface with renewed force.

He had cooped himself in this remote village with the orange roofs, and made himself invisible to the world, nursing his raw broken heart. He had endured long solitary walks through the countryside, vineyards and olive tree fields, grateful for the solitude, trying to come to terms with his situation. Under the shade of the almond tree, with the elegant white and red blossoms, the tight band around his chest loosened and allowed him to breathe. For a few precious minutes. When he strolled along the stretch of the beautiful Congida Beach and stared at the drooping willow trees which bordered its banks, he felt that the river and the trees were communicating with him. Everything he did and heard—the chattering of the birds, the booming sound of the gales through the trees and hills, following the ripples of the river for long hours with the rain falling silently around him—made him realize how lucky he was to have found this beautiful village. Where he could let his heart weep and hope to heal, in tandem… He even took a ferry down the river from Congida Beach and allowed the blend of emerald landscapes and glittering water to fill him with therapeutic energy. He had worn himself out in the hope that his tired body would offer him some respite and a good night's sleep. But to no avail. The terrible pain of memory wouldn't ease.

His mom had phoned him several times in real concern and had even offered to fly out to him, to be with him. But he had firmly refused her company. He knew he wanted to be alone, for a while at least. He had completed some work in Porto, then on an impulse had hired a car and driven all the way to Freixo de Espada à Cinta. The moment he drove into the Manueline village, with its coloured windows and doors, he knew he had arrived at the perfect spot. Tucked away in a corner of North Portugal with breathtaking vistas, Re had walked the little village, exploring narrow isolated winding lanes in peace. He had visited the cathedral and settled there for hours, studying the gilded altar with the eye of an impassioned researcher, then strolled to the cemetery beyond, paying his respects to strangers in beautiful graves. The cemetery overlooked another spectacular country view.

He had climbed up to the tower and even sat praying at the ash tree with its attached sword. Something about the tree had given him a semblance of peace. He didn't know what it was, but seeing the big sword strapped to the ash tree had invoked a sense of momentary harmony. A couple of elderly people had tried to speak to him in Portuguese, but Re couldn't follow what they were saying... although he could sense the kind concern behind their words. He had clicked hundreds of pictures and shot videos, spent hours doing nothing but sit on rocks and meditate with the landscapes. If this didn't heal him, nothing would.

Tomorrow, he planned to walk up the winding road to a small chapel of Senhora Ernos, the patron saint of Freixo. The kind waitress at his hotel had looked him squarely in the eye and stated that he simply had to take Senhora Ernos' blessings. It was as if she could instinctively gauge his inner turmoil. And he had agreed. It was going to be his last day in the village, anyway. He had no choice but to emerge into the real world soon.

With a deep sigh, he turned away from the steep drop and climbed back to the paved landing with the tall pine trees and wooden picnic tables. In a corner of the cliff, Senhora Douro's white statue stood overlooking the wide and deep valley, as if guarding it with her powers. The rays of dawn skimmed over the smooth marble, adding a brush of papaya orange and a glimpse of reality to the folds of her garment and her serene face. Re paused, staring up at the beautiful figure, as she cradled a small child in her arms.

It was in that moment that it happened. A sudden trembling broke all over his body—strong frissons of unease. Re closed his eyes, aware of what was happening and yet unable to control it. The images were strong and powerfully realistic. *The hazy form of a tall monument... rising spires of a cathedral... and sea waves swelling high. Re was walking up a steep path... he could sense the cold biting him and the waves licking his face and suddenly a tightening of the chest, as if someone had gripped him. Then, out of nowhere, a thick dark swirl of smoke blocking his way. He couldn't see the path and he desperately waved away the smoke, but it kept piling higher and higher and thicker and thicker. Finally, Re walked straight into the black wall of smoke, even as it coiled around him, suffocating him.*

With a start, Re's eyes flashed open, his body still quivering. Senhora Douro gazed down at him, her face smooth porcelain, but a hint of warmth in her expression. Inhaling deeply, Re turned around, his heart beating quickly. It was a vision... *his vision.* But it confused him. Where was this place? Why was it calling him? What did the smoke mean, why had it choked him? One thing was certain. He would have to return to the hotel and immediately pack his bags. His self-isolation was over.

He had just entered his hotel room, when his cell phone rang. It was his mother.

"Re, I need your help." His mother's tone was grave.

"What is it, *Maman*?"

"My friend's daughter needs you. It is very urgent. Can you go to Penafiel?"

Minutes later, his WhatsApp pinged. His mother had sent him the pin to the Quinta de Monteiro Estate.

Chapter
2

The air of sombre grief was palpable as Re spotted pockets of people murmuring in low voices, in different parts of the garden. From the little his mother could brief him, Re had grasped the enormity and gravity of the situation. Ricardo Monteiro was an active, pleasant and influential personality, not only in Penafiel, but also in the entire country. Then who could have killed this prominent, almost eighty year old man, on his home turf, with the least regard for getting caught?

He paused for a moment outside the ivy-covered ancient mansion with green shutters on its windows, fleetingly admiring the tenacious spirit of the old stone. Standing tall for more than 200 years, it must have witnessed a whole range of events through history into the present. Re felt an instant affinity with the house which boasted an intricate gothic fountain right at the front entrance.

He walked in through the grand wooden door into a large hall with a high ceiling and multiple boxed windows. Again, more people shuffling around, discussing, wondering how to fit into this atmosphere of grief. Relatives? Employees of the vineyard? His eyes cruised across the long hall with its oversized comfortable red sofas, and wall-to-wall thick cream carpet. His gaze flicked over the uniformed staff, serving water and tea to the guests. Re couldn't spot Filipa Monteiro anywhere. He had tried reaching her earlier on his two hour trip from Freixo de Espada à Cinta to Penafiel. But she hadn't responded.

A middle-aged man in a suit moved towards him with purposeful strides, but with a polite smile on his face.

"Excuse me, are you from the press?" he asked, his accent thick.

It was his well-trimmed beard that Re noticed at once. Must be a task to maintain it, he thought idly, as he habitually took in the man's expensive suit, his thin lips, and direct grey eyes behind black-rimmed spectacles.

"No, not actively so. I am here for Senhorita Filipa Monteiro."

The man's gaze narrowed. "Madam isn't here right now."

"Oh, I guess I will have to wait for her then."

"I am afraid that wouldn't be advisable. As you probably know, something really tragic has happened in the family just a short while ago. By the way, I am her secretary, Tiago. All her appointments have been cancelled. In fact, I don't recall seeing yours in the book. What was your name again?" Tiago enquired as he extracted a leather pocket book and flipped through the pages.

Something flew out of it and Re picked it up. It was a picture of a young kid, standing between an older couple and holding their hands.

"Thank you," he remarked with a half-smile, as he tucked the photo back into the diary. "What was your name again?"

"Re Parkar, and yes, I am aware of the tragedy. That is precisely the reason for my presence—I was asked to get immediately in touch with Senhorita Filipa by Senhora Monteiro. Could you please send the *senhorita* a message saying I am here?"

"Oh, I see," Tiago closed his pocket book. "I am afraid no one knows where Senhorita Filipa is. She has been untraceable for the last hour and a half."

"I see… and her cell phone—?"

"Has been switched off. She has an important event tomorrow evening, but as of now, all meetings and engagements stand postponed until we have clear instructions from madam. You saw the crowd outside, with cameras and tripods? That's the press waiting for a statement from her. She is, after all, the rightful and only heir to the Monteiro Estate. She would have to make a statement eventually, which is what we are all expecting too, but for now, she is probably and understandably in shock. Till she returns, I am afraid, no one would be allowed to stay here."

Re nodded, sensing the dismissal. He strode out of the hall, into the yard, noticing the group of reporters awaiting Filipa. He tried Filipa's number again, but a recorded voice in Portuguese announced her unavailability.

Re moved towards the shops, wondering what to do next. He could stroll through the exquisite gardens and while away his time until she returned. Or he could just sit and watch the peacocks strutting around as if they owned the place. He chose the latter option, settling on a bench under a camellia shrub, observing the restless energy around him.

Quinta de Monteiro grew one of the world's most famous wines, and he knew that their green wine was his mother's favourite. She had sometimes spoken about her friend from Portugal, but Re could never have imagined that something this tragic would bring him to the estate. It was sad, to say the least, and it disturbed him. A good healthy man, whose acts of philanthropy were famous on the internet—why would anyone want to murder him? It was true that money and success always came at the cost of friendship, and there was a likelihood that Ricardo had his fair share of enemies. But did someone really hate him enough to kill him?

Re leaned against the wooden bench and casually took in the scene. Everyone seemed to be on pause, as if waiting for something more to happen—the press, the staff, the guests and even the peacocks stood still, listening to something humming in the breeze. Some uniformed policemen were in deep conversation on one side of the garden. Re longed to know more details, but knew better than to chat with the Portuguese police. Where *was* Filipa?

"Mr. Re Parkar," a low voice interrupted his thoughts.

Re turned to face a man sporting a blazer with an embroidered Monteiro emblem. His hair was sparse and receding, and the candid lines on his face revealed his age to be in the late sixties, perhaps even pushing seventy. The expression on his face was neutral, but his eyes appeared kind.

"Yes?"

"I am Mr. Monteiro's butler, Pedro. Would you please follow me?" he whispered.

Re nodded and fell in step with him as the butler quickly led the investigator down a shady path, tunnelling through thick foliage of trees and bushes. At the end of the path Pedro turned towards a building and opened a huge wooden door. The smell of wine and beer spilled in the open air. It was a cellar!

Pedro turned to the investigator and indicated the door. "Please step in."

Re followed his instructions and walked into the dark interior. The door was quickly shut behind him. Instantly, the low murmur of a Gregorian chant filled his ears, as he surveyed the neat rows of barrels in the soothing dim orange light of the overhanging bulbs.

"Re Parkar?" a soft voice from behind almost startled him.

He swivelled to face a pleasant-looking elegant and well-styled woman in her mid-twenties; there was a mass of cascading highlighted sun-bleached curls which settled around her head like a halo. She was attired in a formal skirt and coat.

"I am sorry for the drama. But I can't go out there," she apologized, her accent thick, part defiantly as she brushed the hair off her face.

"Filipa?" the detective confirmed.

"That's right. Re, thank you for being here. I can't tell you how grateful I am. My mother is in an ashram in India somewhere and unreachable, and I couldn't trust a single person here. Maria, your mother, was the only one I could think of."

"I am glad I could be here," Re replied. "I am deeply sorry for your loss, Filipa." He noticed the vulnerability behind the mask of intelligence. A visual of wind chimes, tinkling in the air, rose in his mind. Wind chimes… suited her perfectly.

"Thank you, but seriously, I never thought in my wildest dreams that I would witness such a day… Avô dying in my arms—something I wouldn't wish on my biggest enemy!"

She paused, struggling to control her emotions, and the silence was occupied with the soothing echoes of the Gregorian chants. She sniffed and touched a handkerchief to her eyes.

"I am sorry—I feel like someone has buried me under a pile of rubble, and I can't breathe."

"I understand."

"I am angry and grieving at the same time. My grandfather—Avô—was my world. He spoke to me at dawn today and told me to follow my heart… I was so surprised. Practical and dynamic Avô being so sentimental… Now suddenly, he is gone, leaving me adrift in a world which right now makes no sense."

This was the first time he had met Filipa, but Re couldn't deny the instant comfort level. As if he understood her innermost anguish in this very moment. The shock, her pain and her immense loss—he could feel it all.

"This is the only place no one will come looking for me. I am hiding out here till I find my bearings, and get my thoughts in order. Tiago is too demanding, and the staff is looking to me to take the reins. Reins! Of an empire Grandpa built almost single-handedly over the last sixty years! Honouring the legacy left to him by his forefathers… And here I am… confused, paranoid, a coward in a state of shock trying to fathom what the heck happened today!"

Filipa perched on a barrel, holding a hand to her forehead. The continuous chanting in the dimly orange-lit cellar added a trace of contradictory surreal calm to the whole episode.

"What *did* happen—you think you can share some details?" Re asked, quietly.

Filipa nodded and took a deep breath. "I have a big event coming up tomorrow evening and it was to be a very busy day today. So, I rose early—I am so glad I did—because I caught Avô in his office just before he went for his ritual morning walk. He has always been an early riser, and I don't remember a day he missed his walk. However, he wanted to share something with me today. I sensed a restlessness in him, and he said an odd thing to me—he said, 'Follow your heart'. At the time, I was surprised, but I didn't think it very odd until what happened later. He asked me to meet him in half an hour at the wedding lawn—which is a family tradition lawn, we have all the Monteiro functions there, in front of the statue of Senhora Mary. Strange because that was the exact spot he was assaulted. As decided, I was almost at the lawn half an hour later, when I heard a loud dull noise, and Grandpa shouting in agony. I rushed through the trees to the spot, and there I found him, at the foot of the steps, semiconscious."

"And you didn't see the attacker?"

"Unfortunately, no. I did hear movement and some running, but it was not yet light, and I didn't dare leave Avô in that state. Which was just as well, because he seemed to want to say something to me. He asked me to look into his pocket... and I did. To my surprise, I found a key. And he said something very strange—he said, *Promise me you will follow the trail of the lenços.*"

"*Lenços?*"

"Handkerchiefs."

"You sure you heard right?"

"Yes, quite sure. His speech was heavy and slurred, but I couldn't have heard him wrong. And then he said—*I love Ana.*" Filipa's voice tapered off on a note of confusion. She glanced at him, a look of bewilderment on her young face.

"Ana is—" Re prompted, gently.

"I don't know. I don't have the slightest clue who Ana is... never heard of her." Filipa shook her head vigorously.

Re frowned, slightly surprised.

"And the key?"

"I believe it is a key to his office drawer."

"And you haven't as yet checked it out."

"No. I couldn't go into his office. It has been a nightmare, what with the police arriving, and all the questioning... and they were only doing their work but I felt like escaping from it all. It feels like a terrible dream that I desperately want to wake up from."

"Have the police taken—?"

Filipa nodded. "Yes, they took him away. You know what worries me? That I don't have the slightest notion what he was talking about—I don't know about any *lenço,* and I have no clue who this mysterious Ana is, and why Avô claimed that he loved her, for the very first time, and that too when he was dying in my arms! And most importantly, why did someone murder my loving and gentle grandfather!"

"If it is of any solace to you, Filipa, I am here to help you find the answers to all your questions." Re's tone was gentle and kind. "But first, tell me—did your grandfather have any enemies? Any incidents that happened in the past or recently which could throw some light on why he was attacked?"

"Had you met and known Avô, you would have never posed this question. Ask any of his staff… ask Pedro. Ricardo Monteiro is a name synonymous with love and caring. He has helped set up hundreds of families, sponsored the education of hundreds of needy children, and his list of philanthropies is endless."

"Right," Re nodded. *A granddaughter's love could not be questioned or doubted,* he thought. And yet, someone had intentionally snatched away the life of the old man with a brutal, murderous blow.

"I think the first thing to do is to check out the drawer, and understand what is in it that your grandpa wanted you to see. And Filipa, it is time for you to step out and face the crowd, and do your duty," Re reminded, quietly.

Filipa glanced up at him, and he saw the pain reflected in her deep brown eyes. She pursed her lips, nodded, and rose.

"Let's do it then. Let's go find out if this key belongs to his drawer."

Chapter
3

Pedro was standing guard outside the cellar door, and turned to glance at Filipa enquiringly.

"Let's take the back entrance to Avô's office," she instructed tersely.

The butler nodded and led the way through a clump of trees which ran along a small pond. Swans swam leisurely in the clear water, and Re couldn't help noticing the air of quaint charm which sat over the entire estate. He felt as if he had stepped into another version of Disney World. Any other time he would have leisurely strolled through the pathways, and enjoyed soaking in the positive vibes of the estate.

Pedro approached a door almost completely hidden by overgrown ivy, and they entered a narrow corridor. Re touched the wooden panels of the walls. A secret entrance, he realized, for the Monteiro family. The narrow passage ended at another door and the three of them stepped into Ricardo Monteiro's office.

It was a grand old place with the stamp of legacy obvious in the colour schemes, ornate sofas and tapestries. And yet it wasn't ostentatious. Ricardo had been a man of elegant tastes, Re thought. Pedro exited quietly, and Filipa headed straight for the opulent desk. Re watched as she turned the key and opened the drawer. He waited, almost impatiently, as she withdrew an envelope.

"It's from Grandpa to me." She sounded surprised as she read her name scrawled on the white envelope, in his handwriting. She hesitated for some seconds, an expression of wonder on her face. Then, with a deep breath, she flipped it open and extracted a set of keys on a keychain.

"Another key," Re remarked, in a matter-of-fact manner.

Filipa nodded, her lips pursed, as her fingers curled over the keys in her palm. At length, she glanced up, her eyes moist.

"You know what opens with that key?" Re asked, astutely.

"Avô's private safe in his room. No one has ever had access to it. Not even Grandma, not even Mãe. So strange that after all these years, he finally wanted *me* to have the key to his most sacrosanct space."

"Obviously, it contains something he wants *only* you to see."

"But what can that be? I have been very close to my grandfather… he is my idol. I have learnt everything that I know of life and business from him. He has been my teacher, mentor, my closest friend. We have shared a lot in life. That is why this perplexes me—this sudden revelation of a stranger called Ana, and this *lenço*…"

"Why not find out? Go open that safe," Re suggested, gently.

"Yes… right away. This way."

Filipa opened a side door and led Re through a small passage into a private sitting room, and then through another door into a large bedroom. This room was flashier and as Re stood in the room, staring at the ornate frescoed ceiling and the painted walls, he experienced a sudden surge of energy. Strong, vibrant, romantic, and yet he could trace something infinitely sad… violins played a melancholy tune in his mind and he shook his head. Ricardo Monteiro had been an unhappy man. But a man with so much luxury, the world at his feet, and a legacy to be proud of… what in heavens could have made him so melancholy? Something told him the answer lay in the safe, and they were about to find out the truth.

Filipa drew aside a thick velvet curtain, exposing a heavy metal old-fashioned safe, resting deep inside a depression in the wall. Re stood discreetly apart, as she inserted the key with a slight tremble to her hand. She turned the carved handle and opened the heavy door. For some moments, she stared inside, and Re noticed her hesitation. He curbed his instinctive impatience and allowed her time. After all, she had opened a chamber that had been Ricardo's own private and personal space. He could only imagine what that space treasured… secrets held not only from the world but from his near and dear ones as well.

Filipa rummaged through the contents of the safe, and at length, she extracted a slim wooden box. She shut the safe, pocketed the key, and turned to her companion.

"I believe this is what he wanted me to find," she said, the slight tremor in her voice revealing a mix of trepidation and excitement.

She carried the wooden box to the table, placed it with unconscious reverence, inhaled a deep breath, and lifted the lid. She gaped at the contents of the box for a long minute. Re frowned as he, too, assessed the contents of the box, with momentary confusion.

"*Handkerchiefs,*" he said, with disbelief.

There were five largish white soft handkerchiefs. They were bordered with a running lace of red hearts. On each kerchief, the intricate embroidery of a variety of drawings— in striking bright colours—was different. Re touched the embroidered articles, most prominently a heart and flowers, musical instruments, trees, and coloured words and short sentences in Portuguese at the centre of the cloth.

Re stared at the pieces of art, a strong aura of fragrance and love reaching out to him, and he closed his eyes in appreciation of the skill and its essence.

"These are not just *any* handkerchiefs," Filipa said, her voice low. "These are the *Lenços dos Namorados.*"

"The *lenços* that Ricardo asked you to follow?" Re confirmed. "What are they?"

"It is a very old Portuguese tradition—the celebrated 'Valentine's handkerchiefs' of Portugal are carefully embroidered kerchiefs with a message of love in them. Almost like a *declaration* of love. As the eighteenth-century tradition goes, girls in the Minho region of Portugal would use a piece of linen or cotton and embroider beautiful messages in Portuguese, as well as motifs of love like hearts, keys, flowers and more, much like what you see on these kerchiefs. They would then send this kerchief secretly to their beloved. At their next public encounter, if their sweetheart openly displayed and flaunted the kerchief, it meant that he had accepted her offer of friendship, and the courtship had begun."

"How beautiful and intriguing! A unique way of sharing affection and avowals. But these kerchiefs… are they also—" Re paused, delicately.

"Yes, these are obviously love kerchiefs." Filipa shrugged, an odd crankiness in her tone.

"Sent by your grandmother to Ricardo?"

Filipa shook her head. "No, definitely not. These beautiful *lenços* are sent by the mysterious Ana to Avô!"

"*I love Ana…*" Re repeated Ricardo's words to Filipa. "And he never mentioned this to you before? No hint? No pictures? Nothing at all?"

"*Absolutamente nada!* Grandma was a strict woman, disciplined and stern. But I always thought they loved each other, in their strange oldish ways that I probably did not understand in my childhood. I never doubted their love for each other, so never suspected otherwise. I had no reason to believe that there was someone else in his life. I am so confused—this has come as a big shock to me. I don't know what Grandpa wants me to do." Filipa suddenly sounded agitated.

Re picked up the kerchiefs and felt the soft linen. A handwritten date was pinned to each of them. He studied the dates closely. 25th April 1977…

"Strangely, there is a gap of several years between two kerchiefs. Each one received on 25th April, sent to him over the years. This is simply amazing… consistently sending

Ricardo these stunning hand-embroidered kerchiefs. It must have taken time and energy, not to mention, determination. You know what, Filipa, I don't think she was in his life at all. I believe that she *wanted* to be in his life. Otherwise, why would she send five kerchiefs over a period of several decades?" Re was thoughtful.

"I am sorry, but I need time to process this." Filipa perched on the bed, a dazed look on her face.

"I understand. It's a big shock on top of the tragic loss of your grandfather this morning. But I do need to ask you questions, and jog your memory for more information." Re was apologetic.

"Yes, of course." Filipa looked abashed.

"Does 25th April have any special significance in Ricardo's life?" the detective asked.

"Only that it is Carnation Revolution Day. One of the most important days in Portugal."

"I have read about it. The peaceful revolution?"

"That's right. 25th April 1974 was the day a coup against the *Estado Novo* took place in Lisbon, but there was no bloodshed. It was celebrated with carnations, and hence called the Carnation Revolution."

Re was silent as he reflected. "*Promise me you will follow the trail of the lenços... I love Ana...*" Re said, softly, his mind beginning to churn with ideas. "Tell me, do you trust Pedro?"

"Pedro—our family butler? Of course! I grew up around him. He was practically Grandpa's right hand and best friend. I would trust him with my life," Filipa remarked. "Why do you ask?"

"Would he not know about Ana and your grandfather?"

Filipa stared at Re, comprehension dawning on her face. "You are right. If any person really understands Avô, it is Pedro. We can find out right away."

She leaned over, and pressed a button on the side of the bed. Within minutes, there was a soft knock on the door, and Pedro entered. With his blazer and his poised bearing, he appeared every bit distinguished. Re's gaze flew over him in a quick study, trying to sense his energy. He felt a whiff of familiarity, of loyalty. The butler glanced from Filipa to Re in carefully guarded curiosity, and then his gaze settled on the *lenços*. The expression on his face rippled for a fraction of a second, before returning to impassivity.

"Pedro, I need to ask you something very confidential. You are the only person Avô would have shared his deepest secrets with. Do you know of any Ana who came into Grandpa's life? Do you know anything about these *lenços*?" Filipa asked, directly.

Pedro pursed his lips momentarily, contemplation on his face as he eyed the *lenços*. Then he sighed. "Yes, Senhorita Filipa, I knew Ana. I had been sworn to secrecy, and at any other time, I wouldn't have said anything. But the situation is different now, and I can see that Senhor Monteiro has led you to those kerchiefs—which means it is time to share his story." Pedro's demeanour was dignified, but his red-rimmed eyes betrayed inner agitation and fondness for his employer and late friend.

"Pedro, please sit down and tell me everything." Filipa patted the chair beside her, and the butler readily sat on it.

"It was the year 1970. Senhor Ricardo had just got married. It was a good match with a reputed family. Senhora Juliet was cultured, classy, and well-versed in the management of wine estates. Which gave Senhor Ricardo some time to get involved with other activities that he believed in."

"Other activities?" Filipa prompted.

Re leaned against a cupboard, his hands folded, and listened with a great deal of interest.

"The authoritarian rule irked him no end, and he slowly began to get involved in the movement for freedom from autocracy. He joined a group of rebels who worked on the inside, with the military. Occasionally, some of the April Captains—as they were called—would have meetings at the estate to discuss strategies, politics, and the future. They were assigned 'errands', and it was on one such errand that Senhor Ricardo met Ana Ribeiro. Perhaps it was shared interest that brought them together. Ana had the same fiery spirit of rebellion inside her, and she kind of joined the group. Or perhaps it was the fact that Ana was unconventional and very beautiful, but whatever the reason, Senhor Ricardo fell madly in love with her.

"It was a passionate and fantastic love, unlike anything I had ever seen. Ricardo would confide in me about their love, and how desperate he was to be with Ana. But he was married, and that complicated his emotional life. In the end, they had to forego their grand love. Senhora Juliet got wind of the affair and was very disturbed. She swore that she would end her life, if the *senhor* did not end his affair. Ricardo had no choice—he was morally and legally bound to Senhora

Juliet. Ricardo and Ana had always known that a time would come when they would have to terminate their affair. Senhora Juliet's threat was too real to ignore. So, he ended it, and Ana accepted it. I still remember that evening. It was 25th April, Carnation Revolution—Portugal was rejoicing, and Senhor Ricardo was in his study, his room dark, with the thick curtains drawn to exclude even a sliver of light. When I entered the study, he said in a dead voice—'*Pedro, I need your help. I need you to help me live.*'"

The butler paused, a catch in his voice. Filipa's eyes welled up again. Re could clearly envision the scenario—the passionate and young Ricardo, and a headstrong, beautiful Ana; their torrid but short-lived affair; the tumultuous emotions of two souls who found each other through shared ideologies, and knew they belonged together, but were forced to part due to unsurmountable circumstances. What must they have gone through? Loving and parting… what agony, what anguish… Re knew it and understood it. Tears pricked at the back of his eyes. Kindred spirits, kindred emotions…

"What happened next?" Filipa asked, her voice a whisper.

"Ana left that day in tears, but there was always something different about her. She was a deeply emotional and sensitive woman, but equally strong and resilient. I felt that she would eventually bounce back and get her life together; but some years later, out of the blue, Ricardo received the first *lenço* with a poem and beautiful embroidery. Ricardo was in a strange mood that day, I remember. Elated but cautious, hiding the thrill of reconnection, yet wondering and confused about his own reactions and actions… And I wondered all the time if it

was a good thing that had happened to him, or the worst…
In Ana's absence, he had, in a way, quietly begun living his
life. Fallen into a certain routine. Then, was it a good thing
to get sucked back into a whirlpool of emotions? It was a
strange time for him."

Pedro paused, a reflective faraway look in his deep-set
wise eyes. Re could understand his concern. Ricardo would
have endured infinite emotional hardship in trying to find
his balance and to get on track again, post his parting with
Ana. And just when he probably had succeeded, Ana had re-
entered his life through the *lenço*. Obviously, with a message
of love in it—which must have led to an emotional setback
for him. But why had she sent the *lenço* in the first place?
What had induced her to send him a *lenço*, on the exact same
date as they had parted?

Re felt himself being siphoned into this strange love
story that was more than 40 years old. But did distance and
time ever matter? He didn't need to answer that question—
experience had taught him that it definitely did not. Being
in love was like being on a musical loop… as soon as its
duration ended, it rolled right back to the beginning… and
the journey continued…

"I thought it would be a one-off thing," Pedro resumed.
"The *lenço* business. But I was wrong. A few years later,
another *lenço* arrived, on the exact same date—25th of April.
With beautiful embroidery, and an elaborate pictorial and
poetic message again. And Ricardo went through another
'state'—of chaotic emotional upheaval. After that, he knew

that sooner than later, the next one would arrive, and so it did. There were five such *lenços* in all, over a period of several decades. But after the fifth *lenço*, the *senhor* waited and waited, almost eagerly, but a sixth *lenço* never appeared. He was restless over the years, his long walks became longer, and the silences between the *senhora* and him just grew lengthier. It was truly sad to see him in this state—of limbo and a kind of anticipation. I have not read the contents of the *lenços*, but I believe that they were some sort of letters to him… with hints… perhaps she believed and hoped that he would go looking for her, and they would be united again."

"Now that you mention it, I sort of recall a bit of those moods when Avô preferred to be by himself—often sitting by the lake, staring at the ducks. I was afraid to disturb him, he appeared so lost and forlorn, even distant," Filipa reminisced. "But if he was so miserable and if he missed Ana so much, did Grandpa not go looking for Ana, or try to reach her at all?"

"I wouldn't be able to say. He was loyal to your grandmother right until the end. He had made up his mind to do right by Senhora Juliet, and I think he stayed loyal to the promise."

"And yet Grandpa's last words mentioned the trail of *lenços,* and were a confession of love for Ana." Filipa sighed.

"Love is a strange emotion, Filipa. Deep and poignant to the point that life without your beloved doesn't make sense. Still, you have to go on, like everything is normal, when deep inside you, all is chaos and joyless," Re spoke up.

Filipa glanced at him, surprised. "But Grandpa seemed to be a happy and content person on the whole, and he loved the estate."

"Which was probably why he immersed himself in his work and the estate. To find joy in his legacy, instead of in his life," Re said.

"He always truly loved Ana. I believe she was his real love," Pedro confirmed, quietly.

Silence ensued, as Filipa stared from the butler to the investigator. She rose and began pacing the room, a little agitatedly, tucking and re-tucking her wavy unruly hair behind her ears.

"Now, what do we do next? Where do I begin my search? Am I supposed to start right away? The timing couldn't have been worse. Tomorrow is my big event, Grandpa is no more, Mãe is in India somewhere, the press is waiting outside, and the police need to ask questions…"

"Breathe!" Re commanded, sensing panic. "Let's go step by step…"

Before Re could complete his sentence, a loud crash echoed, followed by the sound of splintering glass. Re rose, startled.

"It came from the office," Pedro said, and the three of them hastened to the outer room.

It took a few seconds for Re to realize that the window pane on the side of the garden had splintered, and a big hole gaped at him. Lying on the floor, wrapped in a crumpled piece of paper, was a big stone.

"Someone hurled this through the window," he said, picking up the paper. "Something's written on it."

He flattened the paper on the table and Pedro and Filipa stared at it.

Solve the trail of the lenços before 5:00 pm tomorrow, or be responsible for the bloodbath…

Filipa glanced up at Re, fear writ large on her ashen face. "This is what nightmares are made of!" she whispered. "What does this mean, and what in heavens am I to do?"

Re turned his attention to her and looked at her directly. "This is difficult, I know. But you need to focus, and help me understand and solve this. Pedro, is anyone else aware of these *lenços*?"

"Not a soul. Not even Senhora Juliet knew about them, nor Filipa's mother. I seriously doubt that Ricardo talked about it to anyone… they evoked an emotion which he completely blocked off, even within himself."

"But someone is aware of the kerchiefs and wants them desperately enough to cause a bloodbath," Re frowned. "But why 5:00 PM tomorrow, why the deadline?"

"I am not sure if it is connected, but we are launching a world symbol of peace, like an offering from Portugal, in a grand ceremony at the Basílica Santa Luzia tomorrow."

"The note doesn't mention your event… he or she could have, for clarity, so we can't really be sure there is a connection. Is there anything else that is significant about tomorrow?"

"It is Carnation Revolution Day, there would be celebrations all over the country," Pedro pointed out.

"That's it, perhaps! Threaten to turn a day of celebrations into something ugly. But where? Which part of Penafiel?" the detective wondered. He turned to Filipa. "Do you have any reason to believe that tomorrow's event and this threat are connected? Have you ever received any such threats to prevent the event from happening?" Re asked.

Filipa shook her head. "Never. In fact, everyone—mayors of each region, the media, the representatives from other European nations, the locals—all have gone out of their way to ensure the success of the event."

"Given the tragic happening this morning, would you consider cancelling the event?"

Filipa did not respond at once. Her gaze rested on the *lenços* with the beautiful colours, embroidered motifs and words, and her fingers fiddled with the hem. Re noticed the change in skin tone on her left ring finger. Like a ring had been removed after a long period of time. His curiosity was piqued, there had to be story there...

"No," the young lady said, at length. "The event won't be cancelled. It isn't about me alone. The inauguration of the symbol is a world event and cannot be called off—it would inconvenience a lot of people, not to mention causing huge losses of money which we cannot afford. Even with such a horrible situation. Avô wouldn't have wanted that. He was very strict about these matters, and his work ethic was impeccable. I have to respect and follow it."

Pedro expelled a quick sigh of relief. "Good decision, *senhorita*. Ricardo would have been proud of you."

"Well, we have a big puzzle here—the five kerchiefs. Ricardo's last wish was for you to follow the trail of the *lenços,* and an anonymous person also goads us to solve the trail— which means, firstly, there is indeed a path in these kerchiefs, and they are not random gifts sent by Ana to Ricardo. They lead somewhere, and we need to know where. I am assuming that you both have no clue where they lead, right?"

Re glanced from the older man to the younger lady. Both shook their heads in silence.

"Which leaves us with one choice. We need to do some research on Ana—dig up information—like where she lived, what she did after they parted ways, why she did not send the sixth kerchief. Would you be able to help Pedro—are you in possession of any useful info on Ana?"

"Actually, not too much. Only that she lived in Penafiel with her sister in the early days. But I not even sure if that house still stands, or if anyone still lives there. They owned a small wine garden... I am sure I can find the address somewhere."

"Good. That would be the place to begin, then."

The buzz of Pedro's walkie-talkie interrupted Re.

"What is it, Tiago?" Pedro spoke imperiously into the instrument.

"The police are here. They would like to speak to madam at once. In fact, I don't like their tone at all. They would like to take her in for questioning, they say. Apparently, they have found something... unusual and damaging." Tiago's voice crackled through the speaker.

Pedro stared at Re, startled. Filipa too stopped her pacing, surprise flashing across her face. "Hold them there. I will call you back."

"What in heavens!" Filipa burst out, her tone loud and incredulous. "Found something damaging? Like evidence? Do they suspect me of harming my own grandfather?"

"Depends on what they have found," Re said, in a calmly cautious tone.

"What do we do now?" Pedro asked, practically.

Re turned to Filipa. "We have until 5:00 PM tomorrow to solve the trail of the *lenços*. If you meet the police now, they may detain you for questioning, under some whim or pretext, and probably do their best to slap you with a criminal charge. It happens. They may detain you without reason, unconditionally, and we cannot allow that because I need you to solve this trail."

Filipa's eyes flashed with anger. "I am not going to be accused of murdering my own beloved grandfather. Come whim come pretext!"

"Excellent!" Re nodded his approval. "Then pack a light bag, some snacks and a drink. We shall leave unseen by a back door. Do you know any place where we will not be traced? Not a Monteiro home, of course. But a trustworthy friend perhaps? Just as a base for a couple of hours."

"I do—Julieta, my friend. She lives a short distance from here and is the soul of discretion."

"Cool. Then we need to get going, immediately. My car is parked out front. Pedro, can you drive it to a back entrance?

Perhaps take a longish route out and then head to the back, so that no one notices?" Re asked.

Before the butler could respond, his walkie-talkie crackled again.

"Pedro? The police are waiting," Tiago remarked.

"Madam is resting in her room and I dare not disturb her just yet. Tell them we will notify them once she is ready to meet anyone."

"The police are refusing to budge. They say they will wait till madam is ready to meet them," Tiago said.

"Very well. Please request the maid to serve them some tea," Pedro replied calmly, and turned off the walkie-talkie. He glanced at the detective and raised an eyebrow. "Now what?"

"We act fast. Filipa, one other thing. Given that the event tomorrow is so important, do you mind if I invite someone very trusted to oversee things?" Re asked.

"But I have Tiago and Pedro to do the needful. They have been on it since the beginning, they know what's to be done, right down to the last detail," Filipa pointed out.

"No offense Pedro—" Re cut in.

"Not at all," the butler said.

"But given the situation, with the police now after us, I would feel much more in control with a trusted person who can assist Pedro and Tiago."

"Who is this trusted person?"

"My friend, Officer Stefan Weiss. He works with the Austrian Police but is on leave right now; I am sure he will step in for a couple of days to help us with the situation. We have worked on some cases together—he is dependable, and a fireball of action and intelligence."

Filipa glanced at Pedro and raised an eyebrow enquiringly. The butler nodded, with alacrity.

"All right then," the *senhorita* agreed. "We are caught in a terrible situation and the event tomorrow is of utmost importance. There's no harm bringing in an added helping hand. Pedro—you and Tiago will ensure that Stefan gets all the help he needs? Nothing must hinder tomorrow's programme. You will ensure that, won't you?"

"I will, *senhorita*. I promise."

Filipa gave him a grateful, watery smile. "I shall also write out a quick statement for the press, and the committee meeting this afternoon. Also, please send out an email to the mayors of the five counties, briefly explaining the situation, but assuring them that the event will go as per plan—that they have nothing to worry about. I don't want anyone to feel insecure in the present state of affairs."

"That is the right thing to do." Pedro nodded, but his eyes shone with pride.

"Good. Give me ten minutes Re… my laptop is in my room. I will forward Pedro the emails and a press note. And then, he can meet us with the car at the Swan Pond," she suggested.

Then she picked up the box of *lenços* and briskly left the room, her ample hair swinging on her back.

Pedro turned his attention to the investigator.

"I can stall the police for a couple of hours. But what happens when they know she has vanished? And what do I tell them?"

"You say you can't find her. Her car is still parked here, and her phone will be switched off. She left without informing anyone, even you. Grief can do that to a person. It can affect the brain. People can behave irrationally."

Pedro nodded and accepted the car keys Re offered.

"I will share my number with you. Anything important comes up, you send me a message right away. Somehow, we need these 36 hours to solve the trail of the *lenços* and find out who killed Ricardo—*any which way.* It is vital."

Re and Pedro exchanged a long look of tacit understanding, the silence reverberating with suppressed tension. Pedro expelled a big sigh and exited the room.

Re remained in Ricardo's bedroom for some moments, alone, breathing in the smell of polished wood and ancient regal furniture. Light streamed in through the latticed windows, forming a chequered pattern on the red rug and the four-poster bed with its intricately woven silk bedspread. The lush abode of a rich man, and yet, the energy that emanated from the room was that of earthy comfort. Re could smell wet mud and rain. Or was it the smell of tears— those of a man lost in love, yet determined to live? Re closed his eyes and allowed the energy of the room to wash over him. *Wish me luck, Ricardo… wish me luck…* he spoke to the strong aura in the room. An unmitigated desire rose in Re's mind. A desire to see justice done at any cost… but not only for Ricardo's tragic death. It was a yearning to trace the source of the *lenços* and to offer Ricardo some solace for his lovesick heart.

Re sighed. It was time to make a quick phone call to Officer Stefan Weiss.

Chapter
4

In the cradle of the nation
where the ceilings sail...
Beyond the holy tree,
where the 39 smokes trail...
Where the walls listen
to the secrets that it keeps,
But the heart lands
where the chimney speaks.

Filipa drove out the back entrance and smoothly travelled down the thickly wooded area. She had changed into jeans and a black top with a hoodie. A stuffed backpack rested on the backseat. "I have some sandwiches, chocolate and two bottles of water—just in case we don't have time to stop and eat," she explained.

Re's phone pinged, and he glanced at the message and nodded.

"We have Ana's home address in Penafiel. That is our first stop. Someone there may perhaps remember the Ribeiro sisters. I will make the enquiries while you stay in the car. We don't want people recognizing you."

She was quiet as Re switched on the GPS; she manoeuvred the car according to GPS instructions. They passed the *Santuário do Sameiro*, sitting atop the hill, a snow-white Romanesque structure with graceful curves and lines, blessing the town of Penafiel with its serene presence. They passed through the old town and into the countryside, turned a lane and halted by a neat bungalow.

"Are you sure it's here?" Filipa was doubtful. "This seems to be a well-maintained property."

"It is, as per the address sent to us by Pedro. Let me check." Re descended from the car and stood staring at the cream-coloured two-storied bungalow with a large garden circling the house. The windows were shut and dark blue curtains were drawn. He opened the wooden gate and walked down the grassy path to the main door. It seemed obvious that no one was living here, but still he rang the bell and waited. He rang the bell again, but it yielded no result. As Re retraced his steps to the car, a signboard tucked behind a bush caught his eye. *For Sale*. But what did it mean? Was the house sold or had the decision to sell it changed? Or had someone just chucked the sign into the garden?

"No one at home," he reported briefly, as he got into the car.

"Ana can't be living here anymore, so close to the Monteiro Estate, that's for certain. But perhaps her sister?" Filipa guessed.

"The house looks as if it was recently renovated. I wish there was someone here who could give us information. I have an idea—let's go to the local post office, they may have something for us."

"You mean like who lives in this house?" Filipa looked a little incredulous.

"They may know if any letters ever go to this house," Re responded patiently.

But the single young girl handling the Post Office had nothing new to offer. She had no clue who lived at the pretty bungalow, and she couldn't recall ever delivering any letters to that address. Re climbed into the car with a sigh.

"At least we know that the Ribeiro sisters don't live here anymore. Otherwise, the Post Office can't have not known of the existence of one of the oldest families in Penafiel."

"What next?"

"Now we do some reading—of handkerchiefs," the detective said in a practical tone.

Filipa extracted the box from her backpack. Re noticed that her eyes were still red-rimmed and her face puffy. Such a big reminder, that the trajectory of life is so uncertain. Everything can change in a flash. This morning, she had been a content woman, equipped to implement her ambitious plans. Secure in her world of fulfilment, happy in her sense of achievement, the future appearing bright and promising. And then, an anonymous hand had sprung the cruellest joke on her. Like a giant scooping out of the core of her existence. A huge wave of grief had swallowed her completely, but to give the lady credit, she was holding up well. Re appreciated people who fought for justice, and there was no doubt in his mind that Filipa's determined efforts would prove useful.

He focused his attention on the handkerchiefs which were of the softest linen, and Re placed them on the seat, in chronological order.

"These *lenços* have been sent to Ricardo over a period of almost thirty-five years. If we take Pedro's version as our starting point, we can assume that Ana sent each of these handkerchiefs with the hope that Ricardo would go looking for her."

"But why didn't she just call Avô?" Filipa wondered.

"Well, we don't know the exact circumstances under which they parted. Obviously, parting is always traumatic. We don't know either under *what terms* they parted. Perhaps they had mutually decided never to talk to each other again, or even call each other. She may have simply been adhering to their rules."

"And yet she sent these kerchiefs regularly over years, in the hope of—what? That he would divorce my grandmother and pursue her? Sounds absolutely wild to me! And I am so glad and proud that he didn't. I am so glad that he realized the value of his relationship with my grandmother. He was married when he met Ana. She must have known it was just an affair, and that he would never leave grandmother. And that their fling was just that—a premature affair with no future, and a predetermined expiry date! A foregone conclusion to a flighty romance."

Re glanced at Filipa, sensing the bitterness in her tone, and in her heart. It wasn't easy, he knew, to discover that your beloved grandfather loved a complete stranger. A stranger she had never known, or seen, or even knew existed. Had

Ricardo been wrong in revealing his secret right at the end? Would it not have been more sensitive to gradually ease the news to his granddaughter, instead of the manner in which it was slammed into her life? Would it leave a cruel scar? Would she ever get over it, or would she secretly harbour a lifetime grudge against her grandfather for the deception that had left her alone to grapple with hard truths? Rapid questions rose in Re's mind, but he knew that only time would answer them.

"You are angry," he remarked, tersely.

"Of course, I am angry!" Filipa burst out. "I am *furious*. What is this—some kind of a game? This is nothing more than a juvenile means of attracting a man who didn't love her anymore—chasing him for years, with no real reciprocation. Did she have no self-respect? Did she not see that Grandpa didn't love her anymore, or possibly, never loved her?"

"He did love her, Filipa. When Pedro found him in his study, he asked him to help him live. Those words sound like those of a heartbroken lover. And don't forget his last words—I love Ana," Re reminded gently.

"I know… it was possibly regret, of some kind. I am not sure. I am not sure of anything to do with Grandpa anymore. Regardless, the fact that these handkerchiefs are somehow responsible for the death of my dear Grandpa—that angers me even more."

"I understand, but let's not jump to conclusions, nor blame Ana for anything yet," Re admonished quietly. "Let's go step by step. Each of these *lenços* was received on the 25th of April, years apart. April 25th is Carnation Day, as well as the day they parted. Obviously, that left a huge mark on

Ana—hence the importance of the date. The date of the first kerchief is 25th April 1977. Three years after they parted. What was Ana doing in those three years? Where was she? I feel the *lenço* will hold the clue. Can you read what's written on it?"

Filipa angled the kerchief towards herself and stared at it. Little hearts bordered the four sides of the linen, with a tree in the centre. The embroidery was dainty and neat, as each line of a small paragraph was woven in a different colour.

"Is it a letter?"

"A letter of sorts. Let me translate this for you."

Filipa took a pen and paper from her backpack, and began scribbling on it. Her wavy hair partly covered her face as she frowned in concentration, trying to find the best English words. At length, she glanced up and handed him the paper.

"*Dear Ricardo,*
In the cradle of the nation,
where the ceilings sail…
Beyond the holy tree,
where the 39 smokes trail…
Where the walls listen
to the secrets that it keeps,
But the heart lands
where the chimney speaks.
Come find it… Waiting to meet you…"

"This is certainly a description of a place; it is an invitation to come and find something that she has kept for him. And she is hoping to meet him too, of course," Re observed.

"Kind of sad. Because he never went." Filipa's voice was expressionless.

"Any idea which place this could be?"

"Yes, she made it very easy with the first line. Plus, she has embroidered a clue in the corner. AQUI NASCEU PORTUGAL."

"The birthplace of Portugal. She sent this *lenço* from Guimarães?"

"That's right. Although I have no clue what 'ceilings sail' and '39 smokes trail' means."

"We'll figure it out, once we reach the town. It is obvious now that Ana was tempting Ricardo to find her. And she didn't want to make it too difficult. At the same time, I believe that she didn't want to seem desperate. Also, we cannot rule out that this verse perhaps meant something to Ricardo. Some shared memory perhaps? But that is something we may never know."

"Yes, possibly."

"How well do you know Guimarães?"

"Fairly well."

"How far would it be from here?"

"Around half an hour by car."

Re pushed back his sliding glasses and straightened his black jacket. "Let's get going then. It is 11:00 now, we should be there by 11:30. And keep your backpack with you."

Officer Stefan Weiss drove at a steady pace. He had borrowed a friend's car for two days, because he could never refuse Re

Parkar anything. Especially not a significant call for help. And his phone call had been deeply rooted in some sort of panic. Re needed his assistance, and Stefan had to heed it. Although he was on holiday in Spain, and Isabel was just a trifle annoyed. But she acquiesced that the matter had to be of utmost importance if Re had requested his presence, Stefan thought.

In half an hour he would be at the Monteiro Estate, one of the famous wine families of Europe. He had heard so much about their Vinho Verde, and if the circumstances had been happier, he would have enjoyed exploring the estate, and tasting the wine. But for now, he was curious to meet Pedro, Tiago, and Filipa, to oversee one of Portugal's biggest events. The rest he would leave to Re, who worked in a rather eclectic manner. Stefan never questioned Re's method or style of working, he just trusted his friend's instinct. They actually made a good team—while Stefan worked on procedurals, logic and proof, Re worked with energies and visions. And somehow, they both managed to satisfy their own investigative cravings, which culminated in a common deductive conclusion. This time it would be no different, Stefan was confident. He couldn't wait to get to Penafiel and help Re unravel the truth.

Guimarães was situated in north Portugal in the Braga district. Re had been to the ninth-century old town years ago with his mother, but now the memories were a blur of merging images of narrow cobbled streets, uneven large courtyards, colourful houses and cafes. As they drove towards the valley surrounded by scenic hills, he was glad Filipa would be able to steer him.

At around 11:30, Re parked outside the entrance to the pedestrian-only Centro Histórico de Guimarães. They headed to a long narrow cobbled street on foot, a street which seemed to cut through the heart of the historic town.

"Here we are—the Cradle of the Nation. Mostly referred to as such because our country's first king, Afonso Henriques, was born here in the early twelfth-century. Guimarães is associated with the creation of the Portuguese national identity and language. It was the feudal territory of the dukes and it was these dukes who declared Portuguese independence in the mid-twelfth-century." Filipa explained. "The city got the status of a UNESCO World Heritage site some years back… it's a beautiful town—a blend of the old with the modern. I love this street—the Rua de Santa Maria is historic. It cuts through the centre of the town and is the oldest route that narrows down to the main square."

"It's got a certain character to it," Re agreed, as he took quick pictures of the grand Parliament building and the narrow alley which scuttled between the buildings.

"So where are we headed?" Filipa asked.

"For a quick coffee first?" Re suggested.

"Then let's head straight to Largo da Oliveira, the main plaza. There are many cafes at the historic Praça, but my grandfather's dear friend Santiago owns a cafe right opposite the famous holy olive tree at the Church of Our Lady of Oliveira."

They walked through the narrow-cobbled street with the straight cluster of traditional houses leaning into Rua de Santa Maria. Re felt as if he was walking through a narrow coloured tunnel of card box windows and doors which led into Praça de São Tiago, an uneven medieval plaza circled by an unbroken queue of wood-framed brown and white buildings. Cafes had opened up and the Square was filled with coloured patio tables and chairs where young students were grouped together, chatting and laughing. Filipa led the detective through the Square into another irregular-shaped plaza which was dominated by the church—Igreja de Nossa Senhora da Oliveira—with a Manueline canopy on the left, and the olive tree in the centre. Bordering the Square was a prominent yellow heritage building with long box windows and flowerbeds overflowing with attractive flowers.

Instantly, a strong energy rose to meet Re, and he felt the energy pulsate around his head and his ponytail, its powerful sense of belonging and presence almost staggering him. He glanced at Filipa to see if she sensed it, but she seemed calm. Perhaps her grief had dulled her senses? Perhaps she wasn't meant to feel it?

"We could have stopped on the way at the Casa Costinhas, which serves the original *torta de Guimarães*—a secret pastry recipe of the nuns from the convent in the olden days. But I do want to meet Santiago, it's been ages and he would like to know about Grandpa."

Re nodded, "I am not in the mood for pastries."

"Me neither. But do you mind if we just stop by this olive tree? It has a story—many, actually, but one of them is that a century-old olive tree once grew here, right in front of the Church of Our Lady of Oliveira. When the tree began to wither, a sacred cross was erected on the Square in 1342, and suddenly the tree came to life, bearing fruit. That was when this Square got its name *"Largo da Oliveira."* The one you see here, however, was planted in 1985. But I feel that the powerful spirit and energy of this place is still unchanged."

Re smiled at her, feeling a sense of delight and relief. He knew in that moment that he was happy to be helping Filipa. She appeared tough and almost callous in her anger, but on the inside, she was soft and sensitive after all. And he enjoyed working for and with sensitive people. In fact, it was a prerequisite to the successful conclusion of a case.

It was as Filipa stood staring at the tree and praying outside the church that a large group of school children strolled down the Square. Conversation went back and forth in Portuguese, and Re sensed their excitement. A split second later, he saw the tall capped man very close to Senhorita Monteiro. A strong gut instinct rose inside him. "Filipa! Be careful!"

Even as he shouted, he saw Filipa stumble. Some children screamed and scattered. The next moment, the man with the cap sprinted between the crowd of children and vanished round the street.

"Are you okay? What just happened?" Re asked, catching up with Filipa.

The *senhorita* appeared visibly shaken.

"I am fine, mostly. He tried to steal my backpack. But I held on to it for dear life," she remarked.

A frown appeared on the detective's forehead. "Did you catch a glimpse of his face?"

"Nope, only his cap."

"The *lenços* are in the bag. Someone seems to want them desperately, which means that there are others who know about the handkerchiefs too. This is getting more and more intriguing, and needs some serious thinking... Let's go get that coffee."

Filipa nodded, but she still appeared pale. Re realized that he would have to be more attentive. An old gentleman was murdered just this morning, and someone had threatened a bloodbath if the trail of *lenços* was not solved within 36 hours. And then, a rather public attempt at theft. Obviously, someone urgently needed the trail of the *lenços* to be solved. Who and why? Were they also looking for Ana Ribeiro? How was all of it connected?

Who was Ana? Re wondered, a frown on his face. And more importantly, where was she right now? Why were people so interested in the love handkerchiefs she had sent privately to her old flame? What was so special about the *lenços*?

He knew that these questions were too early in the investigation, but the answers to them would be revealed in Ana's journey. He needed to trace her life from the point she and Ricardo parted ways. Reconstructing a journey through a timespan of more than 40 years, a journey fraught with emotional turmoil, was far from being either easy or pleasant. Re felt that he was about to begin a roller-coaster ride through the hills and valleys of the secret minds of two strangers. Because this was not just Ana's life journey—she was intrinsically connected to Ricardo, if the *lenços* were anything to go by. Who knew what this roller-coaster ride would reveal? Re only wished it wasn't sadder than it already was... if only for Filipa's sake.

Senhorita Monteiro pushed open the glass door of the cafe and it tinkled merrily. Re glanced around the neat and charming interiors, designed in touristy ambience for leisure. An old man with a shining bald head was seated comfortably behind the counter, his head immersed in a newspaper.

"Santiago?" Filipa ventured.

The old man's head shot up, and he stared at the *senhorita* from behind his glasses.

"Filipa, my dear! What are you doing here?" Santiago exclaimed, obvious pleasure in his voice.

He rose from behind the counter and hugged the young lady. It was evident to Re that Santiago was fond of Filipa.

"Just felt like meeting you Santiago." Filipa's eyes were moist.

"Ah my dear, always here for you."

"This is Re, a friend of mine."

"Welcome to Guimarães, Re," Santiago beamed. Then he turned to Filipa and his gaze was soft and tender. "I just heard about Ricardo. What ghastly news to wake up to... how did it happen?"

As Filipa shared the tragic details, Re ordered the coffee and glanced around the cafe. Beautiful paintings lined one wall of the cafe and they appeared to document the historic monuments of Guimarães—a painting of the rustic fortification of the Castelo de Guimarães—the tenth-century castle of the king Afonso Henrique on a green hill; the exquisite baroque Igreja Nossa Senhora da Consolação—Church of our lady of Consolation—which stood at the end of the long avenue of a beautiful garden, one of the main churches of Guimarães; the grand fifteenth-century *Paço dos Duques de Bragança* or the Ducal Palace displaying its chimneys... Re's gaze paused at the next painting, curiosity and interest flickering in him. The picture was an elaborate painting of an inverted boat, but it didn't quite seem like a real boat.

"Sorry to interrupt. But what is this?" Re asked, turning to Santiago.

"It's the ceiling of the Ducal Palace. Shaped like a boat. It is very fascinating. Are you planning to visit the Ducal Palace now that you are here?"

Filipa glanced at Re.

"Yes, I believe that we would," Re confirmed, and she appeared surprised.

"Then do meet Sylvie... she used to adore your Grandpa... she is on the advisory of the palace, and refuses to retire." He chuckled.

"Santiago, may I ask you something?" Filipa said. "You were Grandpa's good friend. Did you know anything about Ana?"

"Ah, Ana Ribeiro... hadn't heard that name in a long while... Of course I knew Ana—a beautiful and fiery woman, a little wild if you asked me, but yet so dignified, and so much in love with our Ricardo. She was perfect for him in every way. She matched his wit, intelligence and enthusiasm but could also put some sense into him. They understood each other perfectly. Unfortunately, it was not to be. I feel that was the saddest part of Ricardo's life—I fear he may have never gotten over her."

Re glanced at Filipa to gauge her reaction. She avoided looking at him, concentrating on the old man instead, her hair covering her face and hiding it. Re understood in a flash. Filipa did not quite trust him yet, at least not enough to reveal and confess her deepest emotions. She would take time, and he wouldn't rush her.

"Do you know if she came here?"

"Oh yes, she did, straight after their breakup. Worked at the Ducal Palace for a while, then got another job offer somewhere. Sylvie would probably be able to tell you more. I did meet her on a few occasions, when she dropped by under the pretext of some coffee, but actually hoping for news of Ricardo. It was quite tragic really. I liked her a lot. And I felt that life had been a little unfair to her. But Ricardo was an honourable man. He had made his choice. It was to be with Juliet, who despite everything, stood by him. So he had nothing to complain about." He shrugged. "When do you plan to have the funeral my dear? I would like to be there."

"To be honest, I hadn't even thought of it, Santiago— what with everything, the police and… and other stuff…" Filipa's voice trailed.

"Bound to happen, my dear. Don't worry… this is unthinkably miserable, but Ricardo lived a full life… he had everything—money, fame, family, legacy and ultimately, he knew the 'grand love'. Very few of us encounter that in one lifetime."

Re stared at him, his words touching a core somewhere deep inside him. Images of his one true love rose before his eyes, and sudden emotions surged inside him. He turned away abruptly, and mumbling an excuse, stepped out into the Square. The olive tree and the church, the bustle of tourists, the scraping of chairs and tables, and the cheer of laughter brought back a sense of normalcy to his inner turmoil. He sighed. He would have to gain better control over his emotions. Even the slightest allusion to soul-love, and he seemed to lose it. He was here to help Filipa, not wallow in his own sorrows.

Five minutes later, Filipa joined him. She appeared calmer and looked at him pointedly.

"You OK?" she asked. "You came out rather abruptly from there."

"Yes, all good. Just remembered something that I had to do. I looked up the Ducal Palace—it has 39 chimneys."

"Yes, I kind of remember that now. So?"

"You noticed the painting of the ceiling that looked like an inverted boat?"

"From the Paço dos Duques, yes."

Re extracted the translation from his jacket pocket.

"*In the cradle of the nation
where the ceilings sail...
Beyond the holy tree,
where the 39 smokes trail...
Where the walls listen
to the secrets that it keeps,*

But the heart lands
where the chimney speaks.'

"We are in the cradle of the nation right now, and this here is the holy tree—the Oliviera. 'Where the ceilings sail' has got to be the ceiling of the Ducal Palace... it was an inverted boat, a boat that never actually took sail. '39 smokes trail' would be the 39 chimneys of the palace. Ana worked at the palace. It is now obvious that she sent the *lenço* with these directions because she wanted Ricardo to come meet her at the Paço dos Duques." Re sounded excited.

"That seems accurate," Filipa's eyes lit up. "But what about the next four lines?"

"We will figure those out soon enough. Let's head to the palace."

"It's a short walk from the Historic Centre, right next to the King's Palace."

"Do you want me to hold your backpack?"

Filipa turned to him and looked him fully in the face for the first time, her gaze direct. He noticed her slightly bushy but tamed eyebrows, the intense brown eyes, and curly mass of hair, probably tamped down with serum, and the dimple in her right cheek.

"I appreciate it that you here with me Re, truly I do. I wouldn't have known what to do without you. But you really need to stop treating me with kid gloves. Yes, I lost my beloved grandfather a couple of hours back; yes, I am totally devastated and my world has suddenly gone anti-gravitationally haywire, but I am also totally and relentlessly determined to pursue the truth behind this ghastly tragedy, to find out who did it, and why. And so, if we have to do this together, you would have to trust me. And that means trusting me to take care of this backpack with the precious *lenços!*"

A twinkle rose in Re's deep brown eyes. He pushed back his slipping glasses and nodded. "*Mais oui…* Point noted *senhorita* and accepted gracefully. But may I gently add that it works both ways? If we want this to succeed, *ma chérie*, you would need to trust me implicitly too. And that means sharing your deepest contemplations and doubts with me. Are you game?"

"Do you '*ma chérie*' every girl you meet?"

"Every girl, woman and child I feel protective about."

"That is sweet." Filipa smiled for the first time that day and Re felt warmth radiate inside him.

"It's a pact. We repose infinite, unquestionable faith in each other while on this journey to find the truth," Re concluded.

"Deal. So, I carry my own bag, and I promise you the *lenços* are safe with me."

"I trust you!" Re chuckled.

"It's a good beginning," Filipa smiled as they fell in step.

They strode up the street of Santa Maria, Filipa pointing out an alley that opened into a courtyard.

"This is the entrance to the ancient leather market—the Zona de Couros, the tanning and leather-making district of the city. Once it was a flourishing industry here, and if you walk in, you will find a whole little ancient world in there. But now all that remain are fascinating old buildings with brick chimneys, and tanneries."

"And what about this defence wall. Does it run around the city?" Re pointed to the battlement wall that seemed to run along the street.

"They are the *Muralhas* or Walls of Guimarães, built in the thirteenth-century to protect Guimarães, that had eight 'Ports' or gates. If we had the time, we could have walked all the way on the defence wall. I came once with Avô and we walked the entire length of the wall and enjoyed the lovely views of the city."

"Must have been a special time with him," Re observed.

"It was. Grandpa and I did things together—he took me to many places, shared the history of Portugal with me. He was my best friend and teacher."

Re was silent, allowing her time to reminisce and come to terms with her great loss.

The walk to the palace was short but partly uphill, and Re kept a sharp lookout for anyone following them. Specially a man with a cap but for the moment, all seemed clear.

Right before them stood the Paço dos Duques, the residence of the dukes. Four tall rust-coloured chimneys between two turreted towers formed the top facade of the palace. On the left stood the King's Castle, on a large grassy mound of hill. It appeared more like a battlement with bare stone walls topped with conical structures—like on a fence—bordering the entire castle, but completely hollow on the inside. Tourists walked on top of the walls, taking pictures of the park.

Re and Filipa strode into the impressive large courtyard. Re noticed that the many chimneys that rose from between conical roofs on all four sides resembled chocolate candy sticks. Re hadn't seen so many chimneys in any palace before. They were certainly a unique feature of the palace.

"Filipa!" a voice hailed from behind them.

They turned to face a woman in her late seventies attired in a black dress and a shrug, a snow-white bob sitting tight on a lined face. Her eyes were a deep blue and she now smiled kindly at Filipa.

"Hello Sylvie, so good to see you after so many years," Filipa enthused quietly.

"Likewise, my dear. Come inside, into my office."

They walked past well-illuminated displays in glass cupboards, piles of books and brochures, and settled into comfortable chairs.

"Santiago called and said you were coming. So sorry for your loss my dear, Ricardo was such a special man. I will miss him." Sylvie held Filipa's hands in hers.

"Thank you. It was too sudden and shocking. This is Re, my friend who is also an investigator. We are trying to find out who did it."

Sylvie glanced at Re and nodded. "I am so glad that Re is here to help you."

"Sylvie, you do know about Ana?" Filipa ventured.

"Of course I do. In fact, we have worked together. I was a manager when she came to work with me in 1974, right after the Carnation Rebellion. Apparently, her sister had moved here, so Ana came here too—to live with her sister. I remember her so clearly—a smart young lady with a sensible head, it was clear what Ricardo saw in her."

"Sylvie, we are trying to locate Ana urgently. So please share whatever you do know about her," Re requested.

"She was an excellent and hardworking assistant, she learnt the history of this palace instantly, and did splendid tours. The tourists were always happy with the way she incorporated new methods of sharing the same history. But I knew about her break-up with Ricardo—we all knew, and there was little we could do to alleviate their pain. Love can be a blessing and a curse, but in either case, the euphoria and the grief are both too personal to be shared. At the same time, it gives you a lifeline in the dark."

Re absorbed the words of the older lady—so much wisdom in such few lines. It was almost as if she was speaking to him about his love. *The euphoria and the grief are too personal to share… give you a lifeline in the dark…*

"Did she talk about the relationship with you?" Filipa asked.

"No, I think she was determined to move forward, and not allow her love for him to pull her down. Which was very wise, if you ask me. But I don't believe she ever gave up on him. She was always hopeful that he would return to her one day. But he never did, unfortunately. I mean not in the sense she expected and desired. In her spare time, I would see her working on a *lenço*—beautiful intricate work, and I knew it was for him. She was probably just humouring herself— giving herself a lifeline to keep living.

"She worked here for three years, and then one day she sent in her resignation saying she was leaving Guimarães, as her sister was moving to Viana do Castelo. Who knows what she was going through? And what had compelled her to leave a good job?"

"Why do you say that?" Re asked, leaning forward.

Sylvie frowned, trying to dip into her memory.

"I am not sure if it is at all relevant, but on at least two occasions, I saw an unpleasant interaction between Ana and a man. He came looking for her claiming to be her boyfriend, and they stepped out in the courtyard. I could see that Ana was angry and that she was completely uninterested in this guy. But he refused to see reason, and finally, she had to threaten to call the police. He vanished after that. But it left a sharp image in my mind."

"Would you know his name?" Re asked, feeling hopeful.

"Rod, short for Rodrigo. Not an easy face to forget either. Unpleasant character."

"That is very helpful indeed, Sylvie."

"But I never saw Ana again after she quit the job, which is a pity. And I truly hope that wherever she went, life dealt her a fair deal."

"Did she go to Viana do Castelo then?" Filipa asked eagerly.

"I believe she got a job in Porto in a wine shop. I remember asking her why she wanted to leave, and she said she wanted to be closer to her dream. I believe that she may even have left a forwarding address."

Re and Filipa glanced at each other, a light of excitement in Filipa's eyes.

"Sylvie, one final thing. Would these lines mean anything to you?

'*Where the walls listen*
to the secrets that it keeps,
But the heart lands
where the chimney speaks,'" Re read out the lines of the *lenço*.

Sylvie was thoughtful. "Come, let me show you something."

The two followed her with alacrity. As she led them from chamber to chamber, the grandeur of the palace unfolded gradually. It was a combination of rustic charm and ethnic polish. The flooring was of burnished tiles and the walls were thick grey stone, some of which were covered with magnificent rich tapestries depicting grand battle scenes. Original Chinese blue pottery and vases of varying sizes on ornate cupboards, and invaluable paintings adorned the walls. It was a beautiful palace with its very own rustic appeal and glamour.

Sylvie paused before a beautiful chamber.

"Ana used to love this palace chapel. I love it too. Just feel the energy here…"

Re could. It was a cosy chapel with amazing stained-glass windows that adorned an entire backdrop. The combination of coloured luminescent glass pictures and polished wood gave the chapel an ethereal appearance. Re quickly dipped his head and prayed, then followed the two ladies down the corridor.

It was the ceiling in the great hall that really caught Re's attention. The entire roof was a wooden marvel. Hundreds of thick and long strips of wood curved and intersected, arched and bent, to join at the multiple levels to form the most magnificent wooden boat structure Re had ever witnessed. The painting in the cafe did little justice to the elaborate woodwork, the many strands of wood that went into making an inverted conical boat. It was almost as if Re could see the representation of life in a physical model right above him. Intersecting moments, people, situations at different points in life, blending, bending and moulding of minds, to accommodate diversity, and ultimately all connected, forming the big picture of life and the universe. Re couldn't take his eyes off the fascinating structure. He quickly took a few pictures for his personal reference.

"You can see where the wooden strands touch the walls? Just look below it. You will see two big gaps in the wall… some stones missing? Well, those are actually slits, very cleverly designed into the walls to allow sound from this room and some other rooms to be heard in the duke's room. Which is how the saying goes—walls have ears and they listen," Sylvie explained with a smile. "Isn't that ingenious?"

"Absolutely!" Re agreed and Filipa endorsed this with a nod. "This is certainly 'where the walls listen to the secrets that it keeps'. But what about 'the heart lands where the chimney speaks'? The chimney would speak through the roof… like all chimneys do."

"Ana used to love to visit the roof of the palace. Surprisingly, access to the Ducal Palace roof isn't difficult at all. In fact, every lunch hour she would spend alone on the roof gazing out at the fantastic view of Guimarães, and then again in the evening before departure, when the town stretches far and wide in the setting sun and the twinkling lights. I still remember the expression on her face every single time she would descend from the roof. Awed, yet sad."

"So, if Ana had wanted to keep something for Ricardo…" Re said, contemplatively.

"…it would be on the roof," Sylvie concluded, an almost imperceptible smile on her lips. "Come let me show you the way."

She led them through the palace office to a small door. A narrow flight of steps curved in a spiral. "This will lead you to the roof. Go take a look," she offered.

Re needed no further invitation. With Filipa close at his heels, he ascended the large stone steps. Within minutes, he pushed open the door, and they were at the top of the Ducal Palace. A cold gust of wind met them on the roof, almost blowing them away.

"What a gorgeous view!" Filipa exclaimed, holding on to the jacket and backpack.

Re couldn't agree more. Below them, Guimarães spread far and wide, a mix of orange roofs and tall buildings, merging in the distance into the hills. The roof itself was a sight to see, with the multiple chimneys appearing more like candies on a cake at closer quarters, as they jutted out at strategic points from the slanting roof. It was indeed a fascinating sight. Re could understand why Ana, a heartbroken woman trying to heal, would seek solace on top of a palace amid quaint chimneys which stood around like friends, offering passive support.

"Where do you think is the gift, or whatever it was, that she kept for Avô?" Filipa wondered.

"It can't be too far from the door. I think we should check out this closest chimney. Wait—"

Right next to the door and just opposite the chimney, Re spotted the depression in the wall. It was deep and large enough for his hand to slip in. Filipa waited with bated breath as Re slid his hand in, cautiously. The wind flapped his ponytail and jacket randomly as he struggled to squeeze his fingers through the slit in the wall.

"There is something here," he said, excitement spiralling inside him. Within seconds, he extracted a small packet wrapped in thick plastic. He glanced at his companion.

Filipa stared at the parcel, running a tongue over her dry lips, suddenly afraid to touch it. Suddenly afraid to say anything. Re could gauge the state of her mind—the idea of coming face-to-face with the past for the first time could be daunting.

Re held the packet gingerly, aware that he was actually holding a piece of the *lenço* puzzle. Even a piece of history. How long had the parcel sat here, waiting patiently to be discovered? Forty years? Untouched, unopened and forgotten. Until now… What mystery was it finally going to unravel? Re's heartbeat accelerated in anticipation.

"Let's get out of this wind. With your permission, I would like to open the packet," he suggested.

"Of course. Grandpa's permission actually," she added nervously.

Re carried the box down the narrow stone stairs and into the office. They sat down at the table and Re carefully undid the wrapping. For a few seconds, both of them stared at the beautiful wooden black box, the size of Re's palm. Two exquisite hearts were engraved on the lid of the box; the artwork was so intricate and neat that Re had no doubt the box was an antique.

"It is stunning," Filipa whispered.

"There is something inside." Re opened the lid.

A single sheet of folded paper lay ensconced on a bed of cotton in the otherwise empty box. He unfolded the paper with delicate fingers, careful not to crumple the brittle, fragile sheet. The neat black handwriting had smudged in places, but it was clearly legible.

"I believe it's a letter to your Grandpa."

He handed it to her and she accepted it without a word. Re waited as she read the letter. Reality had suddenly taken on a new turn. Ana had suddenly transformed from a hearsay person and a hazy picture to a flesh and blood person, speaking to them from the past. Were they now actually going to discover the depths of her mind, traversing from the deep dark recesses to healing light? At the least, he hoped so…

At length, when Filipa glanced up, her eyes were moist and she brushed away the tears, betraying a mix of impatience and annoyance.

"It's in Portuguese. I will have to translate it for you. Give me ten minutes."

There was an air of subtle anger around her which puzzled Re—was it the effort of translation, or the letter itself, he wondered as she helped herself to a sheet of paper from the desk and scribbled hastily, often referring to the original. He waited as she gave herself up to the task with furious concentration. Finally, she handed the translated sheet to him and leaned against the chair, staring up at the white ceiling.

Dear Ricardo,

If you are reading this, it means that you followed me to Guimarães… and what can give me more pleasure than the knowledge that you care!

We parted in tears—yes, I saw yours too—and I understood your helplessness. You had to do what you did and I had to accept it. But I cannot accept that you do not love me. I know you do and that is why I sent you the lenço… I hoped that you would decipher it and come looking for me… which you did.

After I left you in Penafiel—I was heartbroken and clueless where life would lead me. I just knew that I had to move away from you… far away from you for the sake of our resolves. For the sake of my sanity… so that I wouldn't be tempted to meet you and her… I promised myself that I would only meet you if you chose to. And I will hold on to that promise, till you come and meet me.

As you may have already realized, I went to live with my sister Sofia who worked in Guimarães. Luckily, because of my love and knowledge of music and the arts, I got a job as an assistant to the manager at the Ducal Palace. Sylvie, your friend, is a great person, and has been such a warm and steady rock in my life. I threw myself into my work because I wanted to make something of myself, and I will continue to do so. Sofia and I tried to make it work, but there is now too much history between us; she and her son moved to Viana do Castelo.

I have a job offer from Porto. The father of one of my students from Penafiel, Marcelo Oliveira, happened to be here and I took him on a palace tour. He loved the tour, and was quick to offer me a manager's job at his wine outlet in Porto. I have not made any decision yet, and I am hoping that you will help me take it.

Rodrigo Tavares—if you remember him—who has always been in love with me, proposed to me. But I love and have loved only one man, and no other has any role in my life. So of course, I said no. I hope that makes you happy.

Three years have passed since I last met you... and I have waited all this while for you to come to me... I hope that wait is now over.

Forever yours,
Ana

By the rise of the bridge,
on the wind of the river,
Through the dark of the cellar,
through the deep swirling colour.
When the journey ends,
the earnest heart calls
for the harvest to pile
on the story on the walls.

"So, she found the first parcel. That is good news," Pedro spoke on the phone in a low tone. "The *lenços* are important to us, so I hope no one was keeping watch or was following them? Anything suspicious at all?"

Pedro listened in for a few minutes, then switched off the phone, a twitch of a smile hinting at his satisfaction. The plan was off to a good start. Or at least he hoped it was. He, of all people, was the first to know how horribly wrong things could go. He had seen too much of it in his lifetime, and earnestly prayed for success this time. Poor Ricardo. He had never really heeded anyone's advice, always gallant, and sometimes fallaciously following his gut instinct. But he had suffered and paid the price for his decisions, and only he, Pedro, knew how much. The lengthy solitary evening hours in the study gazing at her photo, the unbridled pinch of longing and desire in his heart and on the premature lines of his handsome face, but never a word of repentance emerging from his lips. Abiding by duty, but betraying the heart. But in the end, dying with her name on his lips.

A sense of anger and frustration surged in him. Such a waste of a good relationship… and now after his death, there was still no peace. In fact, matters just got more complicated, urgent and tumultuous. With Senhorita Filipa sucked into it all rather unceremoniously, and dangerously. But wasn't it better even *after* death than *never*? A small voice niggled at the back of his mind. Better, yes, much better now than never…

Tiago entered the room, with the phone in his hand.

"The police would like to know where Senhorita Filipa is."

"I told them already. She isn't here. She isn't answering her phone and her car is still parked in the garage. It is obvious that she doesn't want to be found for a while. Give her some time… she is grieving."

"The police don't understand grief. They only understand proof," Tiago spoke stoically.

The secretary was still in his formal coat, and the expression in his eyes, from behind the black square-framed glasses, was grim.

"What proof?" Pedro asked, curious.

"Apparently they found the weapon that took Senhor Ricardo's life."

"And?" Pedro frowned.

"It was his own walking stick."

"So?"

"It has her fingerprints on them."

Pedro stared at the secretary for long moments, a startled expression on his usually impassive face.

"She wouldn't kill her own grandfather, she loved him too much," the butler brushed it off.

"You and I know it. The police don't understand love either, only proof," Tiago was relentless. "However, I agree that this is a mistake. She is an elected mayor of Penafiel. Trusted and respected by leading luminaries of Portugal. She is on the verge of launching a world symbol tomorrow at Basílica Santa Luzia. The police would have to rethink their strategy. They cannot arrest Senhorita Filipa, she is too important a figure."

Pedro reflected, "It is up to us to see that till she is ready to take up her duties again, we run the show, as effectively as we can, and right up to the event tomorrow."

Tiago nodded. "I am on it. She had called a meeting around noon, and I will take it forward."

"I will join you for it," Pedro added. "And Officer Stefan Weiss."

"Who is that?" Tiago frowned.

"Someone Senhorita Filipa has appointed to oversee the event and to be there for us."

"We don't need an outsider to help us with our event. We are perfectly capable," Tiago insisted, his frown deepening.

"I agree, but this is a special case and too much has already disturbed the *senhorita*. Plus, we follow instructions. And with the *senhorita* not here to resolve last minute issues, let's agree to welcome Officer Stefan Weiss amongst us."

A maid entered the room just then.

"Officer Stefan Weiss is here," she announced.

The butler and secretary exchanged a quick glance, and the latter shook his head in exasperation.

"Bring him in," Pedro confirmed.

The door swung open and a man stepped into the cosy interiors of the cafe.

"Santiago?" the man asked, curtly.

The old man glanced up from his newspaper, at the tall stranger with an impassive face. Sunglasses hid his eyes, but Santiago could guess that behind the glasses the eyes were cold and calculating.

"What is it? What do you want?" the cafe owner demanded.

"I'd like to share a glass of de Cruz wine with you," the stranger said.

"Now? In the morning, when the world drinks coffee?" the old man frowned.

"Yes, now!" The stranger placed a bottle of wine on the table and upturned an ice cream glass on the counter.

Santiago noticed that his hand was gloved. He didn't like this stranger barging in with his strange request, bordering on arrogance. *What was all this about?* he wondered, a slight twinge of anxiety pricking him. He glanced at this phone, which was charging at the corner of the table. Could he reach it in time? Sudden perspiration broke out on his forehead.

The stranger poured the red wine in the glass and pushed it towards Santiago. "Drink it!" he ordered.

"Look, I am not much of a wine drinker. Tell me what it is that you want. What is all this about?" Santiago hedged.

"Drink the wine!" the stranger ordered, in a slow and deliberate manner.

Santiago hesitated. The man's tone was haughty and unflinching. The old man tried to hide the rising panic inside him, as his heart began racing with a sense of foreboding. He picked up the glass to stall for time.

"At least tell me what this is about. Do you need money? Is that it? I can give you as much as you want," the old man offered.

The man thrust his hand forward. It was covered with a handkerchief and a gun peeped ominously from underneath it. The expression on the man's face was etched in stone, and a single muscle twitched in his jaw.

"You are Santiago? An AC before the Rebellion? This is retribution. Now drink!"

Santiago paled. His eyes flung wildly to the door, hoping that someone would enter. But the stranger had flipped the OPEN sign to CLOSED.

"You can't force me to drink anything, or shoot me. We are in the middle of a busy Square and there are people around," he stammered.

"Try me. I will count to three. Either you drink or I shoot you! The choice is yours. One…" The man's voice was cold as ice.

Santiago sent a desperate plea to heaven.

Re sat in the car and stared at the beautiful *lenço*, feeling its softness and energy throbbing in his hand. The same hearts bordered round the four sides of the soft linen as in the first *lenço*, with elaborate figures of a boat, train and a butterfly, and the Portuguese sentences woven in colourful threads, plaited with love and affection. A deep yearning reached out to him, crossing the distance of decades, as he held the *lenço*. Sentences which Re knew now, were not just hints to Ana's whereabouts, but her hopes disguised as clues. Received on 25th April 1982, five years after the first *lenço* reached Ricardo.

"Here is the translation," Filipa offered him a paper.

"'By the rise of the bridge,
on the wind of the river,
Through the dark of the cellar,
through the deep swirling colour.
When the journey ends,
the earnest heart calls
for the harvest to pile
on the story on the walls.
Come find it… waiting for you…'" Re read aloud.

He paused as he allowed the words to sink in—descriptive, evocative images of colourful nature—a flowing river under a bridge, and people engaged in harvesting in traditional clothes—rose before his eyes, and the odour of vineyards floated up to tickle his senses. The scene was serene and beckoning...

"Beautiful words and imagery, but since we already know that she left for Porto, I don't think we should second-guess her destination," Re suggested.

"Quite right. In any case, *'dark of the cellar'* and *'deep swirling colour'* definitely indicate a wine connection."

"Assuming she did go to Porto, we should ideally head to the city. So, how far to Porto from here?"

"Around 45 minutes."

Re nodded and turned the ignition of the car. As they headed out of Guimarães, the detective sent out a mental thank you to the spirit of the town. It had not let them down. Apart from its historical significance, the town had offered him a breakthrough in their trail of the *lenços*. Re had learned so much more about the mysterious Ana too. He could imagine her spending her time on the roof of the Paço dos Duques in the company of the 39 chimneys, perhaps sewing the *lenço*, pouring her heart out into each stitch. In his mind's eye, he could visualize a fiery, passionate, and beautiful woman, torn between decisions and desires... whose only big mistake in life was to fall madly, irrefutably and irrevocably in love with a married man. And for that, she had unapologetically suffered.

The road was a scenic long stretch between hills, with the grey and white clouds hanging low overhead, almost touching the road and horizon in front.

"Is it normal for a person to leave a forwarding address?" Filipa frowned, as she glanced at the slip of paper on which Sylvie had copied a Porto address.

"Remember that Ana did not wish to vanish from Ricardo's life. On the contrary, she wanted to be found, and she needed to make it easy for him to find her, whenever he was ready. So, it makes perfect sense to me."

"But to keep the forwarding address for so many years? Wouldn't the office clear out old irrelevant stuff?"

"I believe it must have been in Ana's file as an old employee. Does it matter? I am grateful we have an address—it saves us so much time."

"That's true, of course."

A light drizzle began, but the sun streamed in through the branches turning the leaves to gold. It was a surreal sight, the entire landscape dappled in shades of luminescent gold. Re took it as a sign as he drove through the golden countryside towards Porto. It was as if the universe was sending him a message that he was on the right track. He shot Filipa a glance. Her face was half-turned to the open window, her eyes closed, her curls flapping with the wind, but Re could tell that she wasn't sleeping.

"You didn't react to Ana's letter," he pointed out, softly.

"I didn't because I thought it was a pathetic letter," she responded, sitting up straight in her seat. "It was the letter of a woman desperately seeking attention, like a spoilt child who can't get her way. In my honest opinion, she had no business trying to lure Grandpa. Especially since he had made his choice, and especially since they had parted ways for good."

"Don't you think you are being a bit too harsh on Ana?" Re frowned. "She was a woman in love, she would think with her heart, not her head, don't you agree?"

"That does not excuse her for trying to wreck Avô's marriage, when his choice was made. She was trying to disrupt our household. What did she really expect? That Avô would go waltzing to her, leaving Grandma and the estate? She must have truly been blind, then. Love cannot be forced. Love cannot be 'managed'. It has to be spontaneous and exclusive. I believe that Ana was fully aware of this, and yet she deliberately pursued Avô with the aim of complicating his life."

"Wow," Re whistled. "You have Ana all sorted out in your head."

"I do… I think I do… whatever… let's not discuss Ana. I wish Grandpa had never told me about her!"

A little perplexed, Re allowed silence to slip between them. Filipa's reactions were a little over the top, he felt. She seemed determined to regard Ana as the enemy. Was she placing the blame squarely on Ana, to protect herself from more hurt? Perhaps it was easier to excuse her own grandfather for his actions? Or was it something deeper? More personal?

Officer Stefan Weiss sat in Filipa's office, and glanced at the list of invitees and the tasks to be implemented. He had had a good meeting with Pedro and Tiago, who had brought him up to date with the details of the event. At around 4:00 PM, Filipa had prearranged a staff meeting of the county and the estate. The next morning, a final checklist visit to Basílica Santa Luzia was also planned along with the mayor of Viana do Castelo. He was slowly getting a grip on the entire event. It was an amazingly well-planned affair, with attention afforded to the minutest detail. The actual ceremony was to begin at sharp 5:00 at the basilica, and the general public and audience would be admitted into the courtyard half an hour before the ceremony. The gold symbol of peace would be unveiled by the five mayors of five counties who were especially arriving for the launch, and carnations would be dropped by helicopter.

The event would be broadcast live for all the world to follow and appreciate. Portugal would be the proud presenter of a new world symbol of peace, which would be displayed on all government sites, documents and monuments. The message was clear. Portugal meets the world in peace, and invites other countries to do the same. It was a first step towards global peace. Filipa must be particularly proud of what she was about to achieve, Stefan thought. It was a pity tragedy had struck so close to home, and that other matters had compounded the situation.

The door of the office opened, and Tiago walked in with a police officer. He was stocky with thin brown hair and a clean-shaven pleasant face.

"Officer Weiss, this is Officer Frederico Lusa from the Penafiel Police," Tiago announced. "The officer would like to talk to you about tomorrow's security arrangements at the Santa Luzia, which they would carry out with the help of the local police staff."

Stefan's eyes widened in surprise. "Lusa?" he exclaimed.

"Stefan!"

The police officers looked at each other in surprise, then shook hands warmly. Tiago glanced from one to the other, thrust back his black-framed glasses, and then discreetly exited the room.

"It's been a long time my friend," Lusa smiled.

"It has," Stefan agreed.

"But what are you doing here?"

"I am overseeing the event tomorrow, in an unofficial capacity, of course."

"You mean in the absence of Senhorita Filipa," Lusa added.

"I believe so. She is incapacitated with grief, as you may already be aware." Stefan chose his words carefully.

"We have damaging evidence against Filipa," Lusa said, directly. "I wish she had come up to us and talked."

"What kind of evidence?"

"We found the murder weapon—Ricardo's walking stick—and it has her fingerprints on it."

"You and I both know that evidence can be planted. She's his granddaughter for God's sake. She wouldn't do such a horrendous thing. There was no need," Stefan explained patiently.

"Although I would agree with you in principle, until evidence shows otherwise I will have to continue to search for and arrest her."

"Just imagine what she must be going through. This top-notch event planned tomorrow, and just the morning before, her grandfather is murdered. Even assuming that she did do it, think about the timing of the death if nothing else. It's all wrong! She wouldn't sabotage her own event with such a gruesome act," Stefan pursued.

Lusa was silent for a moment, as the words sunk in. "You are right about that. She wouldn't disrupt her own event, not with deliberate murder."

"There you are!" Stefan felt a sliver of triumph.

"But here's something that is confusing—she was spotted in Guimarães a short while ago. She went to visit her grandfather's old friend, Santiago. Not long after that, he was found dead. How is *that* for timing?"

"*Mein Gott!*" Stefan exclaimed. "What happened?"

"He was slumped over his counter, with a glass of wine in his hand. We are assuming the wine contained poison, because his mouth was frothing."

Stefan was silent. Re and Filipa must have been together, and must have visited Santiago to uncover details of Ana. Had someone followed them? Who would have killed Santiago, and why?

"Any motive? Did anyone see anything suspicious?" Stefan asked.

"My colleagues are still at the crime scene, questioning and trying to find the details. But people distinctly remember spotting Filipa accompanied by a ponytailed man, entering Santiago's coffee shop."

"Not enough evidence there. Could be just a coincidence, or someone is deliberately framing Senhorita Filipa. Come on, you have to agree with me," Stefan cajoled the other officer.

"Although you could be right, I prefer staying neutral right now. Not to mention that I am curious—if she is grieving, what is she doing in Guimarães, meeting people? And who is the man with her? The police are on the lookout for Senhorita Filipa, and will take her into custody once we find her. Now about tomorrow—we have plans for a security tie-up with the local police. It's a big event, and we don't want to take any risks, especially given what happened today."

"Let me invite Pedro and Tiago from the team to understand the details, so that we are all on the same page," Stefan said, and Officer Lusa nodded.

Chapter
7

Re drove down a palm tree-lined road, with the frothy Atlantic Ocean splashing across the rocks and the promenade. The charm of a coastal seaside town on the right side of the road and the rising cluster of colourful hillside houses on the left gave Porto the feel of having the best of both worlds. On a pleasant evening, with a happier mindset, this drive would be a perfect getaway for relaxed dreaming.

Now, as Re turned into an inner alley and combed the lane for parking, all he could do was focus on what lay ahead. Would they finally know Ana's whereabouts, or would they journey deeper into her mysterious life without actually meeting her?

Luckily, the detective found a parking spot just outside the Praça da Ribeira, a historical landmark, the oldest square from the medieval ages. They walked down the paved path, past narrow cobbled alleyways, squashed between buildings with wrought iron balconies, coloured railings, attractive facades and eighteenth-century townhouses. The three-storied iconic fountain from the 1780s in the Square displayed the Portugal

Coat of Arms, and the Square opened up to the river front. It was like stepping into a world where the river, land and houses merged into a splash of gentle colours and shapes.

"I had forgotten how beautiful A Ribeira is." Filipa sighed. "Ribeira means 'riverside' in Portuguese, and is such an apt name for this beautiful Square. Grandpa would often drive to this riverside quarter of Porto for his business—Porto being an important commercial centre for the wine trade—and I always accompanied him. I am particularly fond of this part of the old town, one of the liveliest and most picturesque areas of Porto. It is surprising that life got so busy that I am actually returning to this part of Porto after a couple of years."

"Well, I was here a week ago, staring out at the Rio Douro for hours, watching the sunset and drinking wine to drown my sorrows!" Re grimaced.

"Ah… That comment is a direct invitation to rouse curiosity and questions," Filipa remarked, flashing him a side glance. "Want to talk about it?"

"Perhaps later," Re grinned. "Let's take the Douro taxi across to Gaia."

People were lining up for the taxi, and Re and Filipa joined the queue. The cafes, bars, and restaurants with timber tables and fine dining on the bank were packed to the gills with tourists. Two guitarists were performing some original Portuguese songs, and their music filled the air with charm and cheer. A couple of girls broke into a spontaneous dance, and the tourists encouraged them with claps.

The boat taxi whirred to a halt by the bank and the passengers stepped off the gangway. Re and Filipa strode to a far corner of the boat and settled down for the short 5-minute Ribeira to Gaia bank ride. The blue-grey river was at eye level, and the reflections from the glass doubled the play of the choppy waves.

As the boat moved, slowly cutting across the waters to the other bank, Re idly allowed the chatter of the tourists to take over his mind. How excited and happy they appeared. So completely in the moment of discovery. For a few minutes, Re was glad to let go of the tension which was building up inside him. How precious it was to have an uneventful life with your family and friends, even predictable. His profession had offered him multiple opportunities to witness the many disruptions in life and the havoc they could wreak on one's sanity. It actually took the disruptions to really appreciate the mundane. You realize what a blessing it was, when your life is tossed around in a tragedy or unforeseen cruel circumstances. Yes, the mundane, the routine and the regular was good, he thought with a sigh. He glanced at his companion and found her staring far across the distance, lost in her own world of contemplation.

The boat slowed down and docked on the Gaia bank, and the tourists clattered on the gangway. Re whipped out his phone and turned on the GPS.

"We head left. Keep a sharp lookout for the Wine & Tapas Shop," he said.

Filipa nodded and fell in step as they walked briskly down the broad promenade. The picturesque street was lined with historical stores with elaborate facades, and restaurants facing the river. The promenade was teeming with tourists, shopping at the local flea market. Re read the names of the shops as they progressed down the promenade, until finally, tucked into a corner, he spotted the Wine & Tapas shop.

"Still standing strong." Filipa sounded relieved.

A lone young man stood behind a counter, in a low dimmed oblong room. Racks and racks of port wine of all ages lined the walls. He welcomed Re and Filipa with a warm friendly smile.

"What can I do for you? Are you here for the wine-tasting?" he asked, pleasantly.

"Actually, we are looking for an Ana Ribeiro, who worked in this shop in the '70s. Would you, by any chance, know anything about her?" Re enquired.

"In the '70s! Unfortunately, I wasn't born then!" The young man laughed. "We bought the shop rather recently too, so I wouldn't know the earlier owner either. However, I do know someone who could help you. Marcus—the old manager of this shop—who luckily still works here, may be of some assistance to you." The youngster seemed to be enjoying his own set of contradictions.

A few minutes later, a frail-looking hunched man with thinning hair and spectacles appeared from the interiors of the store.

"Marcus, these tourists are looking for Ana Ribeiro—you often talk about her, don't you?" the young man said.

"Ah Ana, of course, I remember her," Marcus smiled. "A sweet young lady, so hardworking, and learnt so much on the job. When she came here, she had little knowledge of wines, but when she quit the job, she was ready to open her own shop. A warm girl, that one, but so unhappy. She worked like a horse at the shop, but during lunch hour, she would go out and sit staring at the Douro—her image is still fresh in my mind—her curly hair blowing with the wind, least concerned about passers-by who threw her curious and interested looks. Often, I saw her work on a *lenço,* and I teased her about it, asking her the name of her beau, but she merely blushed and never told me her secret."

Filipa shot Re a glance and shook her head almost imperceptibly, pursing her lips in disdain.

"How long did she work here?" she asked.

"I believe it was more than five years. Steady gal, and enthusiastic about a lot of things. On some weekends, she would work at the Livraria Lello—the old bookstore—and some weekends, she would be an assistant at the Casa São Roque Museum, because she loved art, she said. She even joined a tile-making workshop, and became so good that she volunteered to help with some restoration work on tiles at one of the sites."

Re made a mental note of it. Somehow, he felt that it was an important detail. Versatile Ana—books, art, culture—a woman of refined tastes, using her time well, and always keeping herself occupied… if only to be able to forget Ricardo? Or to be able to live for him? Earnest desire, but a fate which seemed just out of reach…

"But poor lady was badly hounded by this rogue of a man," Marcus continued. "He kept turning up at the oddest hours, and it was obvious she did not wish to meet him. I even told him so once, but he was rude and told me that she was a cheat, and to be careful of her. I threw him out of the shop and warned him never to set foot here again. I believe that it was because of him that she eventually left Porto despite being settled here. Boss was unhappy when she left. We were all very fond of her, there was something appealing about her... she *cared*... for all of us. I kind of mentioned this to the man who came looking for her some years ago."

Re was startled. "Someone came looking for her? How long ago was that?"

"Perhaps seven, eight years ago."

"Did he give a name?"

"Not that I remember. He did ask me if Ana had left some packet for a friend, an article, and I said 'No'."

"Do you recall his appearance?"

"Middle-aged, tall, wore a jacket. Nothing out of the ordinary."

"Do you have any idea where Ana went after she left Porto?"

"I believe she was considering a job offer in some school in Amarante. She felt that dabbling in music and arts would do her good. I do hope that you find her. Could you please wait a minute?" Marcus turned around and disappeared into an inner room. When he returned a few minutes later, he was holding a small folded paper bag.

"She forgot to take these when she left. They are some letters and bills. Do give this to her, they are her belongings. I continued to keep them in the hope that she may drop by to say hello."

Re experienced a surge of excitement—what a piece of luck! To actually be able to read something written by Ana herself, and some of her correspondence, was a big jump in their investigation. He hoped that he would find something of value in the material.

"Thank you. You have been a huge help," the detective remarked.

"When you meet Ana, tell her I think of her often. Tell her to come visit me soon."

"We will," Re assured, with a smile. The old man's affection for his former sales assistant was heartwarming.

He and Filipa stepped out of the shop, into the street, which was milling with tourists.

"What a sweet old man, and so fond of Ana," Re commented.

"Completely enamoured of her," Filip agreed, drily. "I am famished. Let's grab a bite."

"Yes, me too. And we'll sit in a quiet spot to check these bills out. What luck to have found some written material. Good job, Marcus."

They found a snack joint under a white canopy and ordered *tapas* and two glasses of wine. Re opened the paper packet impatiently. There were two letters inside, and a bunch of bills clipped together with a pin.

"Letters sent to her by one single person. They are in Portuguese, you will have to read them for me." Re pushed the letters to Filipa.

He sensed a reluctance in her, and he glanced at her in surprise.

"It is her private mail. Are we allowed to read it?" she hedged.

"Ethically, no. But practically, yes, if you want to solve the mystery of the *lenços* and trace the enigmatic Ana Ribeiro," Re replied, wryly. "You don't need to feel guilty—all's fair in deciphering a mystery, *ma chérie*."

"Ok, if you say so," Filipa shrugged. "But for the record, I am doing this under protest."

"*Mais bien*, I understand." Re shook his head mentally, in mild exasperation.

He was finding it a little difficult to comprehend Filipa. She was an intelligent and determined young lady, with presence of mind. Her energy was strong and forceful, and for the most part, Re found it positive. She was reasonable too, except when it came to Ana. It was as if Filipa had made her mind up about the woman, and had decided that she would offer Ana no chance for redemption—she would continue to hate her.

He sank into his chair, a picture of forced patience, as the *senhorita* scanned through the two letters.

"Well?" he quirked an eyebrow.

"Nothing noteworthy," Filipa declared with a shrug. "It's just a job offer from the Tapas & Wine Shop for Ana, when she was in Guimarães. It's brief and concise, requesting Ana to join as soon as she could. The second letter is Ana's acceptance."

Re tried to curb his disappointment, as he took the letters from Filipa. Ana's handwriting was curvy and slanted, like in the other letter she had written to Ricardo. He had hoped that there would be some clue in the letters, but they were a dead end. He turned more hopefully to the bills. As he flicked through them, he was suddenly swamped by an uncharacteristic urge to sit in a quiet corner, away from prying eyes, out of respect to the person.

"I will check the bills a little later," he concluded aloud. "Let's eat first".

"Oh?" Filipa searched his face and smirked. "A belated sense of guilt?"

Re was surprised by her perceptiveness. "Belated sense of respect, perhaps. A detective cannot afford to feel guilty. It would jeopardize the journey to the truth."

A half-smile lifted her lips, and she nodded. They tucked into the tapas in silence for a few minutes.

"This wine, the de Cruz wine, comes from Freixo de Espada à Cinta. A relatively young wine, but it has taken Portugal by storm. And I feel proud to say that Joana de Cruz was my mentor for some months, and I learnt a lot from her. In fact, it was her dream, her symbol, that we plan to launch tomorrow at Basílica Santa Luzia. A universal symbol of peace that we plan to offer to the world. It is just so incredibly sad that neither Joana nor Avô will be present to witness this momentous event of our lives."

"Joana de Cruz?"

"She passed away a few months ago—a sudden short illness. My only solace is that she knew our plan, and was initially a part of it too. So, I'm happy that she died knowing her dream would come true."

Both were silent for a few minutes. Re stared out at the Douro, serene in the early evening sun. The traditional red and black wooden '*rabelo* boats', that originally transported barrels of wine from the inland to Porto, now swayed gently in the water, their oars idle, a sharp contrast to the wild green grass and moss on the bank bordered with tiny red flowers. Re could read their names—*Distinto, Quinta da Foz, Ferrão, Porto Cruz*… representations of an era long gone, and now serving more as a reminder of traditional times. Across the river, the Cais da Ribeira, the waterfront spread like a patchwork quilt of sunlit conical shapes and lines—orange roofs with contrasting white, red, blue and green facades of the historic buildings with colourful terraced houses… In the near distance, the Ponte de Dom Luís was a reminder of the coexistence of the ethnic with the modern.

"Difficult to believe that we are in the oldest part of Porto, and the most medieval," he said reflectively. "But I *can* imagine Ana sitting by the river and working on her embroidery."

"You are a romantic," Filipa observed.

"And you are not?"

"No. I don't have time for such foolhardy emotions. There is too much to do in this world, lots of people to help. In any case, I don't believe in love, I mean I don't believe in love that lasts all your life, and love that you cannot live without. All that to me is just glorified sentiment, candy floss that advertising men have created to fool women."

"How cynical you are, *ma chérie*." Re was surprised.

"Only practical. And now that I have witnessed how Ana frittered away her life sewing *lenços* for a man who was never hers and would never be hers, I am more than ever convinced that love is a wasted emotion. It misleads you in pursuing an illusion, it drags you through life like a sack of unused potatoes!"

"*Mon dieu!* Never heard of that expression before." Re's lips quivered with suppressed laughter. "But would you not call Ana's love, love?"

"No. It is obsession. She couldn't be with Grandpa, so she became obsessed with the *idea* of being with him. She convinced herself that she was in love."

"For years and decades"

"All her life… keeping her illusion of love warm on the remnant of an obsessive memory."

"And yet Ricardo's last words were—*I love Ana.*" Re sighed.

Filipa preferred to maintain silence, and Re assumed that her venting had concluded. He whipped out the message of the *lenço,* and reread it aloud.

"'*By the rise of the bridge,*
on the wind of the river,
Through the dark of the cellar,
through the deep swirling colour.
When the journey ends,
the earnest heart calls
for the harvest to pile
on the story on the walls.'

"*The rise of the bridge on the wind of the Douro river,* we have already visited the shop where she worked and sold wine. What knowledge did we gain from this visit? That she stitched another of her *lenços,* worked at the bookstore

Lirvraria Lello over the weekends, and attended some tile workshops, and volunteered to restore some of the tiles of a monument."

"Also, that her friend or whoever he was—Rod—came looking for her here, and created a scene again."

"And that somebody—some stranger—also enquired if she had left a packet behind. A very strange question indeed, considering it is only now, by following the trail of the *lenços,* that we have begun to fathom Ana's pattern of actions. She left a gift for him at Guimarães, but is there a gift for Ricardo in Porto?"

"There has to be. I've been thinking… Could it be a tile that she left for Grandpa? *Azulejos* are a big thing in Portugal, as you are probably already aware. Porto is full of them—on church walls, house facades, windows, doors, and shops—you name it. The blue azulejos came from the more traditional art form, borrowed from Spain. If I had to make something special for a lover, I would probably make a very special, personalised tile for him as a gift."

"You could be right. Which is why perhaps she actually did attend a tile workshop. But where could she have hidden it from prying eyes?" Re wondered.

"*When the journey ends,*
the earnest heart calls
for the harvest to pile
on the story on the walls.'" Filipa was reflective.

"When life's journey ends, your heart calls out to God… the cathedral? I seem to remember, too, that the cathedral boasts massive azulejos, I mean really amazing. It is located in the Batalha municipality, built on a high rise near the old walls that once protected the town—and it is one of the most important religious monuments of the city. The São Bento station also has some amazing tilework. But my mind seems more inclined towards the cathedral, because I particularly remember this one huge panel of a farmer hosing his hay in a field on the upper terrace."

"So you mean," Re summarized. "Ana was assisting with some tile restoration work at the cathedral, and she may have added a small tile of her own to the panel?"

They both stared at each other as the possibility loomed larger than thought.

"There's one way to find out. I saw a bill paid to an Elsa's Tile Workshop. There's a number too. Want to make a quick call?" Re extracted the yellowed bill and handed it to Filipa. "Use my phone."

Filipa nodded and placed the call, as Re waited in anticipation.

"*Olá? Essa é a Elsa?*" Filipa began and went on in rapid Portuguese. She spoke for some minutes, and listened for a few more, nodding animatedly, and smiling profusely.

Re chuckled mentally—at least something about Ana made Filipa smile.

At length, she cut the call and turned to the detective, handing his phone back to him.

"Well?" Re asked impatiently.

"You were right. It was at Elsa's that Ana did the workshop many years ago. Elsa remembered, because she was in touch with Ana for a short while, and then suddenly Ana went quiet, so Elsa was concerned if Ana was okay. I said I didn't know, but I hoped so."

Re nodded, waiting to hear more.

"She said that it was during the workshop that she made a special tile for her 'loved one', and Elsa helped her make it. She said it was one of the most touching sights of her life— watching Ana make that tile, with eyes moist and a sad smile on her lips. And she thought that it was a very sweet gesture on Ana's part; she hoped that her lover would appreciate what she did for him, and what she had suffered for him."

"Phew… that's a lot of Ana championing," Re remarked.

"A little too much," Filipa snorted. "But we were right. She did leave an azulejo for Grandpa."

Sudden bustle at the end of the street caught Re's attention. Uniformed police clattered towards the Wine & Tapas Shop, and entered the shop that he and Filipa had just exited.

"Filipa, put on your sun glasses and a scarf. It's time to leave this place…" the detective spoke urgently, rising from his seat, and dropping some euros on the table. "Just walk straight to the Douro taxi casually, and get on the boat. I believe that the nature of our investigative journey has just changed… for some strange reason, you are now a wanted person!"

Chapter
8

The water taxi glided smoothly away from the bank, rapidly increasing its distance across the Douro. Re sensed an uncharacteristic sadness as the ancient quay covered with green moss, the rocks bordering the bank in geometric shapes, and the *rabelos* whose idle pedals dipped and danced in the blue-green Douro, turned into a picturesque, almost still painting from the past. The throbbing energy of the present dimmed… *this was how the present froze and became the past. Instantly, with every passing second,* Re thought.

From his mobile vantage point, Re could still catch some activity at the wine shop. How quickly the police had traced Filipa to Porto, and to the Wine Shop. Strange, given that not a soul knew about their whereabouts, not even Pedro. *How, then, was it possible?* he wondered, pushing his glasses back, and zipping up his black jacket. Unless… Re paused in his thinking. Could the police have broadcast a news flash about the VP of Quinta de Monteiro on TV? Had Marcus seen it and hastened to inform the police? That seemed to be the logical explanation. But it also spelled bad news, Re

realized. If the police had broadcast Filipa's photographs, she
could be recognized, which meant that movement for them
would now be difficult and restricted.

As soon as the boat docked, Re and Filipa disembarked
and headed to the Praça da Ribeira. Re knew that the
cathedral wasn't far, but walking would eat into their precious
time. Filipa took the wheel, expertly manoeuvring the car
through the alleys and shortcuts. Within ten minutes, they
arrived at the imposing ninth-century Sé do Porto Cathedral.
Filipa found parking by the colourful rows of buildings at
the bottom of the cathedral. The two of them hastened up
the incline towards the top of the cathedral—which looked
like a fortress—passing a magnificent statue of a soldier. As
Filipa led Re inside, the detective admired the magnificent
architecture which was a blend of the Romanesque, Gothic
and Baroque styles. The archways, the display of gold and
light, and then further on into the interiors, the impressive
azulejos which adorned the towering walls of the cathedral.

"It's breath-taking!" he whistled.

"Wait till you see the cloister and the upper cloister
promenade." Filipa smiled.

She couldn't have been more right. The fourteenth-
century cloister displayed a decoration of detailed blue tile
panels, depicting scenes from the bible. It was like walking
through a surreal conical tunnel of gothic arches, reflective
blue figures, landscapes, and rough stone pillars. But when
they climbed the stairs and arrived at the open square terrace
which overlooked the courtyard below, Re was dazzled. From

the centre, the arches of the cloister below formed a square frame, like an antique garland around an open courtyard.

The pleasant evening light fell on the azulejos that bedecked two sides of the four walls of the massive second level of the cathedral. The sheer magnitude of the blue tile-work took his breath away. Massive panel after panel depicted daily-life scenes of the countryside, with trees, animals, birds and human figures in the fields. Ladies walking in the countryside, men resting on the banks of rivers, hunting scenes, and gentlemen in flowing coats… the imagery was fascinating, and a blend of themes. This was the art of storytelling through pictures at its best and most complex, with an intense amount of detailing that probably even a paint brush couldn't capture. Re was enthralled by the manifestation of art on the walls. From where they stood, the city spread like a colourful chessboard, the Douro river shimmering and gliding between the banks.

"Gorgeous, isn't it?" Filipa couldn't hide the pride in her voice.

"Beautiful," Re agreed. "If Ana had to add an azulejo to these vast landscapes, it would have to be at the bottom of the scene, where she could have had easy access, but where it would also be inconspicuous. Likewise, if it has been added on, it is probably bound to sound hollow, so our best recourse would be to begin tapping the bottom row of tiles. Let's begin at opposite ends."

Filipa nodded and walked to the farthest end of the promenade. The next 15 minutes, they worked in silence. Re tapped, pressed and nudged every single inch of the azulejos, part of his brain admiring the skill and the craft of the tile work, the other part marvelling at the patience it must have required. Finally, they both arrived from opposite ends in the middle of a panel.

"No luck!" Filipa sounded disappointed. "I was so sure that it was a tile she had left for Grandpa."

Re nodded, sharing her emotion. He extracted the translated message from his jacket and reread it. "Perhaps we interpreted it wrong. Let's read it again… '*When the journey ends, the earnest heart calls for the harvest to pile on the story on the walls.*'

"Wait," he said suddenly. "Did you not say that São Bento station has similar azulejos?"

Filipa nodded, appearing a little puzzled.

"This line—'*When the journey ends…*'—where does a journey end in our normal travels? At a station! Perhaps it is not the journey of life, as we assumed, but a simple train trip?"

"Yes, of course, you could be right—there are battle scenes on the station walls, but on the top, almost close to the high ceiling, one can see a depiction of all kinds of vehicles." Filipa's brown eyes began to shine. "Yes, perhaps it *is* São Bento!"

They stared at each other for some minutes, contemplating their next move. Then, with quick tacit understanding, they clattered down the stone stairs, past the gothic archways through the cloister, and into the main temple. Re quickly closed his eyes and prayed, as was his habit. Then he followed Filipa out into the open. Portugal spread far and wide on one side of the hill, a rolling cluster of rust and orange coloured roofs. Grey clouds were now gathering low over the Douro, and far away, thunder rumbled ominously.

"Better to wear your sunglasses and a scarf," Re admonished. "We don't want people to recognize you."

The *senhorita* nodded and wrapped a soft white scarf around her head; she tagged on her sunglasses.

Re and Filipa walked briskly down the hill towards Almeida Garrett Square. Rows and rows of buildings with red and blue facades and windows extended along the left side of the road. Right ahead, loomed the iconic and historic São Bento station, the evening light creating a halo around the monument.

The moment Re stepped into the massive interior foyer of the station, he sensed the vibrant energy. On the left side, huge windows formed the entire wall of the foyer. On the opposite three sides, blue tile azulejos covered the walls from top to bottom. Battle scenes, moments from Portuguese royal history, scenes of country life, the famous Douro vineyards, watermill work, and even the iconic transfer of Port wine in a *rabelo* boat were depicted in the most exquisite detailing. The ceiling in cream yellow was bordered by frescoes, a natural mellow light pervading the foyer.

"Twenty thousand tin-glazed ceramic tiles by Jorge Colaço—it took eleven years to complete the murals. Can you imagine it?" Filipa spoke, wonder in her voice as she glanced around her. "This station never fails to stun me. One of the most beautiful in the world. Basically, the architecture was inspired by nineteenth-century Paris. José Marques da

Silva, the architect, designed the stone facade and roof of the station along the lines of Parisian architecture."

"Wasn't there a legend attached to São Bento? Something about a nun… I seem to have read it somewhere."

"That's right. It's kind of a sad story, actually. On this exact spot of the São Bento station, years ago, was the convent of the Benedictine nuns of Avé Maria. At that time, there were 55 nuns and about 105 staff members in the convent. I think it was around 1834 that a decree was passed by Joaquim António de Aguiar, to remove all religious male orders, and to confiscate the properties. That is why he was known as the 'monks' killer'. No new swearing in was allowed and in any case, religious female orders were struggling to survive. The decree stated that the property would be confiscated after the last nun died. The last nun of the convent of the Benedictine nuns of Avé Maria died in 1892, almost 58 years after the order, and only then could São Bento be constructed. But legend says that the last nun still haunts the São Bento station, and in the quiet hours, people can still hear her saying her prayers."

Re was quiet, sensing the energy of the place. Perhaps on a quiet morning, before the crowds milled the station, he would be able to hear the murmur of prayers echoing in the magnificent foyer of the station.

"Quite a story. In a way, I would understand why Ana would choose São Bento for her gift—she may have felt that it symbolises her own journey, her own haunting story of love and loss. Perhaps she found herself relating with the story of the nuns, who were doomed for extinction, through no fault of theirs."

"And perhaps haunt Avô all his life?" Filipa's voice dripped sarcasm.

"I am sure she didn't have to work hard at that. Ricardo was already in love enough with her."

"I can see you are on Ana's side," she said drily.

"I am on the side of love. And if that means trying to understand what Ricardo and Ana went through, why she left the trail of the *lenços* and where that love landed them, then so be it. Just doing my job, *ma chérie*."

Filipa had the grace to look abashed. "I am sorry. That wasn't fair. But until I can, it's difficult to look at this objectively."

"You'll get there." He smiled reassuringly.

Re glanced around, absorbing the vibrating energy of the historic station. Tourists stared in awe at the towering azulejos, children with their parents tugging at their hands, to be set free to run, lovers with their arms entwined murmured final goodbyes, the low buzz of excitement, the sound of trolley bags and the presence of culture, tradition and history—the energy of it all reached out to Re in a gush.

On his right loomed a large azulejo of a farmer tilling his land, and Re's gaze darted to his companion. She too was staring at the intricate hand-painted enormous tile work. As their eyes locked, realization dawned in her brown eyes. Without another word, they both ran to the lofty azulejo, bang across the main entrance. It took Re only a few seconds to spot the gap at the bottom left corner of the azulejo, just where the hay gathered at the farmer's feet.

"It's gone… but it was here!" Filipa gasped, the ring of disappointment loud in her tone.

For long moments, Re stared at the sullied spot where the small tile should have been, confusion stabbing him. Had they arrived late? Had someone got to it before them? For example, the other man who had enquired at the wine shop?

"My guess is that the tile seems to have been removed recently, because if it had been done years ago, I am positive the cultural centre would have replaced it by now. And if it was removed recently—for example—if it fell off or got damaged or something, then we could probably trace it. Meet the station master, or cultural centre, or something. I am sure we would be able to find it," Re reasoned aloud, more to himself than to Filipa.

"But what if it was stolen?" Filipa asked.

The detective passed her a look of contemplation.

"It's a possibility, no?" she shrugged.

Before Re could respond, sudden movement at the opposite end of the station caught his attention. Two uniformed men entered the station at the far end. The police again! So soon? And at the station? What could be happening? Someone surely had to be tipping them off, but who? And more importantly, how?

Re caught hold of Filipa's hand and swiftly walked towards the nearest exit that led into the interior of the station.

"Don't look, keep walking," he muttered under his breath.

Startled, Filipa fell in step with him, mutely. Re was thinking fast. They needed a place to take quick cover, till the police left the premises… His eyes scouted the station, but nothing seemed to be appropriately safe. For precious seconds, he paused just beside the tracks, wondering which direction to take.

"Come with me," a voice whispered from behind him, and Re swivelled around. His gaze met the solemn eyes of a middle-aged man with a French beard, attired in a uniform and a cap.

Re hesitated for the slightest of seconds, then nodded. He and Filipa followed the railway officer down the platform and in through a door. It was an office. A few people were working on computers, and seemed disinterested in the trio. The man didn't halt but continued to lead them to another room, and shut the door behind him.

"You are Senhorita Filipa Monteiro?" the man asked briefly.

"That's right. And you are—?" Filipa met the officer's curious gaze directly.

"Pedro Lavarez, the station master. I saw you two staring at the azulejo with a great deal of interest—I have web cams trained on the tilework. What were you looking at?" Pedro enquired. His eyes were small and beady but kind, as he stared at them, his fingers caressing his beard.

"I am Re Parkar, an investigative journalist. I am helping Senhorita Filipa find out who killed her grandfather this morning…"

"Yes, I saw the news flash," Pedro said matter-of-factly.

"Really sorry for your loss, *senhorita,* but the news was confusing—they believe that you may have something to do with your grandfather's death."

"That's ridiculous and I will prove my innocence," Filipa scoffed.

"I sure hope so. Which is why I brought you two in here." Pedro smiled for the first time. "My grandfather was a good friend of your grandfather's. They kept in touch for years—they were always there for each other when in need. I have met Ricardo a few times—a fine gentleman. But you still have to answer my question—why were you looking at the azulejo?"

"We believe that an extra small azulejo may have been put there by someone. Like an extension. But it's not there now, and we fear that we may have arrived too late for it," Re explained.

"By someone, do you mean Ana Ribeiro?" Pedro asked, gravely.

Re and Filipa flashed each other startled looks.

"How—?" Filipa began.

"My grandfather knew Ana very well too. She was your grandfather's good friend, from what I heard. When she was in Porto, she helped with some of the tile restoration work here at the station. It was during that time that she put that tile at the bottom, and confided in my grandfather that should Ricardo ever come looking for her, he was to be given the tile. Long after she left Porto, the tile came off, and I have had it in safekeeping in the hope that someone would come to claim it. And I am so glad that you did."

"You have the azulejo here?" Filipa's eyes brightened with hope.

"No, not here. We sent it to Casa São Roque Museum, where Ana did some part-time work. One of the board members, Arno Bandile—he is South African—knew Ricardo well, and was happy to keep it safe along with the other museum artefacts, until Ricardo claimed it. Here, let me give you the address."

He jotted down the address on a slip of paper. "Here you go. From what I have heard, Ana was a wonderful talented lady, and I am so glad that this mission is accomplished. Why don't you wait a few minutes longer here, while I check out if the coast is clear?"

He exited the room, and Re fiddled with the multi-metal Ganesha pendant round his neck. Something was making him uneasy, and he didn't quite know what it was. Once out of here, he planned to check with Stefan.

Pedro was back a few minutes later. "All clear… but you better take this side exit, on your extreme right. Good luck!" He ushered them out, and waved goodbye.

Chapter
9

Officer Stefan Weiss glanced at the faces round the polished table of the conference room at the Monteiro Estate—some eager, some concerned, some worried. He remained a silent support as he sat on the side, and allowed the senior butler to lead the way and take charge.

"A very sad and tragic incident occurred today, as we all know," Pedro began, his glance cruising over the familiar faces of the staff and some guests. "Someone attacked Senhor Ricardo in his own home, on his own land. Such a terrible thing to happen. His death has come as a shock to all of us, but imagine what Senhorita Filipa must be going through. She is probably out there somewhere, trying to deal with it all. But while we give her the time to do what she must, we have a duty to perform here—as loyal members of the Monteiro Estate. We have worked at the estate and the vineyards, and served the family for years, some of us since our childhood, and some for generations. We know no other friend, family and employee—this has been the centre of our existence for a while now. Which is why, we owe the success of tomorrow's event to the Monteiro family—in their time of grief, and in their moment of need. It was Senhorita Filipa's dream to present her mentor's symbol of peace to the world, on behalf of Portugal, and we have to ensure that it all happens the way she wanted it—whether she is present for the event tomorrow or not. That is why tomorrow is an important day for all of us—we have to hold off our mourning, and put our best foot forward. Do we all agree on this?"

A murmur of acceptance and approval rose amidst the staff and the local volunteers.

"Senhorita Filipa has made a statement which I shall read out now. Another one has been sent to the press, and an email has gone to all the participants and guests of tomorrow's event."

While Pedro went on to read Filipa's letter of assurance and request for respect of her privacy in the hour of grief, Stefan sat aside, making some notes. Pedro knew his people; they would listen to him. Stefan's role was to assist, and he was content with observing from the side-lines. He noticed Tiago at the far end of the table, also taking notes, glancing at his phone from time to time, handing out sheets of information and duties. Both he and Pedro seemed to be completely involved with the event. Filipa was lucky to have a dedicated team. The event seemed to be in good hands, and yet a nebulous worrisome emotion seemed to be niggling at the back of Stefan's mind. Lusa and his accusations, Santiago's poisoning and death… he needed to speak to Pedro alone. As soon as the meeting got over. He had a hunch that Pedro might have some answers.

Re brought the car to a halt before they joined the freeway.

"What's up?" Filipa asked, surprised. "The Casa may close for the day."

"I need to make an urgent call. I will be back in a minute."

Re descended from the car and quickly punched in Stefan's number. He could see Filipa turning around and watching him.

"Re," Stefan spoke. "I am so glad you called."

"Why, what's up?" Re's heartbeat quickened.

"The police are on your trail. They are convinced Filipa has a role in her grandfather's murder because they found the murder weapon with her fingerprints on it—his walking stick."

"What? How is that possible?" Re exclaimed.

"Exactly. Sounds like the police are hanging on to scraps. That's not all. Did you visit Santiago today in Guimarães?"

"Yes, how did you know?" the detective frowned, pushing back his spectacles.

"Unfortunately, someone else with deadly intentions also knew that. Because Santiago was found dead, not long after you left—poisoned. There was a glass of wine in his hand, and a small bottle of the de Cruz wine."

"Mon dieu!" Re was taken aback. "So, the wine bottle was spiked, and he drank from the bottle? Was it his own bottle? Did someone slip the poison in, and did he drink by mistake? Or did someone actually make him drink the poisoned wine and leave the bottle behind to tease the police?"

"We'll know soon enough. Although I am quite sure that Santiago did not commit suicide, nor did he drink the poisoned wine by mistake. It was hardcore murder. This is much deeper than we think, Re. Please be careful," Stefan admonished.

"We will. And you too. Trust no one," Re added. "Would you be able to find out some background details on Santiago? Perhaps it will help us understand the motive behind the murder. It seems so out of context in a sense, and rather unexpected."

"Someone is framing Filipa. And there must be a good reason for it. But I am on it."

"*Merci,* Stefan, I am so glad you are at the estate." Re ended the call and returned to the car, deep in thought.

"Everything okay?" she asked.

Re hesitated, wondering how to break the news to Filipa. He turned to face her, observing her puffed eyelids, and the pensive look in her brown eyes.

"I have more bad news. Santiago has been poisoned, in his cafe. Probably minutes after we left him."

Filipa's hand flew to her mouth. "No! Was it because of me… because I… we met him?"

"We don't know. But we will find out. I am so sorry Filipa, this is so hard to take… your Grandpa this morning, and now Santiago… someone is being brutally monstrous."

"This is a nightmare!" Filipa covered her face with her palms, shedding a few quiet tears.

Re allowed the distraught *senhorita* a few minutes to gather herself. Santiago's murder had complicated things. So far, they were on a trail of *lenços*—mostly Ana's love trail for Ricardo. Santiago's death seemed to propel the entire trail in a direction of bloodshed. Were the threat this morning and the old man's death connected? He turned the ignition in silence, driving per GPS instructions, his thoughts churning. Ricardo and Santiago—same age, both knew Ana, probably they all worked together as well? Was there a pattern here? And more importantly, where was the star of this entire scenario? *Where was Ana?*

Casa São Roque Centro de Arte was a beautiful double-storied sunflower yellow-coloured mansion with stylized brown wooden windows. Once the hunting lodge of the noble family of Portugal, it was Portuguese architecture at its best. A group of tourists was walking through the exquisitely maintained interiors, admiring the modern art on display, discussing the artists and art. A painting by the famous modernist painter of Portugal, Amadeo de Souza, was prominently displayed on the cream entrance wall.

"Filipa, my dear!" a voice greeted them.

A tall man in his early seventies, with an athletic build and white beard came forward eagerly, with a warm smile on his face.

"This is for you!" He gallantly offered Filipa a red camellia. "It is a pleasure to finally meet Ricardo's granddaughter."

Filipa accepted the camellia with a shy, reserved smile, and tucked it inside her backpack. "Pleasure meeting you too, Mr. Bandile."

"Oh, call me Arno!"

"I am Re Parkar," the detective introduced himself.

"Welcome to the Casa… I just heard about Ricardo… what awful business this is. Who could have done such a horrible thing and why?" Arno gushed, leading them through doors to the back of the house, and into a sunlit glass garden. The pale peach of the setting evening sun streamed in through the umbrella-patterned grill of the glass, spotlighting a tiled wall and tiled centre-space.

"Let's sit here in this winter garden, my favourite spot in the mansion. Pedro told me that you wanted to know about Ana Ribeiro, is that right?"

Filipa nodded. "She worked with you here, didn't she?"

"Yes, for some years, more like a volunteer, early mornings or some afternoons, in between her other jobs. I had heard about Ana from Ricardo, but I met her for the first time when she appeared in Porto. She knew art and music, and was a great learner. It was a pleasure having her here—she was a natural with people and led the tours with finesse. I was sorry when she left Porto. I tried to persuade her not to leave, you know, even proposed marriage to her, but she laughed it off—she was still madly in love with Ricardo. You can't help a person in love, unreasonable and stubborn, floating in illusions. Foolish young lady. But one thing gave me solace—I knew that no matter where she went, she would do something good with her life. She was too accomplished and dynamic to sit still. Given the right opportunities, I felt that she would make a good life for herself. Did she?"

"We don't know, yet. We are hoping that the azulejo will lead us to her," Filipa replied.

"Ah yes, the azulejo…"

"Pedro said that he gave you the tile for safekeeping," Re reminded gently.

"Oh yes, I did keep it safe. It kind of reminded me of her, and I would gladly guard it forever if you don't particularly want to keep it, now that Ricardo is no more… I mean… you know what I mean." He paused, a little awkward.

Re understood. Here was a man, madly in love with Ana, and holding on to her memory in his old age, any which way possible. Such a strange emotion love was, and added up to such tricky equations. It never knew when to quit, and was characterised by relentless hope. Even when there was none.

"Oh, actually we do want it," Filipa added, hastily.

"Yes, I guessed you would… I will be right back. Till then, enjoy this beautiful winter garden. Do observe keenly the structure of the glass and the pattern. It is unique. And the camellias you see all around the mansion are of the choicest varieties and colours, more than centuries old." His voice was filled with an unconscious pride.

Even from inside the winter garden, the lush vegetation filled with hundreds of camellias was a sight to behold. Red, orange, fuchsia pink—the garden was a splash of colour. Re loved the energy of the space—it was bright, earthy and elevated.

A few minutes later, Arno returned with a slim box that he handed over to Filipa.

"Here you go. You can take a look, while I escort the last batch of tourists to the door," he said, then discreetly exited from the room.

Filipa glanced at Re, and moved her tongue over her dry lips. He nodded.

She lifted the lid of the box, and they both stared at the tile inside. It was no amateur work. It was a beautiful Portuguese traditional design in blue and gold that wove around two entwined red hearts. The strokes were dainty and fine, the colours were muted, yet attractive. Everything about the azulejo spoke of style and elegance.

"Ana was an artist in the true sense of the word. It is a beautiful painting," Re commented, candid admiration in his voice.

"It could be a tracing," Filipa brushed off. "Nicely done, but nothing exquisite. These two hearts in fact make me cringe."

"There's a letter under the tile—addressed to Ricardo."

"Not again!" she whispered, in exasperation.

"I guess you don't have a choice—you would have to translate it even if it pains you," Re remarked, hiding his annoyance.

"Of course, I do know that. It's just… never mind. It will only take a few minutes. Why don't you write it down, while I dictate?"

She handed the detective a pen and paper. Re scribbled the translation, aware of Filipa's emotionless tone of voice, in contrast to Ana's moving letter.

'Dear Ricardo,

If you are reading this, it means that you found the tile. And you are actually here in Porto.

I waited for you to come and meet me in Guimarães but you didn't come. Finally, I took the job as a managing assistant in

Gaia—perhaps one of the best things I did in my life.

I learnt so much on the job, you would be proud of me. Marcus, the manager, has been really kind and helpful, allowing me free time to pursue other interests.

Life hasn't been easy. Trying to make a living in Porto, with Rodrigo constantly hounding me and all I want in life is to be with you. The only thing that keeps me going is the determination not to wallow in self-pity and to make something out of my life. I will not waste it, no matter what. Of course, I want you in it, every second and step of the way. And there will never be another man for me. But I will not let the wait ruin my life. I am right, am I not? You wouldn't want me to sit crying over the past—you would want me to succeed and move on. And move on I will, with you in my heart and mind, supporting me and encouraging me—if not in actual words, in spirit.

But now that you have the tile, my hope goes up.

I am waiting for you… but I don't know how long I shall stay on in Porto… Porto is beautiful… I love the Rio Douro and watching the rabelo gently swaying on the water in the evening, the colourful houses give me joy and the random music that fills the Square acts as a sort of balm to my aching heart… but I am restless. It has been five years now. I am almost 35 years old, and I need to set roots, but not in Porto. The countryside calls me… Luckily, I have another job offer in a school. An old friend of mine, ours—Miguel Carvalho—is now the principal in a nearby county and he would like me to teach there. Strange how the past weaves into your future… I am tempted… working with children, teaching art and music, is more me, although my future lies in wine.

A while back I overheard a conversation between two people about cheap land further up east and north. I was so tempted... who knows, one day...

Please come as soon as you can... the wait is getting more and more painful and unbearable...

Forever yours,
Ana'

Re folded the letter, a deep silence in his heart. He felt as if he was beginning to connect with Ana at a very basic level. Bit by bit, word by word, and emotion by emotion, he could see her clearly in his mind's eye. He admitted that he liked what he saw. A woman with her heart set on a man, yet sensible enough to know that she had to move on, so as to make something of her life. Strong and determined, with an eye on the future and the fulfilment of her own dreams, but with a heart set in the past... A letter filled with sensible thoughts, and yet the yearning and the pain of longing and love underlined each word, like a lie she was telling herself, and desperately wanted to believe in. The long lonely hours of waiting, as days turned into weeks and years, the ticking of her biological and aspirational clock, the contradictory imbalance and tug of war between the yearning and her need to plan for the future... and finally, every single time the dashing of hopes as realization had set in... It was like riding a wave of hope to fall into a sea of disappointment. Was Ricardo to be blamed? Or was Ana solely responsible for the flame of romance that she kept alive inside of her, hoping against hope, with growing years and fading memories? It would be an impossible question to answer.

"What do you think?" Filipa cocked an eyebrow. "Are we any closer to unravelling the trail of the *lenços*?"

"Perhaps, but what I do know is that I am very close to understanding Ana," he remarked. *"Strange how the past weaves into the future…"*

Chapter 10

On the bridge of the Saint,
with blessings and a prayer.
When two hearts join,
there is music in the air.
The painting can dry,
the seasons can change,
but the music of the hearts
can never grow faint.

"Santiago dead?" Pedro was startled. "This is worrying news indeed. He was a good friend of Senhor Ricardo. So very unfortunate…"

"Can you tell me more about him?" Stefan persisted. "Anything that can help us understand why someone would want to kill him?"

They were in Ricardo's office, and Stefan had asked the butler to stay back for a few minutes after the meeting.

Pedro hesitated. "I am just a butler, but I did see and understand things. Back then, Santiago was a young dashing man. He came from an affluent family, they owned restaurants in Porto, I had heard. Handsome and doted on Ricardo. I believe that they studied in the same school, so their friendship was thick. They had their share of girlfriends, and youthful adventures, and escapades."

"Interesting. But do you think that Ricardo's death and Santiago's death are connected?"

"Difficult to say, officer. Ricardo, Santiago, Ana and two or three others were a tight group with common ideologies, and working in their own way against the *Estado Novo*, during the four years before Carnation Revolution. They were a part of a big group called April Captains, and sometimes they had meetings at the estate itself. And then, one evening, something happened, I am not sure what, but they decided to disband, one by one. On 25th April 1974, everyone dispersed. They felt they didn't have any more reason to continue their work. It was also one of the reasons why Ana left, I believe, apart from the fact that she *had* to leave, for the sake of their love. I never saw much of any of them again— including Ana and Santiago. I wasn't even aware that he lived in Guimarães now."

"If Santiago and Ricardo were such good childhood friends, wouldn't they have continued to be in touch?" Stefan frowned.

"Actually, they were, for a while, but not as often as they would have liked, perhaps. But enough for Filipa to get to know Santiago, and enjoy a good bond with him."

"I find it very strange—that such a close friendship suddenly evaporated into a long-distance one. Also, odd that

Santiago never visited the estate again, and more puzzling that Ricardo and Santiago should die on the same day."

Pedro didn't respond, but his forehead was creased in concentration.

"Would you have the names of the other group members?"

"No, but I have a feeling that Senhor Ricardo would have kept a record in a private diary. I am afraid I was never privy to its contents. But with your permission, I could try to find out."

"I think it is the need of the hour. We've got to know if the deaths are connected, or if it's all just a coincidence."

Pedro nodded. "Give me an hour, please."

Re studied the *lenço* with a great deal of interest. Hearts embroidered along the four sides like a delicate lace, a house that appeared to be a church with a cross on it, a curvy bridge, and a guitar with two hearts on its body. Made by the hand of an expert seamstress, the kerchief embodied the culture of love and Portugal. Ana must have spent hours embroidering the *lenço*, a labour of love for sure, but more an act of faith where every stitch pinned a hope and a step to manifest that love.

"Beautifully embroidered as usual. The men in those times must have been so lucky. Imagine being wooed by your beloved in this quaint and charming manner," Re remarked, in candid appreciation.

"Would you have liked to be wooed like that?" Filipa asked, studying Re's face.

"Oh, I am sure I would have loved it. To know that a woman loves you, and has poured her time, energy and love into weaving her heart into the tradition and respecting it, what can be a greater booster for love? I would have cherished such a *lenço,* and the woman, for lifetimes!" Re smiled, self-consciously.

"How gallant you are… you will make some woman lucky one day!" Filipa declared.

"Coming from a cynic, I truly am flattered." Re grinned.

"I am cynical and I don't believe in love, but I do admire those who do. And I can spot a good man from a distance, I have a woman's instinct after all."

"Thank you Senhorita Filipa. If this is your way of saying thank you to me for this shared adventure, I accept it."

"Take it as you like it." Filipa smiled. "Let me translate the *lenço* for you."

Re noticed that she was quite a beautiful woman if she displayed that lovely smile more, and came off her rather high, cynical horse. With her frisky, unruly hair, and her intermittently flashing dimple, she exuded a wild charm and a light-hearted energy. Why wasn't there a boyfriend on the scene? Or was there? But she had not hinted at one, nor had there been any anxious phone calls. His glance involuntarily darted to her finger again, where the light band hinted at a ring. Was she ever going to share the secret of that band with him?

They were sitting on the side of the road, just outside of Porto. A farmhouse nestled against an expansive landscape of rolling hills, its trademark sloping rust-coloured roof standing out against the green. Filipa studied the *lenço* and began scribbling a translation on a notepaper.

"Here you go… cryptic, and at the same time, descriptive and easy." Filipa handed him the translation.

"'*On the bridge of the Saint,*
with blessings and a prayer.
When two hearts join,
there is music in the air.
The painting can dry,
the seasons can change,
but the music of the hearts
can never grow faint.'

"You know the place?" Re raised an eyebrow.

"I think it is fairly obvious. *Bridge of the Saints* has got to be the famous Ponte de São Gonçalo of Amarante which spans the Tâmega river, so we most certainly are headed in the right direction. The bridge has a legend attached to it… with blessings and a prayer would definitely mean São Gonçalo's blessings. So perhaps we should head to it first."

"The music of the hearts—isn't Amarante famous for its two-hearted guitar? I seem to remember reading about it somewhere."

"Yes, it's called the Viola Amarantina, also called *viola de dois corações,* which means two-hearted guitar, because of the two heart-shaped frontal openings. So romantic and typical of Amarante and Northern Portugal. It has ten steel strings in five courses, and is traditionally made from walnut, pine and mahogany. Walnut wood for the sides, pine wood for the soundboard, and the guitar neck is made of mahogany.

"*When two hearts join, there is music in the air… but the music of the hearts can never grow faint…* This has to mean a two-hearted guitar, the Viola Amarantina" Re concluded, pointing to the embroidery on the *lenço*.

"Yes, absolutely. Portuguese people play this guitar all the time, especially during festivals, and to woo their lovers."

"Which explains why Ana embroidered it on the *lenço*. But what should be our first step now? We need to begin our hunt somewhere. What about the school she worked at? I know we don't have a name of the school, but we do know the principal's name, Miguel Carvalho. Let me look up the net." Re did a quick Google search for Miguel Carvalho, Amarante. "Here is one—The Escola Secundária de Amarante, one of the older schools, and prominently led by Miguel Carvalho. I bet he is the one!"

"Good work, let's call the school right away, we may still catch someone in the office, and see if we can get Miguel's number."

A few calls later, Re glanced triumphantly at his companion. "Finally… the school admin has been very kind. Here is Miguel's number. Would you like to do the honours and talk to him? Perhaps he may know of you?"

"I doubt that. I have never heard of Miguel. But let me speak to him." Filipa inhaled deeply. "Let's hope that he responds to an unidentified number."

But Miguel did, and in moments Filipa was talking to the old principal. Re tried to grasp the fluent Portuguese, but his smattering of knowledge could not cope with the speed. Minutes later, Filipa cut the call and glanced at Re.

"He will meet us at the cathedral at around 7:00 PM. Which means we should leave right away."

"Awesome… with some luck, he may be able to tell us where Ana is right now." Re turned on the GPS and the car moved in the direction of Amarante. "I can't help but wonder at the weirdness of the situation. Here we are, trying to solve the trail of the *lenços* and we don't even know where Ana is, and in what condition. None of the people we've met so far have any idea of her present whereabouts either, don't you think that's strange?"

"Do you think Grandpa knew where she lives? Or if he ever met her all these years? It kind of seems impossible that he didn't, yet I know that there was never the slightest mention of Ana in the house. And if he did, he would have himself told her that he loved her. I wish he had shared this part of his life with me much before—it would not have been such a shock then," Filipa confessed.

"He probably wanted to, but may not have found the right moment, or the courage. Who knows now…"

Silence slipped between them as Re drove along the long stretch of road which curved between gradually rising hills. The clouds seemed to be touching the violet-blue horizon ahead, and yet the landscape looked sun-drenched. Re realized that it could rain tonight, and they had much to accomplish before night fell. He didn't wish to mention it to Filipa, but he wondered where exactly this trail of *lenços* was leading. Was it an old man's regret and whim, of things left undone? If it hadn't been for the 'bloodbath' threat, any sensible person would probably have written it off as such, but he knew that such threats could not be taken lightly. They were usually the result of frustrated vindictive minds which could go to any lengths to prove a point. And what about Santiago? Where did he feature in all of this? Was his death connected to the *lenços*, or was it some sort of fluke coincidence that he was killed on the same day as his friend Ricardo? Re found his thoughts vacillating between questions and doubts, and back to questions.

The detective parked the car outside the Amadeo de Souza Cardoso Museum. Re had heard a lot about this Portuguese painter, and any other time, he would have most certainly visited it.

They walked past the touristy 'I love Amarante' display, towards the São Gonçalo bridge. Re had to pause and admire the ancient granite Ponte de São Gonçalo which overlapped the Tâmega river, its two half-moon hollow scoops under the bridge reflecting in the water to form a full O. The sun had set, but the afterglow of the pink and orange sky seemed to pervade Amarante in a luminescence which was powerfully sublime.

"This was once a Roman bridge and road that went through Amarante to Guimarães and Braga. In 1250, Gonçalo rebuilt the bridge with the alms that he received. There's a funny story about it. Once when he went to collect money for the bridge, a man gave him a note and told him to take it to his wife. Gonçalo did as he was told. When the wife read the note which asked her to give him as many gold coins as the paper weighed, she laughed, but São Gonçalo insisted. So, she got a scale, put the paper in one plate and began weighing. To her surprise, the pile of coins kept growing miraculously, but the paper side still did not tilt. Gonçalo got enough coins for his bridge."

"I love such tales," Re chuckled.

"There are supposed to be other miracles too. A cross was put up on the bridge, but in 1763, the river flooded and the bridge fell—but the cross was saved just half an hour before that happened. Now the cross stands in the Church and Convent of São Gonçalo. This bridge was completed in 1791 and has two spires, two ballot box-shaped decorations, and there is also a bench on each balcony. We learnt this in school. In about the 1800s, when the French invaded Portugal the second time, this bridge played its role in defending Amarante for fourteen days against the Napolean troops. That is why it is a hero, and the chief attraction of Amarante," Filipa explained with a smile.

"It looks like a hero too. The energy of a warrior, and the heart of a saviour," Re murmured, and Filipa glanced at him in surprise.

"Well said," she approved, and Re nodded.

They walked past the bridge in silence, as Re allowed the energy of the town to seep into his. Cars and people occupied space on the bridge, and tourists posed and clicked photos. On the right side of the bridge rose the Igreja de São

Gonçalo, its ochre facade and the orange sloping roof simple yet charming.

Re glanced at his watch. It was 6:45, they had 15 minutes to spare, and with mutual understanding, he and Filipa stepped into the church. Re was fascinated by the gilded woodwork altarpieces, and the statues, paintings and azulejo panels from the eighteenth-century.

"São Gonçalo is buried here," Filipa said in a low voice.

Re saw the reclining statue of the Saint Gonçalo and could imagine the level of faith in Amarante for the Saint. As was his habit, he quickly offered a prayer, invoking the blessings of the saints to help him solve the mystery of the *lenços*.

At 7:00 sharp, they stepped out of the church, and Re could sense that Filipa was impatient and a little nervous. Re hoped that Miguel was not late. But he needn't have worried. Within a few minutes, they spotted a tall man in a hat and a long blue jacket striding towards them. He was carrying a large backpack, and he greeted them with a knowing smile.

"Pleasure to meet you Filipa, and you must be Re Parkar." Miguel shook hands with them. "I am so glad we could meet. Your call came in the nick of time. I was about to go home and then on a short trip tomorrow."

"Oh, that was lucky then." Filipa smiled.

"I just work in an honorary capacity now, but it gives me purpose to get up every morning, and see the faces of the future of Portugal," he smiled. "Did you get a chance to go inside the church?"

"It is magnificent," Re acknowledged.

"It is where Ana would volunteer to work over weekends. It was also where she was once accused of stealing a rare artefact."

"What!" Filipa looked startled.

"She didn't steal it, of course; it was that nasty man from her past who was set on making her life miserable. Rodrigo… the artefact was returned and he claimed it was all in fun, but Ana was furious and upset, understandably so. Come, let's go to the Confeitaria da Ponte, at the end of the bridge. Most famous for its variety of cakes."

Re liked Miguel. He seemed to be in his mid-seventies, with a bush of silver hair and beard, and matching silver-rimmed glasses below an intelligent forehead. He possessed an air of casual disregard for the world, which Re found fascinating. He sensed that Miguel's students must have benefitted a lot from interactions with him, and his vision.

The former principal ordered the sweetmeats Papos de Anjo and Bolos de São Gonçalo, then took a corner table by the window, overlooking the bridge and the Tâmega.

"I love this spot. It's my favourite for the past more than 40 years. Something about Amarante and its flair for love and music holds me back in this place. It falls on the Rota do Românico—the Romanesque route—and has so much to offer. Did you know that there are statues of two devils kept in the Museum Amadeo de Souza Cardoso—they come from the church. There is so much colourful culture and history to this place, including the sharing of phallus-shaped cakes with lovers!" He laughed out loud, and Re couldn't help grinning at his infectious laugh. Filipa smiled.

"But here I am blabbering, when actually I am so tremendously sorry about what happened to Ricardo, Filipa. Do accept my deepest condolences. He was such a fine gentleman, a boon to Penafiel and the pride of Portugal. It is sad that he died the way he did."

"Thank you." Filipa nodded.

"I sometimes wonder, though, what life would have been for him with Ana. They were so made for each other, so perfect in every sense of the word—their temperaments, their habits and ideologies. I think they would have made a power couple, and perhaps achieved so much together. They would have probably taken the Vinho Verde to great heights. She had amazing ideas for wine making, she was even developing her own recipe. Fascinating! It is unfortunate the way things turned out for them, but then this is life," Miguel sighed. It was as if he was talking aloud to himself.

"She worked with you in the school, didn't she?" Filipa asked.

"Yes, I made it a point to invite her. She was struggling in Porto, trying to make ends meet. And although we had decided that we would lead independent lives, I couldn't bear the thought of Ana, without Ricardo, trying to make a life for herself."

"That was very considerate of you," Re remarked.

"I was just trying to be a good friend, and I owed it to her. She has always been a good friend to all of us. So, when I got a chance to reciprocate, I did. Luckily, she agreed to come teach art and music at the school. I have to say the students were happy. She has a way with children, and she made the perfect teacher for some years. She lived in the staff quarters, and I remember listening to her sing as she embroidered on a *lenço*. She had a beautiful voice too, and played the *viola amarantina* so well. But when that rascal of a fellow began hounding her, she got restless. When he stole that artefact from the church and she got the brunt of the accusation, she was livid. She realized that it was getting too dangerous. She said she would have to take some decisions once and for all."

"What did she do?" Re leaned forward.

"Her sister had moved to Viana do Castelo and she thought she would settle there eventually. She had received an offer to look after a wine estate by the sea, and she finally decided to accept."

They finished off the sweetmeats. Miguel paid and led them out of the patisserie.

"Let's sit by the bridge," he suggested.

The three of them settled on the stone seat that overlooked the bridge. The waters of the Tâmega glistened in the last glow of the day as it lazed past the houses that bordered the riverbank.

"Did she by any chance leave an article or something for Ricardo?" Re asked.

Miguel smiled and nodded. Something about the way he pursed his lips intrigued Re. Did this man know more about Ana than he was letting on?

The principal opened his bag, and to Re's great surprise, extracted a mini *viola amarantina*. It looked slick and polished, and displayed two heart openings in the front.

"Oh my God!" Filipa exclaimed.

"Yes, it's a beauty. She got it made especially for Ricardo, and sang a song on it too. Many songs actually, in the evenings sometimes, when we would sit out on the porch. She wasn't shy about it and sang really well. She recorded a special song for Ricardo once. I have it on my phone. Would you like to listen to it?"

His eyes were bright, teasing and inviting as he stared at Re and Filipa.

Re's heart skipped a beat. To listen to Ana sing… the first real connection with a physical Ana… a shiver of anticipation ran down his spine.

"I don't believe this," Filipa whispered, in awe.

Miguel shook his head. "I know what you mean."

He fiddled with his phone and paused to stare at the two, his gaze intense.

"Are you ready? Presenting Ana Ribeiro to you."

The light double strumming of a guitar slowly filled the evening. Tentative at first, and then strong and demanding. Then a sweet, mellifluous voice joined in, singing a song which seemed to come straight from the heart. Ana's voice was firm with the slightest of tremors to it, like a sustained twang of a melodious string. Re did not understand the Portuguese words, but then he didn't need to. The unbridled emotion expressed with powerful abandon and yet laced with a sense of yearning sent goose bumps scuttling down his skin. It was as if Ana was pouring all her incandescent love into the words and its melody—the song was a statement, a declaration, and a promise. Mostly a promise to love forever. If this wasn't infinite proof of love, what was, he wondered?

Twilight had fallen on the bridge, the lingering rosy hues luminescent beyond the bridge and the rippling water and the church... like a final goodbye... the clouds hung low like an apple cider-coloured field in the sky. A sharp wind had picked up, flapping Re's pony and Filipa's curly waves. It was as if nature itself was rising to respond to the dulcet sad yet catchy notes in the song, lifting them up and carrying them to her lover's ears, far and beyond to another realm... As the last notes of the song tapered to a slow finish, a deep silence seemed to claim the evening. For seconds, even the birds forgot to chirp. Re's gaze spontaneously darted to Filipa. Her head was bent, and she brushed away a telltale slow trickle from her cheek. He experienced a quiet surge of satisfaction. All was not lost yet...

"Soul-stirring, isn't it? But then Ana was like that— poured herself into every emotion, action, friendship and relationship. I just wish she had got what she desired," Miguel sounded rueful. "Ricardo would have loved to hear this song, if only to realize the kind of rare love he had possessed, but unfortunately lost."

Miguel's words resonated with Re. To love with a full flush of bloom and to be unable to enjoy the reciprocating wave of emotion had to be the saddest trick of fate. Re knew it and understood it extremely well.

"May I keep the guitar?" Filipa asked.

"Yes, of course, she wanted Ricardo to have it, whenever he turned up. So, it is yours now. Also, there is an envelope inside, I believe it is a letter."

Filipa accepted the guitar with implicit reverence in her action. "Thank you so much for taking care of it all these years."

"I had promised Ana that I would hold on to it till the right moment, and I am happy to have fulfilled that promise," Miguel said, brushing off her acknowledgement with his hand. "I shall either email or WhatsApp you her song, Re."

"Thank you. Do you have any idea at all where she could be?" Re asked.

Miguel shook his head. "When we initially parted in Penafiel, we had decided that we would now lead our own lives. But somehow fate seemed to have brought Ana and me together, perhaps because I had some mysterious role to play in her life. But after she left Amarante, she never contacted me again, nor did she enquire if Ricardo ever came for the guitar. It was as if she had decided not to look back. It's been more than 20 years now, I never saw her again after she left for Viana do Castelo."

It was almost dark now and the street lights had come up in the city, setting it aflame with twinkling buttery lights and a golden glow. Re realized that it was time to leave.

"Ana was a special woman. I wish you good luck in finding her, and hope that she is well and safe." Miguel smiled at the two of them.

"Goodbye, thank you for everything," Filipa said.

They shook hands again with the older man and headed down the bridge. Cars passed by and pedestrians dodged them. Re turned to take a last look at Miguel, who was still seated by the bridge, his eyes closed, his head resting against the wall of the bridge.

From a distance, the stranger watched Re and Filipa depart. His eyes remain glued on Miguel, watching his actions with a hawk-like gaze. Miguel rose finally, his shoulders drooping, as he casually strolled down the narrow cobbled street, past the patisserie at the corner. The stranger rose too and began following Miguel, keeping a discreet distance. He was in no hurry. He knew what had to be done, and there was plenty of time to do it. The night was still young and Amarante was beautiful in the night, with the street lights shimmering a golden path.

Pedro was in Ricardo's office, when his phone rang.

"Yes?"

The person at the other end was brief.

"The third gift delivered. Good. What about Miguel? How is he?"

Pedro was quiet as he listened, then nodded. "Our task is not over yet, you know that. We have to see this through till the end. Those gifts are of the utmost importance to us. Keep me posted, I will pay you well."

Pedro switched off the phone, a deep thoughtful expression on his face.

Two policemen were still on guard at the main entrance and he wondered how much longer before they took out an arrest warrant for Senhorita Filipa, if they hadn't already. The absurdity of the accusation almost made him laugh.

He suddenly felt a wave of fatigue. He had loved Ricardo like a brother, being almost of the same age. And Ricardo had relied heavily on him too. Now without his friend and brother, Pedro suddenly felt the pressure of unfinished tasks. The looming responsibility seemed mindboggling. And yet he had no option but to see this through. Even if it was to be his last duty to the Monteiro family. With a deep sigh, he turned to Ricardo's most personal diary, flicked through the pages and began reading it.

In the car, Re brought out the letter. By now, he recognized Ana's handwriting. He quickly began scribbling on the pad, as Filipa translated with swift expertise.

Dear Ricardo,

Hope you are well. I have no clue why you did not come meet me in Porto—can you imagine how I may have waited for you? Every knock on the door, every shadow across the window—I kept thinking that you were finally here. Alas... you didn't come. But as I said before, I moved on. I moved to Amarante.

What a good decision it was, and it was such a relief to finally meet a friend in Miguel. He brought back memories of the time we were all together, bonded in ideology... he took such good care of me, stood by me like a rock. I feel truly blessed. Also my students are wonderful children—how much I enjoy teaching them music and art. Especially the viola amarantina. I had forgotten how much I enjoy singing and playing the guitar—it was amazing to revive it all with the children. There is this one particular student who is specially gifted. Music is his solace; I am so glad that I helped him find it and develop it. His father has vineyards in Viana—you know him, he helped us back then—and is very keen that I take care of the estate there. Even the thought of managing an entire estate gives me a thrill. You remember our plans for the Monteiro? I hope you carried them out…

But Rodrigo hangs over me like a black, black cloud. He is making life very difficult for me, destroying my hard-built reputation with weird and nasty acts. He hopes that when people reject me, I will run to his arms. Foolish man. He never really understood me. I have explained to him time and again that I want to live my life on my own terms, that I don't need him, that love cannot be forced. But he has a strange ego. What does he know about love and sacrifice? What does anyone know of what I have been through in my life? How much I have given up, how much I long for… no one, absolutely no one can understand the long lonely hours as I wait day in and out for a man I love with my whole heart and soul, to return to me.

But now, at least, has the time come? Do I not deserve some love and happiness, Ricardo? We have been through so much together in the 4 years we were together. We were a part of the Rebellion, we endangered our lives, we endured risks, witnessed an iconic freedom and we loved—like crazy. We lived a lifetime together through those years... now it is time to breathe, fully and freely, without inhibitions and encumbrances. And I want to do it with you.

I am touching forty and I am tired. I have to take some major decisions soon. I have dreams—you know about them. I hope that you will help me take my decisions. Come soon...

Only yours,
Ana.

For a few seconds, Re allowed the contents of the letter to seep in—the myriad emotions that seemed to touch a core within him. The lacing of optimism and anticipation amidst the practicality of life. The agony of separation, and yet the healing touch of hope. He wondered what Ricardo would have thought of this letter, had he read it. Perhaps the old man didn't realize that not reading these pieces of Ana's heart would have been his biggest regret. So much pouring of emotion and so much love... a love that would heal any broken heart... even Ricardo's, even one caused by their own doing.

He opened the folded paper again and reread a few lines, glossing over some of the sentences. Then abruptly, he straightened.

"I have to go back. Will you please stay in the car, Filipa?"

"Where are you going?" Filipa glanced at him, confused.

"Miguel. I have to find him. Just don't leave the car, OK? Lock up the doors, keep the key with you, don't unlock them, no matter who it is."

Without further ado, Re stepped out in the dark. He knew his way back. He had to find Miguel. He barely waited for Filipa to lock the doors and wind up the windows, then sprinted across the alley towards the bridge. A gut instinct seemed to be goading him on. He had to reach Miguel, and fast. His heart began to pound, as he crossed the beautifully lit bridge. Strolling passers-by stared at him curiously. Re burst into the patisserie.

"Miguel, do you know where he went?" he asked the man at the counter.

"He has probably gone home."

"Do you know where he lives?" Re asked, trying not to sound panicked.

"Just down this road, in the school campus. You can't miss the school gate on the right. The first house on the right is his."

"*Obrigado!*" Re was grateful.

The cobbled street wound downhill, curving past houses and shops, some of which were open. Moonlight streamed on the cobbled path, even as dark clouds obstructed vision in patches. Re had only one clanging thought on his mind. He had to find Miguel. He had to warn him…

The school gate loomed on the right, with a board which flashed the name of the school, in bold. The metal gate had swung open. A niggling worry wormed into his mind. Re hastened in and spotted the lights on in the first house. Miguel was at home. Then his heart sank. The front door was ajar.

"Miguel! Are you there?" he shouted.

He broke into a sprint and stopped short at the front door, his blood curdling. The old principal lay in the middle of the hall, unconscious, a trickle of white spit in the corner of his lips. His hand was stretched out, and a glass of wine had rolled on the side, the red liquid forming a dark patch on the carpeted floor. Re checked Miguel's pulse, and without a second thought, he began administering CPR. He didn't think, he just acted. A few minutes later, he felt the pulse again—a faint beat… With trembling fingers, he punched the SOS helpline and gave swift instructions as to the situation and their whereabouts. Next, he rolled Miguel on to his side and placed a pillow under his head, in case he vomited. Then he waited… a sudden weary exhaustion caught him unawares, and he touched his Ganesha pendant and prayed.

Filipa sat in the car in the parking lot. The museum had closed long ago, and the building looked solemn and shadowed. Only the 'Amarante' display glowed colourfully in the lights of the Square. The silence was a little unnerving. Without her phone, Filipa felt frustratingly helpless. Where had Re vanished and what was taking him so long? It was getting late… the day's events were beginning to take a toll on her. Although she had kept a tight control over her emotions and followed the trail of the *lenços* without appearing distraught, she knew that deep inside, she was badly rattled. She was distressed, filled with intense grief and anger.

She still did not understand any of it, and she needed time to process it all. She was very worried about the event too, although she knew that Pedro, Tiago and Stefan would see it through. But she wanted to be there, to be able to launch the Peace Symbol—a promise she had made to her mentor Joana de Cruz. And now, with all this happening, and with Grandpa no more, she had no clue where she was headed. Or if she would ever be able to live a normal life again.

A sudden tap on the glass made her jump out of her skin. Her blood curdled, as she saw a face plastered against the window. A cap was pulled low and a face was trying to peer inside the car.

"Senhorita Filipa?" a male voice called.

Filipa shrank into her seat, her heart pounding.

"Filipa, please roll down your window. I want to talk to you."

Fear rose like a sharp wave inside her, choking her. Her palms began sweating and her throat went dry.

"Filipa, open the door, I tell you!" The man rattled the door, trying hard to open it.

If terror had a name, Filipa knew it then. She squeezed her eyes shut, willing the man to go away. *Re, Re where are you?* She murmured a quick prayer.

She heard a shout just then, and the sound of running feet. Instantly, the figure by the door vanished and seconds later, Re peered in through the window.

"Filipa, it's me. It's alright. Unlock the door."

With trembling hands, Filipa leaned forward and

unlocked the car door, and stepped out wildly. The moment she saw Re, she burst into tears.

"Hey, hey, it's alright," Re instantly moved his arms protectively around her, and held her warmly.

"I… I am sorry… that man…" Filipa mumbled, between sobs.

"Don't be, *ma chérie*… you've been through the worst, today. You've been incredibly brave and sensible. Cry as much as you want… let it out." His hand caressed her curls, patting her like a friend.

A few minutes later, she sniffed and stepped away.

"Thank you Re… I don't know what I would have done without you. That man at the door was scary, it was so frightening the way he rattled the door and called out my name… I just lost it, I think."

"He knew that it was you in the car?" Re frowned.

"Yes, he kept saying 'Open the door, Filipa'."

"Did you see his face?"

"I couldn't. He wore a cap, and his face was plastered to the dark window."

"It's all right. He is gone. I think we should take a break and rest a bit. I need to think and make some notes, before we plan our next move. Should we go to your friend Julieta's home now? Do you think it would be safe?"

Filipa nodded, still sniffling.

Re settled into the driving seat and turned on the ignition. Deep lines of worry marred his handsome face. He needed to have a long call with Stefan, things were looking far worse than he had anticipated.

Chapter
11

"Coffee, anyone?" Julieta entered the cosy sitting room, a coffee pot on a tray in her hand, and placed it on the teapoy. A large black and white shaggy-haired dog bounded in and headed straight to Re, staring at the detective with soulful eyes. The detective caressed the soft and shiny fur of the gentle pet.

"Just what I needed. Thank you for doing this, Julieta. I am ever so grateful to you." Filipa rose from her seat and hugged her friend.

"Don't mention it. I am just so very sorry for your loss, Filipa. I wish I could do more. But stay as long as is needed, my home is yours," the tall girl said. "Come on Jota, let me feed you. Let's go!"

"Thank you, Julieta. This requires top secrecy, you do understand?" Re asked.

"Absolutely. My lips are sealed. Just call me if you need anything."

Re watched as the girl and her dog walked down the stairs. Julieta's home was a two-storied solid stone house. She lived downstairs, and rented out the first floor—a gorgeous apartment with wooden furnishings, and quaint windows that overlooked the vegetable garden where the chicken cackled in their pens and squatted on the fence. The bedroom with a massive glass wall for natural light was charming. Re loved the ambience, and could imagine happy tourists returning to the haven after a tiring day.

Julieta had been kind enough to fix them a sandwich and hot coffee, and the detective was glad to see that Filipa appeared almost her normal self again.

"Why don't you rest for an hour. I have to be somewhere, and will be back soon," he suggested.

"Why can't I come with you?" Filipa frowned.

"Because it's been a long day and you've been through a lot. You need some rest. Besides, I am going back to your estate to meet Stefan and you can't be there right now," Re replied, simply.

"Oh well, come back soon. We still have two more *lenços* to wade through," she sounded weary and she yawned.

Re nodded and smiled. "I know but grab your rest while you can. Tomorrow may be busier than today."

He closed the door behind him and stood for some moments in the covered patio. It was past 11:00 and Re realized he needed some rest too. But something was troubling him, and a talk with Stefan would help clear his brain. He stared out at the vegetable garden, dark and shady under a cloudy sky. The moon had vanished, barely peeping from behind thick cover. His mind ran over the day's events, their travel to Guimarães, then to Porto and then to Amarante. And almost every single time, the police had followed them—to the Wine & Tapas Shop, and then to São Bento. How could they have managed it? Not even Pedro and Tiago knew where they were headed, as they tried to unravel the trail of the *lenços*. How did the police know where to find them? Were they being tipped-off? Except for the little incident in the Oliveira Square where someone had tried to steal Filipa's backpack, no one seemed to have followed them. Yet... more than one person knew their whereabouts. First the police, and second the murderer who had killed Santiago, and had almost got rid of Miguel but for a pure stroke of intuition and luck. If Re hadn't trusted his gut instinct, Miguel would have been dead. Someone had followed them to Amarante, and spied on their meeting. It was almost as if Re and Filipa had led the murderer to Miguel. But how could they have led him to the old principal? Re sent a restive hand through his ponytail and pushed his sliding glasses back. Suddenly he paused... the man with the cap in the Guimarães Square... what if he hadn't been *stealing* the bag, but actually been *putting* something in it? Like a small transmitter? A startling comprehension dawned on Re, like a bright flash of light. He turned on his heels and strode right back into the house.

"Back so soon?" Filipa asked, surprised. She was still seated on the sofa.

Re put his finger on his lips. "Shh... give me your backpack," he whispered.

Filipa handed it to him, appearing mystified.

"Excuse me," Re apologized and upturned the entire bag

on the big teapoy. Several articles fell off, including some clothes and a purse, and the *lenço* box… and then Re spotted it. A small black button at the bottom of the backpack.

He pounced on it and flourished it triumphantly. Filipa looked taken aback, as he stepped out into the patio, dug a quick hole in the flowerpot with deft fingers, and buried the button in the mud. With a wide grin of satisfaction, he returned to the hall.

"What was that all about?" the *senhorita* asked, bewildered.

"That was a mini microphone-cum-transmitter that was sharing every action and every movement of ours with some stranger who had the gall to put it in your handbag. That is how the police knew where to find you, and that is how this strange poison-feeder has been trailing us."

"So, you mean the police put it in my bag? But when?"

"Not the police. Someone who is tipping off the police," Re corrected. "Someone who has been following us since we left the estate, then pretended to steal your bag when actually what he did was to place the micro-transmitter in your bag. That gave them easy access to all our movements."

"Oh my God… I feel like my privacy has been violated!" Filipa exclaimed, a shiver running down her spine.

"I am worried about our discussions, and wondering how much of it got carried to this mysterious snoop. Also, the moot point remains—why? Why is he doing all this?"

"Because he wants the gifts that Ana has left for Grandpa."

"What's so special about those gifts that a lover has left for another?" Re frowned. "Unless, there is also another agenda… following the trail is leading us to the people who associated with Ana and Ricardo. Unless—" Re paused.

"Finding them was important because he wanted to kill them," Filipa concluded quietly.

An ominous silence slid between them, as each grappled with this thought. "But why kill them? What is the association with the *lenços*?"

"That's what Stefan and I will try to find out. Will you please stay here and not open the door to anyone? Draw the curtains, keep the lights low?"

"Because now he or she knows we are here?"

Re was quiet. "Yes. But so far, no one has tried to attack you, so as of now I don't believe that there is any direct danger to you. For now, you are more useful in solving the trail of the *lenços* and leading this guy to the 'others'. Who the others may be and why they're important, is what we need to now figure."

"I still feel unsafe, Re, especially since this means he knows where to find us. I think I'd better come with you," Filipa said.

Re considered her suggestion for a few quiet moments, then nodded. "Ok, *ma chérie*. Let's go then. But let's draw the curtains, so if someone is spying on us, let them feel that you are still here."

Driving on the Penafiel roads with the occasional street lamp at midnight felt oddly reassuring, Re thought. The cover of the dark, cloudy night with the occasional streetlight, and not a single soul on the road would make it difficult for anyone to follow them. Re felt easier in mind to be moving, especially now that the transmitter was safely out of the picture.

Half an hour later, the investigator drove from the back lane into the Monteiro Estate. The drive through the dark trees was slow, and Re kept a sharp lookout for anything suspiciously out of the ordinary.

Stefan was waiting for them in Ricardo's office and he shook hands warmly with Re and Filipa.

"So glad to see you both safe," he remarked.

"It was kind of you to step in to take charge of everything at the estate. I know you were on holiday," Filipa said, politely.

"Oh, when Re calls, I know it's a matter of life and death. Duty comes first." Stefan smiled, his blue-grey eyes lighting up. "Please, do tell me what's been happening with you two."

Re brought the officer up to date on the day's happenings, right up to their finding the microphone.

Stefan whistled. "Ingenious of you to figure that out!"

"My only grouse is that it took me longer than necessary to puzzle it out. Inadvertently, we were responsible for leading the predator straight to Santiago and Miguel. Not that I am indulging in some guilt-game, but I do need to be more alert and careful. How is Miguel, by the way?"

"Doing better than expected. He has gained consciousness, but can't speak yet. Miguel was lucky you reached in time and administered CPR. It was touch and go," Stefan acknowledged.

"I am so relieved. But we have to be on the alert—he isn't out of danger yet. The man who did this to him will strike again."

"Yes, we are aware. The police have put a guard outside his room. Miguel is safe for the time being. But what made you go back to him?" Stefan glanced at his friend with candid curiosity.

Re paced the room, his ponytail tucked inside his leather jacket, his face enveloped in contemplation. In the dim light of Ricardo's office, he appeared like a gloomy shadow, as the ancient wooden boards of the flooring creaked periodically. A light drizzle began outside, the sounds of rain interposing on the silence.

"Was it something in the letter?" Filipa asked.

"It's a bit difficult to explain. It was a combination of instinct and facts. I realized that Ana, Ricardo and Miguel had been friends for long, and so was Santiago. All of the same age, and perhaps in their youth did things together. Ricardo died, Santiago died, Ana is missing—at least I presume so, since we know absolutely nothing of her whereabouts… so what about Miguel? As we returned to the car, I felt a sense of unfinished business, like there was more that I could have asked him. So, I thought I would go back and talk to Miguel, and find out some more about their past. But underlying this logic was also a sense of premonition… a sense of impending danger…"

"Glad you trusted your instincts. And you are absolutely right about the friendship thing," Stefan said. "I have been thinking along the same lines, and Pedro told me that all these friends were part of a group called April Captains, before the Carnation Revolution. They worked towards the rebellion, and contributed their bit against the *Estado Novo*."

"Ana and Avô too?" Filipa asked, wonder in her voice.

"Ana and Ricardo were almost like leaders. They would meet occasionally at the estate and sometimes in a pub."

"But what has all this to do with the *lenços*? And Ana… I thought we were following the trail because Grandpa loved Ana and didn't want to leave anything open-ended. But then out of the blue, someone threatens a bloodbath if we don't solve the same trail of the *lenços* too!" Filipa remarked. "The connection fails me."

"Santiago's death and the trail of the *lenços* is definitely connected, and that has been proven by the attack on Miguel," Re said.

"But nothing happened to Arno," Filipa pointed out.

"Arno was Ricardo's friend, not Ana's, which means that the assaulted person has to be a friend of both."

"Which also means that wherever you go next—whoever you meet, could be in danger if he or she has been their friend," Stefan concluded.

"And we need to find out precisely why that is so," Re added.

"But what if we don't meet anyone?" Filipa asked.

"The *lenços* and the gift that Ana has left for Ricardo seem to be linked to a person, somehow. They are people Ana and Ricardo knew and trusted, and that is why the gift has been either consigned to them—like with Miguel, or hidden in their town—like with Santiago."

"Once we know why these people are being attacked, we would know who is doing this," Stefan said.

"Perhaps the police can tell us who has been tipping them off. They followed Filipa to Porto—someone had to have tipped them off."

"I did ask—it was an anonymous call that they traced to a phone booth. As of now, we have two main suspects. The man with the cap, who put the microphone in the backpack, and the man who poisoned Santiago, unless they are the same. What we need to find out is if these two are a team, or are working independently," Stefan said.

"So, the way I see it now, we are working at two levels. Ana and her trail of *lenços*, which to all obvious purposes are her gifts to Ricardo. She sent them in the hope that he would come looking for her, but apparently, he did not; and in the end, Ricardo wanted Filipa to follow the trail because, as per his last words, he loved Ana. On the other hand, we have an anonymous threatening note, which promises to create a bloodbath if the trail of *lenços* is not solved by 5:00 PM tomorrow. Killing Santiago is perhaps the first step of the bloodletting. Miguel, the second, escaped narrowly, but is still not out of danger. There is also a likelihood of there being another casuality," Re summarized.

"So far, your trail has led you to Guimarães, Porto and Amarante. What do you think the next destination would be?" Stefan asked.

"Viana do Castelo," Filipa said. "Because she said so in the letter."

"And do you know if any of Ricardo's friends are in Viana?"

Filipa was thoughtful. "Grandpa had a lot of friends all over Portugal. In fact, the one Ana has mentioned in the letter, the vineyard owner with a gifted musical child—I think I know who she means—Fabio de Sousa. If she did go work for him, then we have to go meet him too."

"Then we would have to warn the police," Stefan said.

"But that means Filipa is exposed to being arrested." Re frowned.

"I think that may change now. Especially after the manner in which you saved Miguel, I think the police are rethinking their strategy. They may be willing to work with us," Stefan clarified.

"That's a relief and splendid then!" Re sounded relieved. "I think we should get an early morning start for Viana do Castelo tomorrow."

"I will be there too, for inspection, along with Pedro and Tiago," the officer said.

"Good… I will take a quick look at the cathedral and the arrangements too, then." Filipa smiled.

"Are you sure?" Re frowned.

"Yes… not only will I be there tomorrow morning, wild horses wouldn't stop me from attending my own event tomorrow evening," Filipa promised.

Re and Stefan exchanged quick glances. The detective saw the look of determination on her face, and experienced an involuntary twinge of admiration. Filipa had guts and was a true-blue Monteiro. He was sure Ricardo would have been proud of her.

From the old fountain,
drink the magic potion,
before you climb the mountain,
by the waves of the ocean.
Come find my heart,
where 16 angels blow their horn,
let your desire be granted,
at the feet of the new dawn.

Julieta's home was shrouded in darkness. Rain fell softly and thunder rumbled like a groaning giant in the sky. Filipa was asleep in her room while Re tossed and turned on the sofa. Sleep seemed to be farthest from his mind which was trapped in a whirl, reliving the day's events and trying to sort the many threads that seemed to interweave between incidents.

Finally, he switched on the light and took out his diary. This investigation had begun with Ricardo's murder, but the person in focus was Ana Ribeiro—right from the beginning with the *lenços*. At first, she had been a hazy form, simply a woman who loved Ricardo. But since their journey all over during this day, Ana had gelled into a clear and sharp image in his mind. Everything seemed to jumble in his head though— her whereabouts, her many passions, her moving from city to city, the varying years that she spent in each town, and most especially, the letters she wrote to Ricardo. They were so full of rich emotion and replete with longing, that Re did not ever doubt her love for him. Yet, at the back of his mind, he was aware of her strength, her will to survive at all costs, and her dreams… Re began penning everything he knew about Ana Ribeiro, and slowly a character sketch began to form in a chronological order to the events in Ana's life.

1. *Born in 1948. Has/Had a sister.*

2. *Lived in Penafiel till 1974. (Till age 26)*

3. *Breakup with Ricardo and they parted ways on 25th April 1974. (Age 26 years)*

   Also Carnation Day.

4. *1974 to 1977 (approximately 3 years, age 26 to 29 years) lived in Guimarães and was an assistant to Sylvie at the Palace of the Dukes of Braganza. Sent a lenço to Ricardo and hid the box on the roof of the Ducal Palace.*

5. *Around 1977 to 1983 (age 29 to 35, approximately 6 to 7 years), she moved to Porto and worked as an Assistant Manager in Wine & Tapas Shop where she learnt about wine, did part time work at the Casa de São Roque and did Azulejo restoration work at the Station São Bento. Sent*

a lenço and hid a special tile for Ricardo at the São Bento, which was later sent to Arno at the Casa São Roque.

6. *Around 1983 to 1985 (approximately 3 years, age 35 to 37) moved to Amarante. Worked at the school with Miguel, was accused of stealing from the church and later found that it was Rodrigo who did it. Played the viola amarantina. Sent a lenço to Ricardo and left a special guitar with a recorded song for Ricardo.*

Re paused and reread the chronology that he had gleaned from following the *lenços* all day, and the letters she had written to Ricardo. What a fascinating woman Ana was… so accomplished, so determined, so much in love, and yet so sensible. Optimism seemed to be her favourite companion through the difficult and dark days of hardship. And yet, she had met kind people who had supported her, and everyone who remembered her had something nice to say about her; they valued her presence in their lives and jobs. Someone like Arno had even proposed to her. There had to be something special about Ana, that even after all these years of absence, Ricardo's last words were about his love for her. A love truly superior and worthy of sacrifice, but where had it eventually led her and Ricardo? Repentance? Only the last of the *lenços* would be able to tell them this.

Perhaps only Ana would be able to share her real journey. But where *was* Ana? All these years, while she moved from city to city, planting love gifts for Ricardo, hoping for him to contact her and be with her, why had she never returned or got in touch with any of her friends? It was almost as if once she moved out of the city, she had promised herself never to look back. And yet she had glanced over her shoulder all her life—to check if Ricardo had followed her. Had he? Would a man who loved Ana so much allow her to disappear from his life forever? Even if he couldn't legally be with her? If life could be so cut and dry, grey areas would never exist. But to all appearances, that was exactly how Ricardo had lived his life. Dutifully married to his wife, mentally pining for Ana, but whom he had neither chased nor sought out. What kind of unimaginable, emotional strength must such a person possess? To defy the hunger of the heart and bury it ten feet beneath daily life, to say goodbye to the one person who mattered the most to you, to live life as if your soulmate had never entered your life—such a person had to have mastered destiny. Had Ricardo done that? *Could Ricardo truly do that?*

Re leaned against the sofa, a sense of clarity in his mind—about Ana and Ricardo. But one thing baffled him. Not once had he seen a single picture of Ana Ribeiro. Nowhere. He quickly switched on his phone and searched for Ana Ribeiro images. A couple of pics came up, but Re knew they were not Ana. She must be in her late seventies today. Settled and probably in good health, but still perhaps not as active as before.

It was while Re was still surfing on the net that he heard the soft sobs, muffled hiccups from Filipa's room. Startled, he headed up the mini-staircase and knocked on the *senhorita's* door.

"Filipa?"

"Come in," she replied, her voice low and cracking.

Re opened the door and peeped in. Filipa was sitting upright on the bed, Ana's three letters strewn on a pillow before her, her hair dishevelled and her eyes red. She glanced at Re, tears streaming down her cheeks.

"Filipa... what happened?" he asked softly, sitting down facing her.

"I... I was reading the letters. They are so... so melancholic... you were right Re... she loved him so much and Avô... what did he do? He wasted his whole life... he wasn't happy, now that I think back. He and Grandma never really did get along. They never even sat at the same table for breakfast. We never had holidays together, it was always just Grandpa and me, while she stayed back to take care of the wine, or went off on her own sometimes. She was never unkind to me, but I knew that the warmth was missing. I was confused growing up, but now, having read Ana's letters, I understand. It's not just that Ana loved Grandpa, it is her confidence in him, her complete belief that he reciprocates her love and that he would come for her—that kind of belief comes when it has been *given*. It is not something she imagined. Grandpa must have made her believe it, and there was real and genuine love between them. And that is why I find this all so ridiculously sad. So wasted. So pointless... this after-thought, this yearning that went on and on for years and years... Poor Ana, poor Grandpa... I miss him..." Filipa spoke in a low tone, her voice breaking into soft sobs again.

Re allowed her the moment of realization, for the dam that had burst. It was time for her to release the frustration and the grief that she had choked back all day, carrying on as if her world hadn't been turned upside down by a swift hand of fate. That she hadn't lost her beloved grandfather who was her sole parent all her growing years.

Finally, when her sobs had tapered into hiccups, Re sat down beside her on the bed and held her hand.

"Don't be too hard on Ricardo and Ana… they were mature adults who chose to love and who chose to part—they knew what they were getting into. If one could control love and whom to love, the meaning of fate would lose its gravitas. Because they are intrinsically connected. And love and fate are larger than us—larger than all of us and our desires put together. But that isn't the end of the road, unless we choose it to be. And we will not choose the end of the road. All these years later, we will try our best to do some kind of justice to the love. I still have no clue what role the handkerchiefs play in the whole scheme of things, or where this trail is leading us, but I do know that together we will ensure that justice is done, in some form or the other. Are you with me on this, Senhorita Filipa?" Re's tone was grave.

She stared into his deep brown eyes, her gaze watery with the unfinished business of her emotions. She nodded, "Every step of the way, Re. I gave Avô a promise, and I will fulfil it to the last ounce of my energy."

"Good girl… so now take a couple of hours of rest. We will leave at dawn. Viana do Castelo awaits us… and a long day which holds the promise of drama and justice," he grinned.

She smiled back and gave him a quick hug. "Thank you."

"'*From the old fountain,*
drink the magic potion,
before you climb the mountain,
by the waves of the ocean.
Come find my heart,
Where 16 angels blow their horn,
let your desire be granted,
at the feet of the new dawn.'

"Sounds like a lovely place by the ocean, where beauty and magic abound," Re sighed as he read the translated *lenço*. He touched the beautiful embroidery, once again fascinated by the minute details, the use of colour, and the choice of words. For that matter, each *lenço* was a lesson in minimalist yet expressive art.

"The ocean mentioned here is the Atlantic ocean—Viana do Castelo is a beautiful town by the ocean, a combination of tradition, religion and culture... I always loved it. Our holidays were spent by a sports hotel very close to the ocean," Filipa reminisced.

"With your Grandpa?"

She nodded.

The pink and peach stains of dawn glowed over Julieta's home and garden as Jota, the huge shaggy dog, merrily sniffed out squirrels from the bushes.

Re felt the soft *lenço* for a minute, then glanced at Filipa.

"Do you mind if I ask you something?"

"Go ahead, we have no secrets," she shrugged. She was attired in jeans and a black cowl-neck top, her hair tousled with the morning wind. Small pouches under her eyes revealed that she had barely slept, much like Re.

"I've noticed that you never speak about your mother. Is everything all right between you two?" The detective studied his companion's face.

Filipa grimaced, a hint of a blush on her cheeks. "You noticed right. My mother left the estate when she was in her twenties. Something happened—Grandpa never told me what exactly, and we never really spoke about it—but she left, never to return. She had a falling-out with him, I think. It was only when she got married to her university boyfriend that she came to meet Grandpa once. Then some years later, when Dad fell seriously sick, mom brought me to the estate. She told me that I would now have to live here, and be my grandfather's support, and take care of the estate. She said that she couldn't do that, but I could; that I should be proud of my legacy and help raise it to great heights. Then onwards, she came a few times, just to check on me, but Grandpa and I clicked famously, and I was very happy to live here. I felt a kinship, a pride, which is what I suppose she meant when she said that she couldn't, but I could."

"But you have no clue why she left home and didn't want to return to Portugal?"

"No, and I didn't ask, because there seemed to be some kind of a secret pact between her and Grandpa—and I didn't wish to be caught in the middle of anything unpleasant. I was too young to understand, and later, I was too unconcerned and busy."

Re nodded and turned the car ignition.

"But surely your Grandpa must have been disappointed and upset that his only daughter did not wish to call her actual home, the Estate de Monteiro, her home. She apparently didn't wish to have anything to do with it, either. In other words, she forsook her claim on her invaluable inheritance. And that is huge too."

"I am sure he did initially try to coax her to change her mind, but my mother can be stubborn—once she's made up her mind, she never changes it. Much like Grandpa, although she hates the comparison. And once Grandpa took me under his wing, I think he was happier and willing to let Mother go her way. He trained me well, took me to conferences and field trips, and sent me to wine tastings and trainings. It was he who sent me to Joana de Cruz—the then mayor of Freixo Espada à Cinta—for mentorship, because she had launched a new wine, and he wanted me to experience the entire process of branding and marketing. She took me under her wing, too, making me feel an important part of her venture, and freely sharing her knowledge; I shall be ever grateful to her skill and vision. As a token of my gratitude, I have collated all my resources to organize the event tomorrow. She always longed to offer the world a Portuguese symbol of peace. She designed it herself, and it has so much meaning. I simply love it. My only regret is that she won't be there to see the launch, and the world welcoming it with love and warmth."

Re was quiet as Filipa slipped into a reminiscent silence. The road wove between rolling hills and long stretches of fields, with hardly any habitation. The colours of spring merged into a rain-washed saffron daylight as the sun rose over the horizon, and a cool breeze streamed through their hair.

Filipa read the *lenço* message again.

"*Magic of the fountain* undoubtedly refers to the old eighteenth-century granite fountain in the middle of the Viana do Castelo Republic Square, bang opposite the Church of Mercy and Old Town Hall. It has all these animal figures on its column and is a national monument, but still provides drinking water to the Square. Hence, I believe, the words— *the magic potion of the fountain*," Filipa explained.

"So, do we head there first?"

Filipa was thoughtful. "I think we better go to Fabio de Sousa's home first. I know he won't be expecting us, but since Ana worked on his estate, he may be able to guide us to the next step."

Re agreed with a nod. He'd had a restless night, trying to figure out the many threads that seemed to be running through their trip. At least the microphone was no more a threat, although their plans may have already been conveyed to their anonymous assailant. But with Stefan and the police now in support of their quest, the detective felt an inkling of relief. Since last night, he had felt an instinctive protectiveness towards Filipa—which, to him, was kind of strange. In all his investigations, he had never experienced an urge to protect someone. Contradictorily, Filipa was a strong dynamic woman, who really needed no protection. And yet her vulnerability peeped through at odd moments, and Re knew that even strong people needed the occasional show of support.

He switched on some music, and the next hour passed in reflection and in listening to soulful Portuguese music as the landscape changed from soft pastels to patchworked emerald and sandy hills. As they approached Viana do Castelo, the sky looked overcast, and the sun vanished into the dull blue hues of the horizon.

It was just as they approached the Sousa residence that Re spotted the car behind him.

The Sousa house was a grand display of Portuguese splendour. The car drove through fields of grape plantations, and came to a halt in front of a white stone house with green wooden windows. Inside, a maid seated them in a cool patio with loads of ferns and plants.

"Filipa, my dear!" the voice boomed.

An elderly man entered the patio, leaning on a stick, a wide beaming smile on his handsome lined face.

"Mr. Sousa… so lovely to see you after ages. Sorry to appear unannounced, so early in the morning." Filipa rose and embraced him on his cheeks.

"No apologies needed, my dear. A cheerful start to the day of an old man—a young and pretty face first thing in the morning. In fact, I had planned to come by tomorrow—to say how sorry I was to hear about Ricardo."

"Thank you. Meet Re Parkar who is helping me find out who killed Grandpa."

Sousa shook hands with the detective.

"Re, what do you think of this whole business?" Sousa

asked, as he settled down on the sofa, placing his stick handy, leaning against his right leg.

Re shook his head. "Messy, but we hope we will have some clarity by this evening."

"This evening! That is wonderful—I hadn't met Ricardo in years, but he was an aristocrat. Who could do such a horrendous thing to that kind old man? Not that Ricardo had a sheltered life with no enemies. In fact, he led a colourful life full of risks. I remember that particular time, way back, when the *Estado Novo* raided their meeting and someone got caught, and they all scattered and went into hiding. Ricardo and his companion came here for a couple of days, and then moved somewhere else till the weather cleared and it was safe for them to return home."

"Grandpa and his companion?" Filipa frowned.

"Yes… Ana… his friend, and everything. Such a beautiful girl… too beautiful to be involved in all that pre-independence rebellion business. But she was dynamic, and she and Ricardo had similar ideologies and work ethics. They stood by each other through that rough period. But in the end, they all had to part ways. It was sad, but crucial for their safety too."

"What exactly happened?" Re asked, his curiosity aflame.

"No one really spoke out loud about it and it was all swept under the carpet, but I know that one of them never returned from the *Estado Novo*. It was upsetting and dangerous, and it forever changed their relationships."

Re and Filipa exchanged a quick glance.

"But did not Ana come here later to manage your estate?" Filipa asked.

"Yes, for a couple of years. I offered her a post here, since she wanted to move out of Amarante. She was a great teacher, taught my son to believe in himself. But she was also a great manager and very responsible—taught me a thing or two about diplomacy and handling staff." He laughed. "But she was ambitious and wanted to own her own vineyards one day. I don't blame her for that. Aristocracy and legacy is one thing, and capability is another. She may not have been born into the vineyard legacy, but she sure was more than capable, and more than a match for any of the heirs with century-old legacies. Unfortunately, she did have a past which caught up with her every now and then."

"Rodrigo?"

Sousa nodded. "An evil man if I knew one. Caught me in the fields one afternoon and tried to fill my head with all kinds of crap about Ana—that she was a thief and a spy, and that she had even killed a person. A load of bullshit and I threw him out of my estate. But Ana was very upset. It was not long after that that she quit, and I heard that she worked for a while in the town in the filigree store by the fountain, it was owned by another of her friends. A year or so later, she left Viana, and I never heard of her again. It's been more than 20 years now. Is she fine? Do you know how she is doing?"

Filipa shook her head. "We are trying to find out where Ana is. Did Ana ever work on a *lenço* while she was here? Did she speak of any gift that she wanted to leave for Grandpa?"

"Not that I remember."

Re and Filipa glanced at each other. Was this a dead end?

A few minutes later, they said their goodbyes and headed to their car. As Filipa settled in her seat, Re gave Stefan a quick call.

"We are leaving this place," Re spoke to the officer.

"Ok. The police will be keeping an eye on him, don't worry. Where are you headed now?"

"To the town. We haven't yet found Ana's gift, and there is a filigree store near the fountain where she worked. We are going there now."

"Right, be careful," Stefan said.

Re switched off the phone and turned the ignition. As he reversed the car and joined the main road that led to the town, he glanced at Filipa, who was frowning.

"What are you thinking?"

"About what Sousa said. About Avô and Ana, and that they were in hiding. He never mentioned this to me."

"He never mentioned *anything* to you which involved Ana," Re pointed out.

"That's true. I just wish he had, I would have understood his work, his need to be a part of the rebellion. His love for Portugal—I would have understood all of it."

"But what about his love for Ana? Would you have understood that? Probably that was your grandfather's biggest fear—that you may not understand."

Filipa pursed her lips. "You mean because I don't believe in love? The kind of love the world goes gaga over? The eternal love for souls? You are probably right. But there is reason for that, too."

Her gaze darted to her ring finger with the shadowy mark on it. Re's heart picked up pace. Was Filipa finally going to come out with her deepest feelings?

"But that's a story for a rainy day," she shrugged. "Let's go find that filigree shop. It is already nine o' clock, the shop should be open by now."

As soon as Re drove past, Stefan Weiss and Officer Lusa parked their car behind some bushes and walked the rest of the way up the drive to Fabio's house. The view into the hall was clear through the transparent windows, and they stationed themselves on some rocks and waited. They could see Fabio move around the hall, reading a paper, and a maid bringing in the tea. The casual morning activity added a surreal sense of normalcy to an otherwise volatile situation. Stefan knew that both the previous attacks had taken place immediately after Filipa had departed. Which meant that Fabio could be targeted any minute now. But twenty minutes later, Stefan glanced impatiently at Lusa.

"Something is not right. By now, there should have been some kind of attempt to contact Fabio. He seems pretty relaxed in there, drinking his tea," Stefan remarked.

"Are they meeting anybody else today?" Lusa asked.

Stefan pursed his lips in thought. "I am not sure. They are headed to a filigree jewellery store in the Fountain Square but—" Stefan shrugged. "Let's wait for another ten minutes and then assign someone for the watch here, for a couple of hours."

The Town Square was a picturesque wide space surrounded by old buildings. In the centre stood the old fountain, and tired tourists sat around it, drinking water from its outlet. Opposite the fountain was the former sixteenth-century Town Hall, and the Misericórdia Church with its beautiful arches and upper balconies. Filipa led Re into a cobbled lane, flanked by the Viana do Castelo Cathedral and lined with shops. She paused at the third shop in the lane and glanced up at the name. *Filigree from Tomaz.* They stepped into a well-lit store, filled with attractive handmade filigree articles and jewellery, displayed in glass showcases and on the walls.

"Filigree is an art which came from Mesopotamia to Europe via the Mediterranean Sea, and has been in Portugal since at least the eighth-century. It is the beautiful art of joining gold threads to make a piece of jewellery. The famous Viana Heart was first commissioned by the Queen Dona Maria, in honour of the sacred heart of Jesus," Filipa moved around the shop as she explained. "I have tried my hand at it like a good Portuguese—unfortunately, I realized early on that I can't sew to save my estate, leave alone tweak two gold wires to make meaning."

Re didn't quite believe that. Filipa seemed to be good at everything—a complete all-rounder. Her energy was healthy and grounded.

A young girl appeared from an inside door, and smiled at Filipa.

"*Bom dia,*" she greeted.

"*Bom dia,*" Filipa nodded, as she studied the glass counters under which shone dainty and handmade filigree hearts.

"I am Tania and we are one of the oldest shops in Viana," the girl said softly, with pride in her voice. "We are known for our filigree hearts, made with a lot of love and devotion."

"They are beautiful," Filipa agreed. "Actually, is there anyone here who can tell us a bit about someone who probably worked here long ago?"

The girl frowned. "Long ago... I have been working here for five years now."

"Oh, much longer than that," Re smiled. "Around more than 20 years ago."

"Ah, you need to then speak to my grandfather. My grandmother is no more, but Grandpa may probably remember something. He's gone out for a walk, he should be back any minute now. Would you like to come and wait?"

"We'll wait," Re replied.

Stefan's phone rang then. It was Pedro.

"Yes Pedro, is this urgent?"

"I have found an entry in Ricardo's journal, a half-torn slip of paper stuck in the middle. I almost overlooked it."

Something in his voice alerted Stefan, "What is it?"

"There are six names under the heading 'Core Group'," Pedro said. "Ricardo, Ana, Miguel, Santiago, Tomaz and Agostinho. No other explanation, and no more notes."

"Thank you Pedro. This is an importance piece of information. Do you know all of them?"

"I interacted with each of them briefly at some point of time, when they came to the estate… everyone except Agostinho. But then Ricardo never really confided in me about any of this. So…"

"Thank you, Pedro. I will talk to you later," Stefan said.

He glanced at Lusa and shook his head, "I think we have been protecting the wrong man!"

"What?"

"I shall explain in the car. First, let's head to the Republic Square and I will try to reach Re to warn him," Stefan said briefly, as they hastened to their car.

Re and Filipa had barely studied the filigree hearts behind the counter when a shortish man with a long overcoat and thick glasses entered the store. The moment he saw them, he paused. Then he stared at Filipa.

"Do I know you?" he asked. "You look familiar."

"I am Filipa, Ricardo de Monteiro's granddaughter. And you are Uncle Tomaz?"

"Filipa! Of course, I know you. You came often when you were a wee child, to play on the beach, and you fiddled and tried to work on the hearts, but you were very poor with the craft." Tomaz laughed.

Filipa smiled. "I remember now, too."

"Come in, come in, what can I do for you?"

Re and Filipa explained their errand. He appeared shocked at the news of Ricardo's death.

"Someone killed him?" he repeated, visibly shaken, as he stumbled into a chair. "That is the saddest thing I have heard. I was in touch with him for years, and then in the last five or six years, life became too difficult to keep up with. I am so terribly sorry my dear. I wish I had met him recently—so much to talk about, so much to reminisce. Old age teaches you to value old friends. Only they know you well and can understand what you are going through. Your fears, the demons... but now with Ricardo gone, an era is over. Life will never be the same for us friends again."

Filipa gulped, sudden tears rising to her eyes. She brushed them away hastily with the back of her hand.

"Do you remember Ana Ribeiro? Ricardo's friend?" Re asked.

"Ana? Of course, I do! She worked at the store for a couple of years. A bundle of complete contradictions, that one. Of course, I knew her from before... when we... I mean way back when we were in Penafiel. So, when she reached out, I was happy to have her help me out at the shop. She helped raise it to a different level altogether, ensured that it got publicity, arranged display tables and live demos of the craft. She was the one who began the export business for us—today my filigree hearts go to all corners of the world, thanks to her. The staff loved her, and my wife too. Considering she was deeply sad, she never allowed it to affect her work and in fact, even her life. Earlier, when I had worked with her in Penafiel, I had found her hard and brash—but time changes you. Love changes you, and she was a woman in love."

"With Avô," Filipa filled in softly.

"Yes. Ricardo and she shared a rare bond. Very special. I have yet to see that kind of love where, when you enter, your partner's eyes and face light up a room. And they were unabashed about it. Fearless and unconcerned, till Juliet put her foot down, and life and some incidents kind of forced them apart."

Re shot Filipa a glance to gauge her reaction. Her face was soft and receptive, and Re sensed the change in her. Last night's dam burst had brought about a miraculous change to her mindset.

"Did you ever see her embroidering a *lenço*?" Re asked.

"I believe that my wife did, and she mentioned it to me. Ana had a beautiful hand. The filigree hearts she worked on, some of the pieces, I have still retained and treasured to showcase the best work of the shop. Delicate and intricate work, but the best part was that she did everything with a smile on her face. I remember thinking mentally that the filigree work brought her the same kind of peace that her trips to Santa Luzia brought to her face."

"The Basílica Santa Luzia?" Filipa confirmed.

"Yes, our religious site. You can see it from the Republic Square, and just about anywhere from Viana, perched on the hill. Ana went every Sunday. She prayed there and she loved it. She always returned with a peaceful smile on her face. Although one evening, I particularly remember that it was late and she hadn't come down for long. I was worried and I was about to go look for her, when she came rushing in and there were tears in her eyes. She never said what happened, but her hair was dishevelled and she looked very disturbed. A week after that, she said goodbye to all of us."

"Do you know where she went?"

"Absolutely no idea. I never saw her again." The old man sounded sad and dejected, and Re felt a wave of sympathy for him.

Was it nostalgia for days gone by, or was it that the excitement of youth no longer filled the heart, or worse, that the lack of energy no more supported the young at heart... Re couldn't answer the question. He merely sensed the energy of the old man as dim and dull...

A step on the creaking board made Re swing around. He saw the silhouette of a tall man, sunglasses on his face, and a hand raised, straight at the old man and Filipa. The energy of the room swirled in slow motion, electric and sparking with menace.

"Duck!" Re shouted, and flung himself at the hitman.

As the others watched in horror, Re struggled with the attacker, holding his hand up, the gun swerving in all directions.

The two figures crashed into the furniture and the cupboards, their bodies writhing in agitated struggle. The shot that rang out a split second later in the room was loud and ear-shattering, drowning the wild screams of terror that rent the shop.

Chapter
13

Officer Stefan Weiss stepped into the shop, followed by Officer Lusa.

"The ambulance has just left, taking Tomaz to the hospital for immediate surgery. The bullet has lodged in his shoulder, and the poor old man is in pain. But at least he will live," Stefan informed them.

Re pursed his lips. Perched on the chair, he shut his eyes for a few minutes, commanding his dizzying thoughts to return to balance, and to calm down.

"Are you and Filipa ok?" Stefan sat down beside Re, while Filipa sat in a corner and leaned against the wall with her eyes closed. She looked ashen and shaken.

"I think we are ok. Luckily the bullet narrowly missed and grazed my arm—it is a surface wound. I was given painkillers, so I should be fine. I am more worried about Filipa though," Re said in a low voice. "I wish I could have protected her better."

"No, don't blame yourself. You did your best," Stefan reassured him at once.

"This was unexpected," Officer Lusa agreed. "We were keeping a watch on Fabio, and didn't expect Tomaz to be the next target, until Stefan had a talk with Pedro… But we are glad you are both safe."

"And you have nothing against Senhorita Filipa now?" Re raised an eyebrow.

"I am sorry we were so determined in the beginning. We had to go with the evidence. But things have escalated much beyond that initial piece of evidence; we have to look for other options and give the *senhorita* the benefit of doubt."

"I am glad that good thinking prevailed. My biggest regret, though, is that the hitman escaped," the detective sighed. "He was really stronger than me, and I was torn between attending to Tomaz and Filipa, or chasing him, and I chose the former. I had no clue of the extent of his injuries and feared the worst."

"Don't worry. We will hunt him down," Lusa averred.

"Pedro called me while we were on guard at Fabio's. He finally found an entry in the diary, inconspicuous and barely legible—it was a list of names in Ricardo's diary."

Re's interest piqued at once.

"Six names to be precise, under the heading 'Core Group'."

"Core Group?" Re frowned.

"Probably for whatever activity they were involved in at that point. There were no details, only names. Ricardo, Ana, Santiago, Miguel, Tomaz and Agostinho. No mention of Arno, Sylvie or Fabio. The moment I heard this, Lusa and I rushed to our car, and drove away from Fabio's house in search of the filigree store. I tried to call to warn you, but couldn't get through. We just narrowly missed catching him—it's fortunate you saved the day. At least, all are alive."

"So, Ricardo and Santiago are dead, Miguel and Tomaz were attacked and saved in the nick of time, and Ana is missing. The only person remaining is Agostinho. Who is he and where is he?" Re frowned. "More importantly, is he the next target?"

"Or is he the one organizing the killings, and if so, why?" Stefan completed.

The officer and Re exchanged reflective glances. Re couldn't help feeling that the worst wasn't over. Two deaths already, and two attempts at murder. Filipa could have died too. The enemy was closer than he thought, and constantly at their heels. But why was he doing all this? What did he hope to achieve? The hitman's cold, unconcerned attempt at killing Tomaz was brutal, and displayed a casual disregard for consequences. There was no fear in his heart, and his hand was steady and committed. Obviously, the person who had assigned him the cruel job was even more so. A cold-blooded murderer. And what had Ana's *lenços* to do with it all? Was this a simple love story, or were they on the trail of something deeper and darker than he had initially imagined? And then there was his vision. It hadn't recurred, mercifully, but he still remembered it. Was it just yesterday morning in Freixo? A shiver ran down his spine. Where was the spot that he saw in his vision? And more than the vision, the 'feeling of evil' that swept through and crawled into his heart was more terrifying. He glanced at his watch. It was almost nine. They had very few hours left to solve this mystery. And they hadn't even found the gift Ana may have left Ricardo in Viana do Castelo. For a few seconds, the idea of treachery entered his thoughts. Ana had left a gift for Ricardo, hadn't she? What if she hadn't, and that *lenço* meant something else? Re shook his head. His mind was wedged between contrasting thoughts and ideas, leading him in circles. The injury on his right arm was raw and hurting, and it was beginning to affect his thinking. It was time to get back to the *lenço*.

He glanced at Filipa and their eyes locked in tacit understanding. It was time to make their next move. She rose and approached him.

"Do you think you can continue with that wound on your arm?" she asked, solicitously.

Re read genuine concern in her eyes. He glanced at his bandaged hand where the sleeve was rolled up. It singed where the bullet had grazed and tore his skin, but the painkiller was taking effect.

"I have seen worse," the detective assured her, rolling down his sleeve gingerly. "But more than that, what is important now is to find out what and who is behind this whole racket. Attempting to kill someone in broad daylight, without the least care of being recognized, is the height of cold brutality. He or she means business, and if we don't solve the trail of *lenços* before 5:00 PM today, there indeed could be another bloodbath, I am quite sure of that now. Also, we still haven't found the gift she may have kept in Viana for Ricardo, and I think that should be our top priority now, before someone else gets to it."

Filipa nodded, brushing a hand through her curls. "Let's go then."

While Filipa said a few consoling and assuring words to Tania who seemed to be in a daze, and gave her Re's number in case she needed any help, Re exchanged a few words with Stefan, explaining their next move. As he stepped out of the shop and into the cobbled street, Tomaz's warm friendly face swam before his eyes. The detective felt the old man's pain and was disturbed. *We will get to the bottom of this affair soon,* he promised himself.

Once at the car, Filipa glanced at Re doubtfully.

"You think you can drive with that hand?"

"Yes, absolutely. It is a surface wound, relax. Perhaps we should read the message on the *lenço* again?"

Filipa nodded and extracted the sheet of translated paper.

"'*From the old fountain,*
drink the magic potion,
before you climb the mountain,
by the waves of the ocean.
Come find my heart,
where 16 angels blow their horn,
let your desire be granted,
at the feet of the new dawn.'"

"So, Fabio wasn't aware of the gifts, and Tomaz knew about the *lenço* but doesn't know about the gift," Re said, as he slowly drove out of the narrow alley where he had parked the car. "*From the old fountain, drink the magic potion…* we already did that. *Before you climb the mountain by the ocean.* Do you know a place where wishes are granted and where *16 angels blow their horn* on a mountain by the ocean?"

Filipa was silent for a few seconds before she glanced at Re, her eyes bright with excitement. "Santa Luzia. Cathedral Santa Luzia. On a hilltop by the ocean where your desires are granted. I am not sure about the 16 angels blowing their horn, but there are several murals and frescoes inside the cathedral…"

"That's it, that's the place!" Re banged an excited hand on the wheel, and instantly winced.

"You better be careful with that hand!" Filipa exclaimed. "I have enough worries already than to add more to it."

"Yes, I am sorry, I forgot," Re grinned sheepishly. "But Filipa, you aren't blaming yourself for what happened to Tomaz are you?"

"How can I not?" she remarked. "You got hurt, Tomaz almost died… I have dragged everyone into this charade of a love story… all everyone does is talk about how wonderful Ana was, and how she made a difference to their lives. But what is the end result? She made life hell for Avô and he died because of her *lenços,* and Santiago died because of it, and… and…"

"Hey, stop it!" Re brought the car to an abrupt halt in a lane, and turned to Filipa. "You are in shock, *ma chérie,* because you almost witnessed cold-blooded murder. It would weaken the strongest of hearts. It is understandable. But before we know all the facts, there is no point blaming Ana, or anyone. Look at it this way, *ma chérie*—what if those *lenços* actually *helped* Ricardo live his life? We don't know why your grandfather died the way he did, but Ricardo probably lived longer because of the *lenços* rather than them being a reason for his death. Think about it. For all you know, those *lenços* were like a ray of hope in his life. He may have waited for one to arrive, and been excited and happy that Ana still cared enough, although years had passed. They may have been his lifeline and his will to go on to do his duties. Don't you think that is possible? And isn't that a wonderful thing, then? Those *lenços* should be protected and preserved as a legacy too, of a relationship that distance and time could not prevent from bonding," Re stared keenly at his companion. "Love is like a potion that can help you endure a lot. The lack of it can lead you to the depths of misery, but once you have it, no matter what the situation, however far from you, love can be your guiding light, your power and strength. I think for Ricardo and Ana, although they were separated, love became their strength and their reason to live. And I can't imagine anything more beautiful than that."

Filipa was quiet for long moments, unable to respond, but silent tears found their way through the corners of her eyes. Re inhaled deeply, his own words offering a sudden semblance of peace within him.

He turned the ignition and tilted his head towards the heiress, "So Senhorita Filipa, is it the Cathedral Santa Luzia now?"

She smiled a watery smile, brushed away her tears, and rested her hand on his arm. "Before we do, I want to tell you that you have been an awesome support to me. You are so right. Avô probably lived longer in the hope given by the *lenços*. I have been foolish and angry because I lost him. But I do understand what you mean."

"Wonderful!"

"So, let's go and take blessings from Santa Luzia!"

As they crossed the metal Eiffel bridge over the water, the Lima river shimmered a tranquil gold in the morning freshness, lazing along the banks and meeting the ocean at the north end.

"This bridge was made by Gustave Eiffel of the Parisian Eiffel Tower fame. You can recognize the exclusive metallic style, can't you? It had once been a wooden bridge joining the two banks of the Lima River, but now is this metal landmark."

"It somehow seems to fit right into the surroundings," Re observed.

Immediately after the bridge ended, the road began winding up the hill. The landscape turned from concrete to sandy, and on the left, the river and the ocean gleamed in the morning sunlight. The road seemed vaguely familiar to Re, but he knew he had never been here before. Slogans and colourful banners were hung from fences and trees—*Paz em nosso coração, paz em nosso mundo.*

"Is this in prepration for this evening?" Re asked.

"Yes," Filipa said, with pride in her voice. "'*Paz em nosso coração, paz em nosso mundo.*' It means 'peace in the heart, peace in the world'. It was Joana's favourite phrase, and that will become our motto when we release the Peace Symbol."

"That's beautiful and so meaningful," Re commented.

As the car crawled higher, the cathedral rose from between tall trees, almost like a sun rising on the horizon. The four turrets of the basilica, the peak of the centre dome, sloping orange roofs—all stood silouttetted against the glittering silver-gold ocean curves, and the verdant fields and hills. It was picturesque and Re paused momentarily to breathe in his fill of the stunning panoramic landscape.

Gradually, they reached the top of the Monte Santa Luzia, and the detective left the car in the parking lot. They strode up the steps, and for some moments, stood by the ledge which served as a half-wall curving round the open space in front of the cathedral. It overlooked the Lima river valley, and the coastline stretched from the north to the south of the estuary bordered by the green, tree-covered mountain range. The magnificent vista took Re's breath away.

"Amazing view, isn't it? It's even more stunning from the top of the cathedral—the National Geographic Magazine has labelled it as the third most beautiful in the world," Filipa explained, her gaze far out on the ocean. The wind played with her ample hair, lifting it like a curtain. "But for me, it is special because Avô would bring me here, quite often. I have spent happy hours sketching and colouring this scene in my little book. That was the time when I knew every curve of the hill, every bend in the estuary, and the colour of the Lima where it merged with the Atlantic. I remember I could never get the shade right—was it blue, green, translucent blue-green, brown sand and watery olive? Avô never laughed at my confusion. He said the colour I drew would be the right colour, of *my* ocean in *my* book. This was his favourite view too."

"Wise man, Ricardo." Re smiled.

"Always. I shall miss him forever—his passing has created a hole in my existence."

They both fell silent. Re had no words to console her, because he understood perfectly well what she meant, and did not wish to ease her misery. He wanted her to bring it all out, talk about it, and allow it to dissipate slowly into the universe—the anguish, the longing, the absence and his presence. The infallible truth was that the aura of sorrow around Filipa would take a long time to get dispelled, and he hoped he could help her in the process.

The Eiffel bridge on the left, the lazy Lima meeting the ocean in a gradual shape of the crescent moon, the meeting and mingling of flowing waters, and then the vast stretch of the ocean, hazy and milky in the cloudy gray of the filtered sunrays offered a modicum of peace. In contrast, the wind was sharp and invaded their personal space, pricking the eyes, and flapping the hair around. It was actually invigorating, and made Re impatient.

He turned to stare at the towering presence before him. Basílica Santa Luzia stood against the backdrop of sheer sky and sea; it exuded so much power and energy, that Re was speechless. He sensed the vibrations of the universe strongest on the top of the hill, and in a flash, he understood what

Santa Luzia meant to Portugal and Viana do Castelo. It was also the perfect place to launch the Portugal World Peace Symbol. The blessings of this energy centre would follow the symbol into the world, and vibrate the same frequency.

"A revivalist Romanesque Byzantine architecture," Filipa commented, as they walked across the open terrace. "The basilica is dedicated to the Sacred Heart of Jesus, and the name of the cathedral comes from a small chapel, called Capela de Santa Luzia, which existed at the top of the hill until 1926. That bronze green statue in front of the sanctuary that you see is of the Sacred Heart of Jesus, by the sculptor Aleixo de Queirós Ribeiro, dated I believe around 1898 or some such year, but inside the church, on the right side, there is an image of Santa Luzia too. And don't miss the rose windows—you can see the backside of one on the front facade, right above the green statue—they are very impressive, and known to be the second largest in all of Europe."

Re smiled. He detected a spark of enthusiasm in his companion, and it pleased him.

Multiple steps that wrapped around all four sides of the off-white stone structure led to the cathedral. Right at the centre of the facade bloomed the huge rose window that Filipa had pointed out. As they walked in through the black entrance, Re inhaled deeply, breathing in the gust of energy that met him. Three huge rose windows dominated the three walls of the cathedral, and were the first to greet them with ornate and colourful stained glass petals. Ahead of them, in a semicircle of wall painting, rose the the tall altar with the statue of Jesus staring down at them...

"*Templo do Sagrado Coração de Jesus*—Temple of the Sacred Heart of Jesus," Filipa murmured, her eyes shining with emotion. "I love this place."

A large chandelier hung from the centre of the cathedral, and a long red carpet ran from between the benches to head up a flight of steps, to the beautiful ornate altar. On top of the multi-level altar, along with the statue of Jesus, two angels kneeled on either side of him, and gazed up at him.

And right above, another dome displayed a painting of Jesus descending on earth, supported by four beams of light. It was magical—the atmosphere in the cathedral.

Fiipa gasped suddenly, and clutched Re's hand.

"Look at the dome!" she whispered in awe. "The angels with the trumpets. Now I remember them distinctly. This painting on the dome, it is by the painter Manuel Pereira da Silva, and symbolizes the moment of the Ascension of Christ."

They were indeed beautiful—the painting of Jesus and the four beams of light set against a sky-blue dome; and on the outer circle of the coloured roof ran a ring of dainty, fairy cherubs, with gold and off-white robes and large wings, blowing on clarinets or trumpets in various positions. It was a lovely lively scene... cherubs heralding the ascension of Jesus... in the Temple of the Sacred Heart of Jesus.

Re counted and there were exactly 16 angels etched on the ceiling, in a circular fashion. *Ana's message on the lenço.* This was the very spot.

"'*Come find my heart*
where 16 angels blow their horn
let your desire be granted
at the feet of the new dawn,'" Re quoted.

"It's perfect… it has to be right under the cherubs," Filipa said, staring up at the ceiling, and then at the statue of Jesus right below it. "But how…" her voice trailed in thought and confusion.

"*Come find the heart…*" Re repeated. "This basilica is dedicated to the sacred heart of Jesus. Ana was involved in making filigree hearts—is there a connection?"

"The Viana heart is an extremely popular symbol of Viana do Castelo," Filipa said.

"There are a hundred places in this cathedral where Ana could have hidden a gift for Ricardo," Re said. "Why would Ana think that Ricardo would be allowed access to the nooks and crevices of this cathedral to search for her gift?"

"Avô was an influential man in Portugal. People knew him and respected him. If he wanted, he could be granted special access."

"You may be right. But… wait…" A glint caught Re's eyes, like the sun shining on a piece of metal, and he blinked. His heartbeat quickened, and he squinted his eyes to focus. "I can see… Filipa, do you see what I see? Come closer to the altar," the detective's voice was aquiver.

Confused, Filipa followed him, as he literally ran to the head of the cathedral and gazed at the statue of Jesus. *Could it be? Was it possible?* Re frowned. Around the neck of the statue of Jesus was a long chain, and a large heart pendant shone in the soft lights of the cathedral.

He and Filipa exchanged quick glances. The latter appeared stunned.

"*Come find my heart,*" Filipa whispered.

"The gift," Re was subdued.

"But in broad daylight? All these years?"

"Very intelligent, and I'm sure Ana had some kind of an understanding with the priest or the caretaker. She has managed this *lenço* business with great detailed thought… enlisting people's help all along. Sylvie, Marcus, Pedro's grandfather in Porto, so why not here? But the important question is —how do we get that heart?"

"By sharing the password with me?" a voice suggested.

Startled, Re wheeled around, his gaze colliding with the piercing stare of a tall man. Sporting a silver beard, sparse hair receding from a broad forehead, and attired in a white robe, his seniority reflected in the aura he carried.

"I am Adriano, a humble servant of this basilica. And you are?" Adriano asked, a gentle smile appearing on his thin lips.

"Filipa Monteiro—VP of Quinta de Monteiro. I have organized a big event here, this evening," Filipa remarked.

"Ah yes, Senhorita Monteiro. I am afraid I've never had the pleasure of meeting you before. The preparations are on, and it will be such a beautiful event for the cathedral," Adriano enthused.

"We need a password to obtain that heart?" Re asked, his tone laced with surprise.

"I am afraid you do. As you can see, that pendant has been there for years now. We were told that someone would come for it. We have been taking care of that beautiful pendant—a symbol of love, religion and bonding—for many years now.

It's not real gold, of course, but still, we would need to have a password or rather a passcode, to release it to you."

Re and Filipa glanced at each other, perplexed. Re was thoughtful. He wondered if Ricardo was in possession of any special password or number that would allow him to obtain the neckpiece.

"If I may ask, did Ana Ribeiro place that heart there?" the detective asked.

"She did. She made it herself and she requested the cathedral to place it there, to be given to the one person who knew the passcode. I wasn't there then, but I heard that she was a lovely warm person and she was focused on what she was doing. Apparently, she would come every Sunday, and help with the cleaning of the artefacts and the altar. She believed in this temple... I believe that it gave her the kind of peace she desired. Before departing from Viana do Castelo, she made this strange request to the team here, and we continued to honour it all these years. But now we would be happy to be released from this duty, provided we hand it over to the person with a passcode." His tone was firm, although he smiled a pleasant smile.

"Can you please give us a few minutes?" Re requested.

"Go ahead. I am sitting right in the front, reading. I will be here for an hour, then I have other duties." Adriano nodded and glided towards the altar.

Re led his companion to the far corner of the cathedral and settled down. The entire monument stretched out before them—a display of energy, strength, power and colour.

"A passcode… What a strange request! What was Ana thinking?" Filipa frowned.

"Rather unexpected, for sure. None of the other gifts had any such condition, so why now?" Re wondered.

"Because she wanted to ensure that Avô was the only person who could get that heart?"

Re nodded, "All these years, that heart has stayed round the neck of the Jesus statue. Just imagine how energized it must be now, it must contain so much positive power. She wanted only Ricardo to have it."

"But wouldn't only Grandpa come for it? The *lenço* was addressed to him, he would be the one to go get it."

"And yet she didn't trust that it would be only him. Or perhaps, she wanted to add a double gate to it. Why?"

"Her stalker, that evil Rodrigo… he had created several problems for her, including stealing from the Amarante Cathedral. Perhaps she felt he would interfere and mess it up again, and steal what was meant for Grandpa."

"Brilliant. Yes, that must be one of the reasons. A precautionary measure to keep Rodrigo out of the picture," Re agreed instantly, then fell silent.

He closed his eyes, thoughts swirling in his head. Ana was a smart, intelligent woman. Very accomplished, and a team worker. Placing the heart pendant, the symbol of Viana and a love gift for Ricardo on the statue, for all the world to see, was a brilliant idea. And yet, she had a lock for it. A lock she had ensured only Ricardo would have a key to. Obviously, because she believed that he loved her. Or was it because he

was in possession of some special knowledge that would lead
him to Viana do Castelo? The trail of the *lenços,* of course,
but also the gifts that he had already found? A passcode to
unlock the fourth gift… which would also ensure that he
had received the other three gifts, and preserved them over
the years.

"This is a check point in the trail of the *lenços!*" Re
exclaimed. "A check point which can be passed through with
a passcode. Ricardo or any person who ventured this far
would have the other three gifts… the fourth gift can only
be accessed because of the journey undertaken so far."

"Meaning?" Filipa frowned.

"This is a pause in the journey. A time to ensure that
Ricardo had indeed received all the three gifts. Only then
could he access the fourth one, with the help of the previous
three. Could you show me the first gift?"

Filipa readily brought out the box with the two hearts
carved on it. Re held it with care and studied it carefully. The
beautiful carving, the polished black of the box… was it only
a love gift, or did it hold a secret? By now, Re had an insight
into Ana's thinking. She had a fine mind, just as practical
as emotional, as thorough as spontaneous. Her journey so
far, the beautiful *lenços* with their love messages, the manner
in which she teamed up with friends and acquaintances
to further her goal, the letters which spoke to the heart—
all brought out diverse emotions, but invariably a strong
steady streak of determination. Ana had promised herself a
destination. She was simply leading Ricardo to it, with firm
tenderness, gentle reminders, and an unhurried pace.

Re turned the box in his hands, studying it minutely. And then a hint of light caught it—two numbers neatly entwined within the curves of the two hearts. Re pushed back his silver-rimmed glasses, and his eyes narrowed as he traced the numbers with his finger. Beautifully carved... Excitement and hope spiralled inside him.

"You see this? 2 and a 5. The first number in the passcode is 25!" he exclaimed.

Filipa stared at the carving and the 25, which now stood out in sharp focus.

"Amazing. I can't believe it. So much thought has gone into making this box. She meant business when she began the trail of the *lenços*."

Re searched for a trace of sarcasm in her voice, but only found genuine admiration.

"Ana truly had something in her," he agreed. "The hearts are her personal motifs. And she has used them to convey so much more than just love. Let's see the other two gifts. I bet there would more numbers on them."

Filipa brought out the azulejo with the two simple hearts drawn very much like the picture on the box. Re spotted the number at once.

"04! I am surprised I did not see it before. They are so intelligently embedded within the hearts, its mind-boggling. I would so love to meet Ana and have a long chat with her... I do hope we can."

"Do I sense some fan talk here?" Filipa cocked an eyebrow, a twinkle in her brown eyes.

"Yes, absolutely." Re laughed sheepishly.

"At this point, I have to admit, I don't blame you." Filipa shrugged.

"Why don't you spot the numbers on the *viola amarantina*?" the detective suggested.

Filipa brought out the guitar, and observed the musical instrument for long minutes. It was an exquisite piece of art, the two hearts forming a perfect central attraction below the strings.

Ana's song with the slightest tremor to her voice echoed in Re's mind. He waited patiently, allowing Filipa her own journey of discovery. The sounds in the cathedral were muted, but an organ played somewhere, deep inside the thick walls of the cathedral. Tourists strolled around the basilica, their cameras trained on the ceiling and the multi-coloured stained-glass rose windows. Re could sense their wonder and understand their awe.

"Any luck?"

Filipa held the guitar close to her eyes.

"Ah ha! Found it… 1 and 9!" she exclaimed. "See, just above both the hearts, painted in brown, the number 1 along the line of the heart and 9 along the curve of the next heart. I almost missed it, because it kind of merges with the polished wood."

"Good job. So now we have the number 250419. That has got to be the passcode," Re grinned.

"Let's go and get Ana's heart!" Filipa almost jumped up.

Re caught her excitement, and nodded. The moment of revelation was here…

Adriano was reading in a quiet corner, oblivious to the

excited whispered chatter of the tourists. He glanced up expectantly as Re and Filipa approached him, and rose to greet them.

"Do you have the passcode?" he asked, pointedly.

"We do. It is 250419," Re said.

Adriano was visibly taken aback. His sharp eyes darted from Re to Filipa, and a slow smile curved his lips. "I won't ask you how you figured that out. But I am glad you did. The gift should rightfully go to you, Filipa. Will you please wait here?"

As Adriano vanished inside the cathedral, Filipa sighed.

"I just remembered the legend behind the Viana heart. It was a story Avô had told me. Centuries ago, there was a beautiful girl named Ana who fell in love with a poor craftsman called Thomas. But her father, Don Florentin, was dead against their marriage, because he wanted his daughter to marry into money and nobility. Once, when he found the two of them meeting secretly, he was so angry that he sentenced Thomas to death. Ana was devastated, and to please her father and save Thomas, she agreed to marry the man her father chose for her. Don Florentin wanted to find the perfect match for Ana, and announced that any man who presented her with the most beautiful jewellery set would marry her. The villagers all united because they believed in Ana and Thomas. Each woman in the village gave Thomas a small piece of gold, to support their love. And thus, Thomas created an exquisite heart as a symbol and proof of his love; it was so awesome that Don Florentin had to accept his hand in marriage for Ana. Apparently, to celebrate their love, the women from the village would gather outside Ana's window, where she would display the golden hearts as proof of their eternal love. The legend continued to grow, and to date, the women of Viana do Castelo still use the symbol of a golden heart to celebrate eternal love."

Re whistled. "What a lovely legend. And what a coincidence that her name was Ana too."

Filipa nodded, "Strikingly odd."

Re saw a couple of men removing the pendant from around the statue's neck with a hooked stick. For years, that pendant had graced the statue, and now perhaps it was going to its rightful owner. However the energy it would possess would be priceless.

A few minutes later, Adriano returned, holding the pendant gingerly on his palm.

"Here you go. I shall miss seeing this on the statue, but perhaps we will get another one made." He smiled disarmingly, handing the pendant to Filipa.

She gently turned it in her hand, an expression of candid awe on her face. It was truly exquisitely made, with the curves and interlaced wires forming a gossamer lace.

"Thank you for taking care of it all these years," she whispered.

"It was all the members of the entire church, not me. They were very particular; I just took it forward. And this is an envelope that goes with that pendant," Adriano added.

Another letter from Ana to Ricardo. Re's heart skipped a beat. Another piece of emotional history, a piece of her heart, cocooned in the warmth and solace of words and wrapped in the folds of a 25 years old sheet of paper… He couldn't wait for Filipa to translate it so that he could read it.

As soon as Adriano retraced his steps to the interiors of the basilica, Filipa pocketed the envelope, but continued to hold on to the pendant.

"This is exceptional work. A Viana heart is usually made of four parts. The heart, which is the largest part, and looks like a real heart but with a little left twist to its tail. Then what is called the four flames on the top. And these two parts are soldered together and the joint is hidden by this attractive flower. And finally, of course, a ring on the top for a chain. This heart ensemble is beautifully made, and would truly make Portugal proud."

Re held the pendant for a few minutes and felt strangely intimidated in its presence. Tingles ran up his arm, and his hand felt warmer as he sensed the vibrations. This was not just a pendant. It was a powerful portal that carried the wisdom of the divine and the sacred love of the celestial energy that could transform and lead the keenest disbeliever into a profound experience.

He held the pendant for long moments and inhaled deeply, savouring the connection. Then he placed it on Filipa's palm and closed her fingers over it.

"Keep it safe," he suggested, briefly. "This is rare and precious."

She nodded, and tucked the necklace carefully in an inner compartment of the backpack. They walked down the central red carpet and headed out of the cathedral. Outside, the weather had changed. Clouds had gathered in the sky and the cathedral was shrouded in a shadowy luminescence. Chairs were being arranged and banners were being put up. Video cameras were being set up in strategic spots with large screens, and Re spotted bulky umbrellas for protection, in case it rained. At the half-wall ledge, across the open space of the basilica, Filipa turned and observed the preparations for the evening, a look of pride on her face.

"We have lots to achieve before you can come back for this event," Re replied, glancing at her and reading her mind.

"I know," she nodded. "Just can't help feeling emotional. This was to be a happy triumphant event for me, now all of it is laced with sadness. I will never be able to disassociate Grandpa's death from this event now."

Re squeezed her hand in comfort.

Filipa leaned against the half-wall and gazed out at the sea. She was silent for some minutes, and Re felt compelled to give her some time alone. He turned to head towards the car when she spoke, her voice low, but laced with emotion.

"You know, I've always felt a special connection to this place because of Grandpa. As I mentioned, we would come here quite often. But I now suddenly recall something very clearly... one morning in particular that we drove to Viana do Castelo... I was very young, around seven or maybe eight, but the memory is still so clear in my head. It was a Sunday and Avô, out of the blue, suggested that we go for a drive to Viana. I was delighted. It was a beautiful day in spring and Pedro too came with us. We hung out by the old town, then in the evening, we came here and gazed at this view which never changes, for hours. I drew in my sketch book, content.

Then Grandpa went inside the cathedral to talk to someone, and Pedro stood by the car down at the parking lot. And I sat here staring at the sea, trying to get the colours right. There was this old lady, a very beautiful old lady, who was strolling by and taking pictures. She asked me if I would take one of her. I was shy because no one had ever asked me to do such an important thing in my life. She gently persuaded me, and I did take a wobbly pic of hers, but she was delighted and gave me a quick hug. She glanced at my sketches and said she loved them, and that I was very talented. I liked her so much, she reminded me of my mama," Filipa said.

Re stared at her, comprehension slowly dawning on him. "Which year would that be?"

"I think maybe 1992 or '91?"

"Anything else that you remember about the meeting?"

Filipa shook her head. "Not about the meeting but something that happened afterwards. A hazy memory, more like pictures put together. I saw that lady at the door of the cathedral talking to a man, and suddenly he shoved her and she fell. And then Grandpa was there and he punched the man in the face, and a crowd began to gather. The other man ran away and Grandpa waved to me to tell me all was ok. Pedro came up and sat with me. I saw Grandpa talking to the nice lady, and they went inside the cathedral. I wanted to go to them, but Pedro chatted about dinner and kept me engaged. It was a while later that Grandpa came out alone and then we drove home. He was very quiet and I didn't want to disturb him. Pedro, too, was quiet. Now that I think back, I realize how strange it all was."

Filipa glanced at Re, her eyes moist and shining.

"You met Ana," Re concluded. "You met Ana, Filipa, and you are telling me this now."

"It *came* to me just *now*, being in this place, like a flash of memory." Filipa appeared frustrated and defensive. "And I was just seven years old, how was I to know that I met Ana?"

"And Ricardo too met Ana!" Re exclaimed. "*Mon dieu*, that changes the perspective on this whole thing."

"It was a chance meeting… I am sure Avô hadn't planned it… I mean—" Filipa halted mid-sentence.

"We don't know that. But Pedro would. Why didn't he say anything?" Re was flustered and angry.

"I feel it was a one-off thing. It never happened again. I never saw Ana again."

Re was silent. He recalled what Tomaz had said. How Ana came home one evening, looking upset and messy. She left Viana do Castelo suddenly after that, within a week's time. So, this was what had happened. Rodrigo had attacked her, and Ricardo had been there to rescue her. Then they had talked. Probably one last time? What had they said to each other? How had they parted? Amicably again… or reluctantly? How had Ana taken it all? A woman who had already given the major part of her adult life to waiting and pining? Re paused in his train of thought, to focus on what was important. Did this mean that Ricardo had followed the trail of the *lenços*, after all? Or had he simply found out where she was, and got in touch with Ana? But then, if he had followed the *lenços*, she would not have sent the remaining last *lenço*. Which meant that he probably met her for the first and last time in Viana do Castelo, Re concluded.

So many questions cluttered his brain, the answers to some now stepping into focus, but some largely hidden under dark clouds of confusion. Re wished he could brush the darkness away and extract clarity out of all that he had seen and experienced since yesterday.

He glanced at Filipa. She was gazing at the basilica, anxiety written on her face. Memory was such a strange phenomenon. It cropped up when you least expected it to. Sometimes to help you along in life, but often laced with nostalgia and regret.

"I am sorry. It's a good thing your memory lit up like it did. And it was wonderful that you met Ana," Re smiled kindly at her. "Did you never ask Pedro or Ricardo who the woman was?"

Filipa shook her head. "It didn't really occur to me that she was anyone important, and then I forgot," she confessed.

"They probably wanted you to forget the incident too. It was unfortunate that you witnessed the brawl anyway. You were too young to understand what was happening."

Re's phone rang just then, and the detective frowned at the unknown number. Who could it be?

"Re Parkar? This is… Tomaz's granddaughter."

Re's heartbeat quickened, with hope the old man was fine, and that there were no more complications. Stefan would have called him, if there had been…

"Grandpa gained consciousness for a short while, and

I was right there. He was swinging between delirium and sudden bouts of clarity. So, I kind of pieced this together. He mentioned Filipa, and then he kept saying that there's something you need to know." The young girl's voice was low and sober.

"What is it?" the detective asked.

"He kept mumbling a name actually… I think it was something like Agostinho. And he said, they need to know… does the name make any sense to you?" she asked.

"Yes, it does. Did he say anything else?"

"No, it was mostly this name, and that you need to know. And then Grandpa took for the worse. He is now in the ICU, and I am really scared for him."

"Sorry to hear that; we are praying that he recovers soon. Be strong, all will be well before long," the detective consoled.

He ended the call and glanced at Filipa, who was listening curiously. The detective told her what he had just learned.

"Agostinho again. Strangely, I have no memory of this person. He never visited the estate, neither did Grandpa ever introduce me to him. And yet he is a part of the Core Group, whatever that is," Filipa remarked, a thoughtful expression on her face.

"The most important question is—is he the next victim? Or is he the perpetrator? And where is he? Which part of Portugal, and how do we reach him? And what did Tomaz want us to know about him? If he weren't in the ICU, we could have probably spoken to him…"

"Perhaps there is some mention in Ana's last letter to Grandpa. We haven't read it yet," she reminded.

"Yes, the letter may have some answers. Let's go somewhere quiet to read it? Perhaps even have a coffee," Re suggested.

As they walked to the parking lot, Re turned around and threw a last look at the cathedral. With the bustling activity and people in action, there was a new energy around it. Excitement and exhilaration. Re only hoped that it would remain that way...

Pedro sat in a chair, looking thoughtful. Tiago had offered to go to the event venue to oversee things for a couple of hours. Officer Stefan Weiss was already on his way there. Pedro was in touch with the five mayors and their secretaries, and had run over the schedules for the evening with them. Everyone would be present at the cathedral at 4:45 sharp. *Except, perhaps, Filipa?* he wondered. He suddenly felt immensely sorry for the heiress of the Monteiro Estate. Ricardo had led an unhappy life, always living in the past, allowing his past to overshadow his present. But now it had overshadowed Filipa's future too, through no fault of hers. It was really unfair.

On an impulse, he switched on his phone and punched in a number.

"Yeah, it's me. How is it going there?" Pedro listened carefully to the response at the other end of the line, his expression softening. "So, they found the fourth gift. That is such a huge relief. Perhaps it is time now... whenever you think it is right."

Pedro nodded and ended the call. Involuntary tears sprung in his eyes, and he brushed them off impatiently. The time to shed tears would be later.

Dearest Ricardo,

So, you got the heart… but then you always had it. This also means that you have all my other 3 gifts too and yet you haven't done anything about them.

This is probably my last letter to you. I have waited for an eternity for you to come to me—from Guimarães, to Porto, to Amarante… and so many years in Viana do Castelo. Now I know that perhaps you may read this letter and yet not come to me. What can be sadder than this reality for me? That you love me—yes I do know that—but you stop yourself from reaching out to me. By your actions, you have sent out a message to the universe. That no matter what you feel for me, you are content to stay connected through our spirits… I wish I was more content… and yet I know that our bond is stronger than before. I can feel it. I know you think of me and want to meet me, but you stop yourself… for whatever reason.

I have mixed feelings for Viana do Castelo. It's a place I connected to the most. Working with Fabio was actually quite fun, and he brought back some good memories… in a way Viana mellowed me, as well as prepared me for my life path. It was always wine, and will always remain wine. I have been offered a partnership in a land by my former employer, and it is an opportunity of a lifetime. Let's see… it would be a dream come true to finally own my own land… after moving from city to city like a nomad with no roots, and trying to find my purpose in life, I may finally have reached the end of my journey. I pray as usual that you will be there with me to help me achieve my dreams. You know that I am 43, almost 44. Too old for just hopes, and perhaps it would be too late now if I don't take action still. I need some peace now... before the start of another big journey...

One sad news... my sister passed away and her son moved to Coimbra. Unfortunately, we never made up, and she always blamed me for what happened. I couldn't explain and she couldn't understand, so things ended on a bitter note.

Rodrigo refuses to leave me alone. He has been following me from Penafiel, and his actions are getting more and more desperate, and in fact quite frightening even. My last resort is to complain to the police and I will, if it comes to that. But now I have to get him out of my life... he has messed it up enough, and my patience and tolerance have worn out.

Waiting for you as always.
Forever yours,
Ana.

Filipa placed the letter on the table beside her coffee and sandwich, and for a few moments, stared at the Lima river.

From the glass wall, they could see the locals gathering around the 16 metre high steel monument built to commemorate the 25th anniversary of the Carnation Revolution, but also as a gateway to the Lima river. They placed carnations at the foot of the gateway and cheered loudly. Re had read the plaque which said, "Viana do Castelo

City Hall tribute to the Citizens who suffered and died victims of injustice and oppression and praise to the noble generation of April who, 25 years ago broke the chains and opened the gates of liberty". Today was a day of celebration.

Now as they sat in the quaint cafe along the riverside at the Praça da Liberdade, the cultural centre, Re thought fleetingly of the Carnation Revolution—the day Ana and Ricardo had parted ways forever. The day the country had found freedom and the day two lovers had forsaken freedom to be eternally bonded in spirit.

"So, this letter must have been written before Ana and Avô met at the cathedral," Filipa observed, interrupting Re's thoughts. "Since there is no mention of the fight."

"No mention of Agostinho either," Re stated, pursing his lips. "But did you notice the change of tone in the letter?"

"Is there one? She is still pining for him," Ana said, flatly.

"But there is a ring of reconciliation to it. Like she has now given up on Ricardo and knows that he will never really seek her out. And yet, despite all her cajoling, she seems to be a little upbeat about it."

"Because she has finally found her path in life?"

Re nodded. "You are right. Partnership in a land is a big thing. What a stroke of luck that her ex-employer offered her this incredible opportunity."

"We are assuming that she took it."

"Ana would have been a fool not to take it. And I feel that she did, because she left immediately after her meeting with Ricardo. She herself says that this is could be her last letter.

Which means she really was moving on, and was letting Ricardo know that he has left it till too late."

"Yes, but it is all still kind of sad," Filipa shook her head and took a sip of her coffee.

Re was silent. Ana's letters in her neat blue penned handwriting had touched a core in him. Ana's energy reflected in her words and in her emotions. She wasn't shy in voicing her thoughts. She wasn't bashful in inviting Ricardo to her. She was a determined woman, who in her journey through life, had known exactly what she wanted.

"What about Rodrigo? What do you think she did after he assaulted her, and Grandpa came to her rescue? Did she go to the police? Did she get rid of him?" Filipa wondered.

"Stefan and Lusa would be able to help with that. They can find out through old records, perhaps if she ever did file a complaint against him. Let me call him right away. Stefan may have returned to Penafiel, but Lusa would be here still."

Re rose and went out of the cafe. It was at the door of the cafe that he saw the man with a cap, his head low, immersed in a paper. Re frowned. He paused at the table deliberately. The man glanced up.

"Good morning. Do I know you?" the detective asked.

For a moment, the man was taken aback. Then he removed his cap and Re noticed that he was a much older man, probably in his late seventies.

The man rose hastily, and Re placed a strong restraining hand on his shoulder.

"Who are you? Why are you following us?" the detective muttered under his breath.

"I am following you because you are trying to find Ana, and I want to find Ana," the man hissed.

In a flash, Re understood. "You are Rodrigo!"

"Yes, her boyfriend."

"Let's step out, we don't want to create a scene in the cafe," Re insisted, and flung an arm over his shoulder.

Filipa rose and followed them, confusion on her face.

They stood out on the bank, with the Lima flowing quietly on the right. Tourists took pictures of the April Monument with its hanging thick chain, while some students had settled on the long broad steps of the banks, and were chattering and laughing.

"Did you say you are Ana's boyfriend?" Re confirmed, his hands on his hips.

"Yes, since we were at the university. She is my first love and girlfriend," Rodrigo declared.

His teeth had a black edge and his gums showed when he spoke.

"If she is your girlfriend, how is it that you don't know where she is," Filipa asked.

"Look, you have to understand this… there has been so much said about our relationship. She has spread so many lies about me over the years. And all I have ever tried to do, is to propose marriage to her, and offer her my protection," Rodrigo said, his voice slightly grating.

"Protection? From what?" Re asked.

"From all her shady activities. She and that Ricardo—with due respect, *senhorita,* to your feelings, I know he was your Grandpa—for years they were on the wrong side of the law.

He was a bad influence on her, he led her down this path which was dangerous and risky, and she followed him blindly. I accept that Ana was spirited, but that was all the more reason why she needed protection. He tempted her down a path she was never supposed to go. But she did, and since then, it has been up to me to try to bring her back to safety."

"So why couldn't you, all these almost 50 years?"

"Because she wouldn't listen. Very strong-minded is my Ana. I tried every technique in the book to show her that the life she has chosen is no good for her."

"You even stole from the Amarante church," Filipa accused.

Rodrigo looked taken aback. "That was years ago and I didn't steal it—that's a lie! It was Ana who dared me to bring that artefact out of the church to prove my love for her. And I did! I lifted it one night—it was a small candelabra, and I showed her I would do anything for her."

Re and Filipa exchanged quick glances.

"But it was Ana who got accused for stealing the artefact, not you."

"That was bad luck. It was never supposed to happen like that. The dare was that I would steal it and return it the next morning, but before I could, the caretaker raised an alarm. Anyway I did return it, saying I found it lying outside the cathedral window, and the matter was hushed. But honestly, I think Ana enjoyed the thrill. She didn't care a jot if her name was dragged into the mud even innocently. She loved the experience. No one knows Ana the way I do…"

"And yet, she rejected you every single time, and told you not to follow her, didn't she?" Re asked.

Rodrigo averted his gaze, taking his time to respond. "How do you know that? Ah yes, all those phony friends of hers... from Porto and wherever... I tried to warn them that Ana was not the person they thought she was. She was involved in shady activities against the government, and I warned them. But they all got taken in by her—she is smart and knows how to use people. But they didn't listen to me... why would she ask me to leave? She needed me as much as I did her. We were in love, and then Ricardo came between us. But that was temporary. The moment she left Penafiel, I followed her, and I knew that it was a matter of time before she forgot him and returned to me."

"But she didn't, did she?" Filipa nudged. "Fifty years, Rodrigo, that's a long time for a person to know her mind. The indisputable fact is that she did not love you."

"She pretended that she didn't when actually I know that she waited for me to find her and cajole her to return. Every single city, every single time," Rodrigo said confidently. "I told you, I know Ana like no one else."

"Then why don't you know where she is now?"

The older man looked a little flummoxed. "I admit I am trying to figure that out. It's difficult sometimes, to follow the way she thinks. I met her when she was in Viana and then she moved town. But I am still looking for her and I will find her."

"Perhaps she doesn't want to be found, have you thought of that? It's been, what, more than 20 years now? She doesn't want to be found, Rodrigo. specially because of the way you assaulted her at the cathedral, all those years back," Filipa accused.

Rodrigo shifted uncomfortably. "I didn't assault her."

"Don't lie, I was there, I saw you!"

"You were there?" For a moment he appeared confused and taken aback. He ran his tongue over his dry lips. "Ana has always been headstrong, and I had waited years for her to come back home to Penafiel. So, when she refused to listen, I just had had enough. I tried to drag her to the car. And it all just turned ugly. And then out of the blue, Ricardo appeared, and it got even more dirty. He punched me in the face, and I swear if it hadn't been for Ana, I would have killed that man, right then and there!" Rodrigo's eyes turned bloodshot and his face changed colour.

"So, it was you who killed Grandpa!"

"No... I would have loved to, mind you. He stole my girlfriend, and turned her against me; I waited all these years in the hope that one day, she would realize how much she loves and needs me. But Ricardo didn't let that happen. And for that alone, I could have murdered him. But I didn't. And certainly not after all these years, I would have done it right there and then. So no, I didn't murder your grandfather, believe me!"

Re stared at the man, desperate and aging, and strangely, felt sorry for him. Another wasted life? In love with Ana, who loved Ricardo. And love led them all on a journey and to the point of no return. Had Ana led Rodrigo on? Had she really dared him to steal? Was she involved in shady activities like he accused? These were doubts more than questions, and voiced probably to cast suspicion and contaminate minds. The fact was that no matter what the truth was, Rodrigo was still looking for Ana for more than 40 years, loving her in his own twisted way, but loving her nevertheless. Rodrigo's entire life played before Re's eyes—the life of a lonely man, obsessed with possessing a woman who didn't love him, and who had somehow managed to slip out of his life forever. But was it really forever? Rodrigo was still looking for Ana, after all these years… to what length would he still go to get her back? Would he hire a hitman to kill Ana's and Ricardo's friends? And perhaps Ana herself too? Would revenge and misplaced love consume his and all their lives?

"Did you kill Santiago?" the detective asked the old man sharply.

Rodrigo looked taken aback. Then his head tilted up, and a sense of pride and hurt crossed his wrinkled face. "I think I am done here," he declared sullenly. "I don't have to respond to any accusations, and I don't want to talk to you about anything else."

Before Re and Filipa could react, the man turned on his heel and walked briskly away.

"But…" Filipa began, and Re restrained her with a hand.

"Let him go. He will be following us again in the hope that we reach Ana."

Chapter
15

The river flows by the trees of our land,
the earth has flourished in its duty.
Life is steady and heady
as we slowly sip its deep beauty.
But it's almost time, my heart,
time to breathe and rest.
Where the sword hugs the tree,
it's time to end this quest.

Stefan stared at the laptop as he sat in the car. There was absolutely no online reference to the 'Core Group', and especially none for Agostinho. Where was he, and what role did he have in the murders and attempted murders? Who had planted a hitman to kill people? And would he stop, or would he continue to chase his targets? Who would be his last victim? Stefan didn't like the virtual intractability of these people. Ricardo dead, Ana missing, Santiago dead, Miguel and Tomaz both fighting for their lives in the hospital. Who would be the next target?

Something else troubled him. Santiago and Miguel were forced to drink poison, from wine. Was there a rival wine connection here? But Tomaz, on the other hand, was shot at point blank. Was it because the hitman was running out of time and did not get an opportunity to pour him poisonous wine? Or... Stefan paused. What if the hitman wanted to shoot not just Tomaz, but also someone else? Filipa? *Mein Gott...* what if Filipa was one of the targets? Why hadn't they thought of it? He better warn Re... but perhaps he had already figured it out?

"So far, we have always had some clue as to where Ana went next. But this time, there is nothing in the letter to indicate her next move, is there?" Re wondered, aloud.

"Except that she now planned to settle down and do what she loved best," Filipa said.

"Wines and wine making? And that this is the beginning of another long journey... she has mentioned that. But this time, there is no forwarding address, and no hint at her next halt. Did she finally decide to walk out of Ricardo's life, for good? "

"If she did, she wouldn't have sent this last *lenço*," Filipa reminded.

"Ah yes... but isn't there a huge gap between the last two *lenços*? What are the dates?"

Filipa extracted the kerchiefs and glanced at the dates that Ricardo had pinned to the top of each *lenço*.

"There is a gap of at least 15 years between the two kerchiefs, and wait…" she glanced at the detective, a glint of excitement in her eyes.

"What?"

"The date on this last kerchief. Its 25th April 2015!" she exclaimed.

"That's just four years ago. Which means…" Re's eyes gleamed behind his spectacles.

"That Ana is alive!" Filipa completed.

"This is exciting," Re admitted. The realization that the trail of the *lenços* may finally lead right up to the real-life Ana, was intriguing. Re couldn't wait to meet her—this fascinating lady whose life he had slowly witnessed through the voices of other people, and her own letters and gifts to Ricardo. "The 15-year gap between the two kerchiefs means that Ana had indeed moved on, but her love for Ricardo had proved stronger than all her resolve."

"Or that she had heard that Grandma was no more, and was perhaps inclined to try one last time with Grandpa?"

Re laughed, "Ah, the cynical *senhorita*."

"You don't think so?" she raised an eyebrow.

"How old do you think Ana is right now? She must be in her early seventies. You think she may still be pining for Ricardo? How do you think she has lived her life in these last 25 years? In my opinion, she must have worked hard on her dream, embarked on the new journey, tried to lay roots like she mentioned in the letter. She may have even married? To my mind that sounds unlikely, but it is a possibility, *n'est-ce pas*? And then, when she eventually did settle, she may have sent a *lenço* to Ricardo, to now witness her glory."

"Or perhaps she failed to settle down, and that is why she thought of Ricardo as a final resort?"

"You mean that she is out there somewhere, drifting, wallowing in self-pity, unaware of her future at the age of seventy?" Re frowned. "Really?"

Filipa pursed her lips. "Yeah, now that you say it, it does seem unlikely."

"Totally. Ana is a dynamic woman, determined yet caring, she went out of her way to help people. Look how she helped Tomaz build his business to make his filigree hearts an international product. And her ex-employer liked her work so much, he even offered her a partnership in his land. I am sure she is somewhere in Portugal, enjoying her wine plantations, and living a happy retired life."

"You are right, of course. So, what do we do next?"

Re opened his pad and glanced at the notes he had made.

1. *Born in 1948. Has/Had a sister.*

2. *Lived in Penafiel till 1974. (Till age 26)*

3. *Breakup with Ricardo and they parted ways on 25th April 1974. (Age 26 years)*

   Also Carnation Day.

4. *1974 to 1977 (approximately 3 years, age 26 to 29 years) lived in Guimarães and was an assistant to Sylvie at the Ducal Palace. Sent a lenço to Ricardo and hid the box on the roof of the Ducal Palace.*

5. *Around 1977 to 1983, (Age 29 to 35, approximately 6 to 7 years), she moved to Porto and worked as an Assistant Manager in Wine & Tapas Shop where she learnt about wine, did part time work at the Casa de São Roque and did Azulejo restoration work at the Station São Bento. Sent a lenço and hid a special tile for Ricardo at the São Bento which was later sent to Arno at the Casa São Roque.*

6. *Around 1983 to 1985, (approximately 3 years, Age 35 to 37) moved to Amarante. Worked at the school with Miguel, was accused of stealing from the church and later found that it was Rodrigo who did it. Played the viola amarantina. Sent a lenço to Ricardo and left a special guitar with a recorded song for Ricardo.*

He needed to add the Viana do Castelo notes, he reminded himself.

"Let's see the last *lenço*, what does it say?"

Filipa held up the beautiful kerchief. If anything, the embroidery had gotten better and more beautiful, like Ana had honed her craft even more. Interspersed between the words was a bowl of fruit, with what looked like cut olives and almonds. Another corner displayed a sword and a wine glass, along with the trademark double hearts.

Filipa translated the colourful threaded words.

*"'The river flows by the trees of our land,
the earth has flourished in its duty.
Life is steady and heady
as we slowly sip its deep beauty.*

But it's almost time, my heart,
time to breathe and rest.
Where the sword hugs the tree,
it's time to end this quest.'"

Silence slipped in after Filipa finished reading the poem. A small slice of country heaven… images of tranquil countryside rose before Re's eyes. The beautiful words, the embroidered pictures, and the loving hearts, all came together to express Ana's deepest desires.

"Such beautiful lines. *The river flows by the trees of our land…* so she is near a river, and *the earth has flourished in its duty…* sounds like fields, plantations?" Re analysed.

"*Life is steady and heady as we slowly sip its deep beauty* sounds like she is enjoying her life," Filipa frowned.

"Exactly. And the words *heady* and *sip* definitely indicate intoxication, perhaps of two kinds. Intoxicatedly content and …"

"Wine. That's what she always wanted to do. Make wine," Filipa concluded.

"That's right. She is in some vineyard, making wine, and is happy about it."

"But where? She could be anywhere in the entirety of Portugal!" Filipa suddenly sounded impatient.

"Wait… these last lines… *But it's almost time, my heart, time to breathe and rest. Where the sword hugs the tree, it's time to end this quest.*" More images rose spontaneously in his mind—long walks in the sleepy old town just yesterday morning, with the perfect landscapes to soothe the tired heart. "Freixo de Espada à Cinta!"

"What?" Filipa sounded incredulous. "That's the other end of Portugal. Ana was mostly on the west coast of Northern Portugal. Freixo is far east, bordering Spain. That's too far for her to go."

"Not if she got a partnership in land to grow her own wine."

"But I've been in those parts for many months, working with Joana. I never saw or heard of an Ana Ribeiro," Filipa still seemed doubtful. "How can you be so sure?"

"*Where the sword hugs the tree…* I have been in Freixo for the last few days, and I have sat before this sword that hugs the tree. The ash tree sword. I am positive that is where Ana is."

"It's a three-hour drive to Freixo. The programme begins at five. We will never be able to drive to Freixo and back in time for the event. I am not going to Freixo! In any case, we are no way closer to solving this. I am not sure where this is leading us!" Filipa said, distressed.

"Your grandfather was murdered yesterday at dawn, Santiago was murdered a few hours later. Miguel and Tomaz barely escaped an assassin's attack on the same day, and Freixo seems to be our last hope of finding Ana, to glean the truth. This is it. The end of the trail of *lenços*—there are no more *lenços* to guide us. We have to go to Freixo, no matter what, because it is leading us to the truth."

Filipa still appeared doubtful and shook her head. "I don't know if this is the right decision. What if we simply waste time?"

Re inhaled deeply and held her gently by the shoulder. Their eyes locked for long moments. Her ample hair framed her heart-shaped face, and her brown eyes filled with a mix of deep concern and anguish.

"Filipa, we don't have a choice. I am afraid you will have to trust my gut instinct, *ma chérie,*" the detective spoke with gentle firmness.

She sighed and nodded. "In that case, you'll have to let me drive. I wouldn't want you to drive this far with an injured arm. Plus, you need a magical maniac right now to expand time, and I will do it with speed."

Filipa was true to her word. She drove in silent determination and Re was content to sit back and ruminate.

"What I don't understand is why Ana didn't try to connect with Grandpa for 15 years. That's a really long time, don't you think?" Filipa reflected aloud.

"She may have been busy."

"Doing what? If she had really followed her wine-making dreams, then I would have known about her. I was in Freixo some years ago, and very active in community life. Joana was a fireball. She had these amazing ideas, knew everyone in Freixo, she showed me the details and taught me the ropes of the business. Of course, I wasn't a novice, but still I learnt some tricks of the trade from her. And her vision for peace and Portugal and the symbol she designed... I know that Joana was incomparable. But how is it that in all those years that I mentored under her, I never ever heard the name Ana Ribeiro? That is why I feel that we may be heading to the wrong place."

"No, we are not." Re was quiet. "You know what, I have an idea. I believe that you would know the current mayor of Freixo, and although she would already have left for Viana do Castelo for your event this evening, you probably know some of her office staff. They can help us look up the city records, and find out if Ana ever lived there."

Filipa hesitated, and Re noticed that her fingers clutched the wheel tightly.

"I am not sure," she hedged.

"Why not? It's a good idea and we are strapped for time. Why not call up some favours just now, to save time?" Re frowned.

Filipa drove to the side of the road. "OK, if you insist… Let me make a few calls."

She descended from the car, and Re saw her speak into the phone, pacing along the road, a forced, pleasant smile on her face. Minutes later, she returned to the car and sat down.

"Done." She turned the ignition and they were moving again.

Re turned to face her. He had sensed her resistance and reluctance, and he couldn't ignore it any more. "Why were you hesitant to call the mayor's office? In fact, now that I think of it, you have been reluctant to drive down to Freixo de Espada à Cinta, haven't you?" he observed. "And it has nothing to do with the *lenços*."

Filipa passed him a quick glance and pursed her lips. "I have my reasons."

"Ah, if there ever was a good time to share all of your reasons, secrets and promises, it is now, *ma chérie*… we have three whole hours to pass before we reach Freixo de Espada à Cinta. We are in this together, so I need to know every single thing. And by everything, I mean everything!"

"No, you don't! My personal life has nothing to do with any of this," she protested.

"Wrong, *ma chérie*. Unfortunately, your personal life is a hot topic of discussion, all over Portugal, right this moment!" Re snorted.

"Put that way, you are right of course. I am in a soup, much bigger than the world's largest cauldron can hold." Filipa sighed.

"And we are going to swim out of it, clean and unharmed. But…"

"*Está bien!* I get it. I will come clean, although I have to warn you, there is nothing much to tell. I met this man some years ago—Fabio—in Joana's office. He was a decent person, quite okay looking too, but with a lot of sense and clarity for life. I liked him. We were different but quite similar too… like black olives and green olives." She laughed. "We hit it off really well. Instant attraction and all that stuff, and I felt that we had something. Fabio proposed to me, and for the first time in my life, I took an impractical decision, with my heart, not my head. It was beautiful for a while, I told Grandpa too, and he was delighted, just surprised because I had been so hasty, and it was so unlike me. But Fabio and I— we are from different parts of Portugal, and when the time came for me to leave, we faced a wall. He never wanted to leave Freixo de Espada à Cinta, and I couldn't imagine a life without the estate. It was an impasse. So, I returned the ring to him. End of the tale."

"Ah, sorry to hear that... but now I get it... all that cynicism stems from this one incomplete love story."

"Hardly a love story!" Filipa scoffed. "It was wrong choices and decisions, and the heart playing a trick—that's all. Leading you to believe that this could have been a story worth telling your grandchildren. It wasn't the kind of love Ana felt for Grandpa, which is really epic. And I am just beginning to wrap my head around the intensity of that emotion."

"Hmm... and you two aren't in touch anymore."

"Nope. The last I heard, he no more worked at the mayor's office."

"Is that relief or regret I hear in your voice?" Re quirked an eyebrow.

"Neither."

"What about now? Would you like to meet him? What would you feel if he showed up suddenly?"

Filipa's gaze darted to him, a look of reflection in her eyes. "Honestly, I don't care anymore," she said, with a shrug.

"Right," Re hid a smile.

The landscape was changing as white-coloured hillocks began rising on either side. Re recognized the soothing green and white countryside he had just passed the day before. Was it only yesterday morning that he had driven from the Manueline village to Penafiel? So much had happened in these 24 hours... Not just the fact that people had lost their lives, but that he had witnessed the unfolding of a love story like none before. All-consuming, rippling with a strange kind of almost sacrosanct passion and drive. But the moot question was—was this only a love story, or was it something more? Was Ana trying to reach out to Ricardo out of the deep, unshakeable love within her, or was there another message in the love letters? Especially that code block that they had faced in the Santa Luzia Cathedral. The sudden demand for a password—at that time, he had thought the purpose of the password was to ensure it was Ricardo who found all the three gifts. But what if it hadn't been Ricardo, but someone else who had found the gifts? Would the heart necklace have remained forever around the statue's neck? What was the purpose of the password? Re went over the troubling thoughts over and over again. He felt he had missed something, an angle... Something that he should be able to spot at once, but couldn't. And the thought disturbed him.

Olive trees scaled the slopes on either side, as the car wound between curves. Clusters of orange roofs appeared ahead, and they sped smoothly towards Freixo de Espada à Cinta.

"Since the *lenço* mentions the ash tree, let's head there first," Re suggested.

Freixo was a beautiful old medieval village, and Re felt as if he had come home, as the car edged its way through narrow cobbled streets with houses overlooking the street. The green windows were shut, and once again, Re got the feeling of a sleepy, laid-back town. Yet it was so peaceful...

The narrow lane opened into the Square of Igreja Matriz, dedicated to São Miguel. Right in the front rose the cathedral, Igreja de Matriz de Freixo de Espada à Cinta, with the ash tree on its left, and the cemetery opening into a big yard right behind it.

A flex in front of the cathedral offered a quick write up— *sixteenth-century rectangular church with three naves, chancel, apses and sacristy. The main elevation is a Manueline portal, with a depressed arch flanked by pilasters and decoration in relief.*

The interior space is of a hall-church type, with a remarkable stone vault with invaluable Baroque carved altarpieces. The chancel has sixteen sixteenth-century panels accredited to the school of Grão Vasco.

The Igreja de Matriz de Freixo de Espada à Cinta is a hall-church built by King Manuel on the same spot of an old Gothic temple, which was initially built in the reign of King D. Sancho II, between 1520-1550, with single cylinder pillars that support ribbed vaults.

"It's beautiful inside but let's focus on the ash tree."

Re led Filipa to the tree standing tall on the left of the cathedral. A big sword was strapped vertically, on an ash coloured strap.

But it's almost time, my heart, time to breathe and rest. Where the sword hugs the tree, it's time to end this quest... Ana's words on the *lenço* popped up in his mind.

"The name of the town literally means ash-tree girded with sword or sword on the belt of an ash. There are at least three legends that explain this phenomenon. But I think, by far the most popular one that appeals to me, is that the name was derived from a Gothic nobleman Espadacinta. Apparently, after war with the Arabs by the Douro River, he was tired, and he came into this region and strapped his sword to the ash tree and rested under it. Another one propagates that the King of Portugal tied his sword to the tree and leaned against it, when he founded this town in the fourteenth-century."

"Yes, I kind of know of the legends," Filipa smiled. "I have worked in this town for many months, remember?"

"Yes, I was simply revising my knowledge. But I like this tree and the atmosphere of stealthy calm. Is it because there is a cemetery right behind it which overlooks a magnificent view? I can understand why Ana finally chose to settle in this Manueline town, with sprawling hills covered with olive and almond trees. Her words on the *lenço*—*it's almost time, my heart, time to breathe and rest. Where the sword hugs the tree, it's time to end this quest*—are an indication that she has finally chosen Freixo as the place to rest."

"The Bragança district is beautiful. And by now, it is obvious that Ana liked and appreciated beauty and nature. Even I am beginning to understand how she would think," Filipa added.

"Which means that Ana has to be in this town, and we have to find her," the detective concluded. "There is a post office here. Let's go ask a few questions. It's a small town and people know each other."

Re strode towards the building standing on the right of the cathedral. An oldish woman was behind a counter which also served as a tourist information office. Filipa greeted her and they spoke in rapid Portuguese. At length, Filipa mumbled her *gracias* and turned to Re.

"She has never heard of an Ana Ribeiro, and she was born and raised here, except for the few years she tried to be a waitress in Paris."

"Oh," Re frowned.

"But she did know an Ana Cardosa, a warm person who was her friend. But she passed away last year after a sudden and brief illness. The lady suggested that we ought to go check out the cemetery," Filipa added in a low voice.

Re stared at her, an uneasy feeling in his pit.

"You think she changed her name to Cardosa, when she came here?"

"Possibly."

"Ana is a pretty common name."

"Yes."

They stepped out of the office in silence, deep in thought. Filipa's phone rang just then, and Re perched on one of the benches outside the office while she spoke on her cell. Could Ana really be dead? He breathed in deeply, allowing the energy of Freixo de Espada à Cinta to guide him. Could two days of intense search for Ana, following her trail of *lenços*, living her anxieties with her, and dreaming her desires through her letters and her gifts, lead to such a flat and disappointing end? Re felt let down. He had built up his hopes. He had an earnest and compelling desire to meet Ana, to see her in the flesh and study what had become of the passionate woman in love. How would she look now? Had she still retained her fiery beauty, or had it faded into a warm memory? What emotions coursed through her body and heart, and how would she react as she glanced back on her journey? With regret or pride? Re not only wanted to learn every single detail of her life, but he also wanted her to fill the gaps in her story, and satisfy his own curiosity. He had in a way become obsessed with Ana of the letters. And he simply wasn't able to accept that he wouldn't be able to do so. *Ana was dead?* The thought distressed him.

Filipa ended her call and sat down beside him on the bench, staring out at the cobbled street and Square in the afternoon light.

"The mayor's office did a quick search on their computers and data, and found the same Ana Cardosa. No Ana Rebeiro," she confirmed briefly. "Ana is indeed dead."

Re pushed back his glasses. "So, when she wrote on the *lenço—it's almost time, my heart, time to breathe and rest. Where the sword hugs the tree, it's time to end this quest*—did she mean that she was dying and that her time had come? Was that why, after a gap of more than 15 years, she suddenly wrote to him, willing him to come meet her one last time?"

"Possibly. But what interests me more is—did he? Did Avô come to Freixo to meet her?" Filipa wondered.

"No, he didn't," a voice cut in.

Startled, Re and Filipa glanced at the man who seemed to have appeared from nowhere. He was tall, muscular and balding, with a French beard, and his black eyes were piercing.

"You are—?" Re blinked at him.

"Private Detective Felixe. I was appointed by Ricardo

Monteiro many years ago." Felixe shook hands with Re and Filipa.

"Appointed to do what?" Filipa frowned.

"Should we go sit by the ash tree? It's a long story," Felixe suggested.

Re and Filipa exchanged quick looks and the former nodded. Suddenly, he felt a frisson of excitement. If Felixe was appointed by Ricardo, were they finally going to learn some of Ricardo's secrets? Even his side of the story, perhaps?

"Appointed to do what?" Filipa repeated, as they sat on the benches by the tree.

"Assigned to keep an eye on Ana."

"I don't understand," Filipa shook her head.

"When Ana and Ricardo parted ways, they had decided never to meet again. At least not unless Ricardo reached out to Ana. But when she sent the first *lenço*—yes, I know all about them—Ricardo was curious, and yet torn by his loyalty to his wife. So, he hired me. All he wanted to know was if Ana was safe."

"So, Ricardo knew where Ana was, all along?" Re asked.

"Kind of. He never attempted to meet her—his only wish was for her to be safe and managing well on her own. That's the only information he demanded. Until his wife passed away. He was a free man then, although he was in his fifties."

"Did he seek Ana out then?" Filipa was curious.

"No. But he did go on the trail of the *lenços*."

"What? Grandpa had already solved it?" she exclaimed, incredulity in her tone.

"Only until Viana do Castelo," Felixe recalled.

"Then why did he not accept the gifts and keep the letters? Why was the trail made to appear as if it was untouched?" Filipa was confused.

"I think I know why," Re cut in quietly. "All along I have wondered how people held on to the gifts after so many years. It was almost like a commitment, a promise that they had made to someone. And that someone was Ricardo! All the people involved were Ana and Ricardo's friends and I think what Ricardo did was to ensure that the trail remained intact for one person. And that person is you, Filipa."

Filipa appeared perplexed, "But why?"

"He must have requested his friends to hold on to the gifts and the letters till you came looking for them at the right time. And they kept their promise. He wanted you to solve the trail of the love *lenços*, just the way he did. He wanted you to read Ana's letters, sense her passion and love, see her gifts, witness her love for him. I think he wanted you to understand his grand love, and live it with him."

"That's right," Felixe agreed.

"He wanted you to love his Ana and help you appreciate why he loved her so much."

Filipa's eyes were moist and she brushed a hand over them. "If that was his intention, he succeeded."

Re swung a comforting arm over her shoulders and squeezed them.

"But what about Viana do Castelo? He did meet her there, did he not?" Re commented.

Felixe nodded. "I arranged that meeting for them. Ana wanted to leave Viana and Ricardo wanted to meet her one last time, before she followed her dream. That was the time Rodrigo also followed her to the cathedral and created a scene. Ricardo had to intervene and drive him away. Ricardo and Ana had a long talk that evening. I don't know what they spoke about, but I do know that he felt the timing was again wrong, for several reasons. They parted once more, never to meet again. And I was told that my duty was over."

"So, you didn't follow Ana after Viana? You don't know where she went?"

"No. I moved on to other assignments."

"Then what are you doing here now? And how did you know where to find us?" Re asked, studying the detective keenly.

"I was hired again yesterday, to keep an eye on you two."

"By whom?" Filipa appeared shocked.

"Pedro."

"Pedro!" she exclaimed, incredulously. "Did everyone know about the *lenços*, except me?"

"Ah, now I get it. Pedro knew that Ricardo had left his trail intact for Filipa, it was his job to ensure that she followed it and found the gifts," Re reflected aloud.

"That's right."

"Well, quite a tale of the *lenços*!" Filipa sighed.

The detective rose. "My job was to share the details with you. I am staying at the Freixo Inn, if you need any assistance just reach out."

"We will be heading back to Viana do Castelo in a short while," Re informed.

Felixe nodded and strode down the narrow lane.

"Why was it so important to Grandpa for me to know Ana?" Filipa wondered.

"Because you are his granddaughter, and you needed to understand what Ana meant in his life."

"Why did he not just share his feelings with me? Tell me his whole story?"

"Share it with you, who doesn't believe in the saga of epic love? Who feels that love doesn't exist? Would you have given a fair, non-judgemental hearing to Ricardo's tale of pining and yearning? I don't think so, Filipa."

She was quiet for some time, staring at the cathedral, and then her gaze travelled unfocused to a spot in space. She sighed, a long sigh of exhaustion.

"You are probably right. I wouldn't have. I would have asked him to stop being ridiculous. I would have scoffed, or probably not. I would have tried to make amends, gone looking for his big love—Ana—tried to unite them. I don't know how I would have reacted. And now I never will know. Avô did not trust me at all."

"I believe it was more his fear of losing you that drove his decisions. He loved you too much to take the risk," Re cut in quietly.

"Too late for everything," Filipa pursed her lips, brushing a hand brusquely over her eyes. "What next? Is Ana Cardosa actually Ana Ribeiro? And is she dead?"

"For some strange reason, I am not yet ready to accept that. In her letter, Ana says that she may be going into partnership with her former employer. What is his name again?"

Filipa dipped into her backpack and brought out the sheaf of letters. She scanned through them quickly.

"Marcelo Oliveira."

"Could you please read that last Viana do Castelo letter again? There was something in it, I feel."

Filipa nodded and translated quickly.

"Wait—" Re stopped her. "Here is what she said—*I have been offered a partnership in a land by my former employer, and it is an opportunity of a lifetime.* Let's see… *it would be a dream come true to finally own my own land…* If Ana went into partnership with Marcelo, she would be owning half of his land, and would have some existence on his property. Why don't we look up Marcelo? He can lead us to Ana."

Filipa nodded. "That makes sense. But we will have to act fast now, if at all I have to catch my own event."

"I understand. But our priority lies in completing this trail of the *lenços*, to prevent the threatened bloodbath. Although I am not yet sure what that means, either. Because the slaughter already began with Ricardo's death." Re shook his head in frustration.

"Wait here, I will be back," Filipa remarked and rose.

Re watched her as she went inside the Information Office. He turned to gaze at the ash tree and its loyal sword, exuding a contradictory sense of restful peace. Like it was the journey's end. Like all roads, emotions and decisions curved inwards…

A sudden frisson ran down his spine, and his fingers tingled.

The towering monument took on a hue of orange and red as the sea waves rose high and crashed against the cliff. Re trudged up the steep path… the cold biting him and the waves licking his face, but the sensation was hot and burning… he sensed a tightening of the chest, as if someone had gripped him. Then, suddenly, a thick dark swirl of smoke blocked his way, blurring his vision and stinging his eyes. He couldn't see his path and he brushed away the smoke desperately, and rubbed his eyes, but smoke kept getting thicker and thicker like a spiralling tunnel. Feeling helpless, Re walked straight into the black tunnel and it instantly coiled around him, choking and suffocating him.

Re's eyes flew open, a sharp pain shooting up his wounded arm. He gasped, his hand involuntarily grasping his throat. He coughed and shook his head, trying to drive away the frightening vision. *His vision.* Warning him and leading him. His heartbeat accelerated because he now knew exactly where to. *To Basílica Santa Luzia. The cathedral where the event was to happen… The cathedral and event were in danger!*

Chapter

16

Filipa exited the office and brandished a piece of paper. With a sudden uplifting of his spirits, Re headed towards her. He contemplated warning her about his vision, then decided he would delay it. There was already a lot on her plate. He didn't wish to reveal his discovery just yet to her. First, they had to find Ana…

"Marcelo owns acres of land, on the other side of town, a bit on the outskirts. The good lady in the office told me to head towards Senhora Ernos' Cathedral. It is en route, she said we can't miss it," Filipa explained.

"Senhora Ernos—the patron saint of Freixo de Espada à Cinta. I almost went that way yesterday."

They climbed into the car and as curious passersby watched, Filipa once again drove through the narrow cobbled lanes with the windows peering into the streets. They passed the main Square with the 'I love Freixo de Espada à Cinta' sign, and Filipa took a right to head into the hills. It was picturesque with the countryside rolling into gentle terraced fields of olive and almond trees. The sky was azure and clear, and the road curved uphill into thick wooded areas. Ten minutes later, a large signboard loomed ahead, which read 'Oliveira Wine Yards'.

"Here's the gate," Re announced.

A uniformed watchman strode towards the car and peered at Filipa, who broke into fluid Portuguese. The man nodded and opened the gates, and the car sped through.

"What did you say to him?" Re asked curiously.

"Only who I am, and that I urgently need to meet Mr. Oliviera." Filipa smiled.

"Smart. Oliveira must be quite old now, he was older than Ana, so probably Ricardo's age? Around eighty? The watchman didn't seem to find it odd at all," Re pondered.

The car drove to a halt in front of a sprawling country house with a huge open patio, lined with comfortable maroon sofas. Hills chequered with olive trees rose gently, surrounding the house in a semi-circle. The sweet-pungent odour of olives filled the air.

Re and Filipa glanced at each other briefly and Re nodded.

Filipa rang the bell at the door and the two of them waited. Re sensed his pulse racing. This was the last stop in their search. If this didn't lead them to Ana, they would be at a dead-end. Literally. And they would have to head back, without answers, and he didn't like the thought at all.

"That's a lovely view. Imagine sitting here in the evenings, with a glass of wine," Re said, idly.

"May I help you?" a deep voice spoke behind them.

Filipa and Re turned to face the middle-aged man staring curiously at them. His face changed reaction when his light brown eyes rested on Filipa, and she simultaneously gasped.

"Fabio!"

"Filipa, what a surprise!"

Re's eyes darted from his companion to Fabio. This was *Fabio?* Filipa's shocked reaction spoke volumes.

"We are looking for Marcelo Oliviera," Re cut in quickly.

"He is my grandfather. Or was, he passed away some years ago. I am his grandson. But Filipa, it's so good to see you again. Please, please sit down." Fabio appeared to be flustered and excited at the same time.

Filipa was trying her best to avoid Re's gaze, forcing herself to be calm as she perched on the sofa.

"Sorry to hear about your grandfather, but you never said you were the grandson of the one of the oldest wine-makers in the country," she remarked.

"It would have just added to all our cross-purposes, wouldn't it? I just thought I would talk about it when the time came." Fabio thrust a hand consciously through his thick flick of hair.

He couldn't boast of traditional handsome looks, but he oozed confidence—Re could understand why Filipa found him attractive. He had an old-devilish charm, and his smile was one of cocky intelligence.

"May I offer you some wine? It's a relatively new brand, but still one of the best Port wines of the country."

Re noticed then the open bar sitting quietly in a niche, with rows of bottles in wooden slits.

"De Cruz wine," he frowned.

"Yes, it's our partner wine."

"Joana de Cruz's wine? She is—was—your partner?" Filipa confirmed.

"That's right. The land you see beyond ours is all Joana's— acres and acres of land producing amazing grapes. But why did you need to meet my grandfather?"

"Wait, let me get this straight," Filipa interrupted. "Since when has Joana been your grandfather's partner?"

"For a long time now, since I was a child. She has been a part of my house ever since I remember. She was very fond of me and my dad, and we loved her! That is how I assisted her in her elections and generally was around when you arrived for your mentorship."

"I can't wrap my head around this. Joana…" Filipa closed her eyes momentarily, trying to steady her thoughts.

"Have you heard of Ana Ribeiro?" Re intervened, his pulse racing.

"No. Why, what's wrong?" Fabio's gaze darted from one to the other.

Filipa suddenly rose and began pacing, and Re could sense her agitation.

"Almost 25 years ago, Ana Ribeiro, whom we are looking for, and who was Ricardo Monteiro's friend, moved to Freixo de Espada à Cinta to be in partnership with your grandfather, Marcelo Oliviera."

"The only person grandfather ever went into partnership with was Joana. I don't know the details, and I never asked because she was always like family and had our best interests at heart. Even after Grandpa passed away, she ensured that our legacy stayed with us and was well looked after, because Dad was kind of only interested in the business aspect. She has been an important part of our lives. You know how Joana was, Filipa, a wonderful person, and I am so glad Grandpa went into partnership with her."

This time Re rose, took a restless turn round the patio, and stood before Filipa. "You know what this means, don't you?"

Filipa did not respond, but stared at the detective with eyes wide, her face pale.

"We have two distinct options before us. The first one is that Ana Ribeiro never came to Freixo like you insisted. She went to another part of the country and did something else, but I still think that is highly improbable. Which brings us to the second option. "

Filipa did not utter a single word. A wild, almost frightened look crossed her eyes.

"That Ana changed her name to Joana de Cruz. And Joana is—was—your grandfather's great love!"

"Oh my god!" the words burst out of Filipa's mouth like bullet shots.

She slumped on the sofa, palms over her face, as if shutting out the world from her life.

Re stood beside her, an intense wave of sympathy cresting inside him. He had a sudden desire to weave an aura of protection around her. But even the thought was futile. No one could protect Filipa from the onslaught of shocks and heartbreaks. She simply had no choice but to be brave.

Because this wasn't over yet, Re knew. He sensed the cloudy and opaque energy around them… it disturbed him… there was worse to come.

"What is happening?" Fabio appeared bewildered. "Filipa, are you okay?"

"She is in shock," Re explained briefly. "Fabio, where did Joana live? Is there anyone in her house now?"

"It is the estate just after ours, but the house is shut right now. As Filipa knows, Joana never married. She mentored a lot of aspiring politicians and wine makers, but she was fiercely private. If you want to know anything about Joana, you have to meet her lawyer, who lives in town. He handled all her affairs right till the end, and even now is managing everything for her."

"Did she leave a will?" Re asked.

"Surprisingly, no, at least not that I know of. She left the estate in Francisco's care because, as she once said to me, she trusted him explicitly. It kind of surprised me, but Francisco apparently has been following her instructions, and so far, there have been no issues. But there seems to be a lot of secrecy involved in it."

"Where can we find him? We need to meet him at once." The urgency in Re's voice made Filipa look up.

"I will take you there," Fabio assured him.

Chapter 17

Francisco of Francisco & Sons, an established law firm on the quaint main street of the small town, was a tall grave man with thick white hair and a surprisingly unlined face. In fact, Re felt that he projected the personality of a well-bred, distinguished and widely travelled man.

The room was a combination of leather, polished wood and glass—the office of a prosperous law firm. Now, as Francisco stared at them across his ostentatious table, Re got the distinct feeling that he was being minutely assessed and gauged by the hawk-like eyes.

"So, you are Filipa, her favourite intern. She always spoke fondly of you, and now you are the one who will be releasing her symbol of peace."

The *senhorita* nodded.

"Very sorry to hear about Ricardo de Monteiro, your grandfather was much loved by Portugal," he said, his voice deep and sympathetic.

"Thank you," Filipa murmured, a little consciously.

"Please tell me what I can do for you."

"Mr. Francisco, we need to give you a quick background of why we are here," Re said. He launched into a concise narration of the events since the day before, and even Fabio listened in astonishment. When at length Re finished his narration, Francisco appeared a little disturbed.

"Sir, Joana trusted you and left you in charge of her estate. Could you please tell us, is Joana actually Ana Ribeiro?"

An uneasy silence seemed to swell in the room the moment Re posed his question. All eyes were trained on the older man, whose gaze flitted from Re to Filipa. Only the low whirr of the air-conditioning punctured the inflated silence.

"Yes, she is," Francisco stated, flatly.

Filipa gasped, and even Re felt a momentary stab of shock. The implications of Francisco's announcement were many. So Joana was Ana, all along. The woman who had devotedly loved Ricardo, who had spent years pining for him, sending him intricate *lenços*, trying to lead him to her—she was no more a mysterious Ana, she now had a startlingly familiar face. Their trail of *lenços* had somehow taken on a thrilling story-bookish hue as they had moved from city to city trying to discover the truth... but now, suddenly, everything had changed. The truth had taken on a dangerously realistic turn, too close for comfort, too tragic to imagine.

And the worst part of it was that Joana too was dead! Re sensed an uncharacteristic, acute grief, the slow uncoiling of a deep pain. Joana and Ricardo never got together. Their intense love story, which lasted for decades, ended on a sad note. Re mentally moaned the loss of love, as well as the chance of meeting an incredible person.

That was his personal loss. For two days, he had lived with Ana, and he had rooted for her. He had wanted her to succeed, no matter what. At least that was a relief. Ana had found her calling, turned her life around, she had been a mayor and a successful entrepreneur, growing and branding her own wine. She had lived to the fullest. And yet... the sense of incompletion was like an abyss which would never be filled.

"This has come as a shock to you," Francisco glanced at them, concerned.

Filipa nodded.

"Joana and I had no secrets, and I knew all about her past. She was such a warm and wonderful person. She knew how to live and let others live," Francisco said, his voice affectionate.

Filipa gulped, unable to speak. Re could only guess what she was going through. Fabio glanced at her repeatedly, genuine concern in his light brown eyes. The spark was still alive, Re thought at the back of his mind.

"How did Joana die?" he asked.

"She passed away suddenly. We found her cold in her bed, one morning. Apparently, she had taken an overdose of sleeping pills, with a glass of her own de Cruz wine. We were all deeply shocked."

"What!" Re exclaimed.

His mind crowded with swirling thoughts, as he instantly saw the pattern—Santiago, Miguel... So whoever had threatened the bloodbath knew that Joana was Ana! Had the hitman been responsible for Joana's death too?

"It not only shocked us, it disturbed us. We all loved Joana," Fabio added, his tone sad.

"Very unlike Joana to take sleeping pills with wine, and the police are still investigating her death. Anyway, a couple of years before her death, Joana had purchased a safe and told me that it could only be opened by a special person."

"Special person?" Fabio frowned.

"Did she mean grandpa? What is in the safe?" Filipa asked.

"I have no clue. All she said was that the right person would open it, and all the contents in the safe were his or hers."

Re and Filipa exchanged quick glances.

"Where is the safe and can we see it?" the detective asked.

Francisco hesitated for a fraction of a second. His wise old eyes rested on Filipa for a while and Re wondered what was going through his head. He had obviously been very fond of Joana, and perhaps protective too. His assessing look was proof of his loyalty towards his friend.

"It is upstairs. But you can only open the safe if you have the code."

The code again! Re felt a frisson of excitement. So, Ana had been leading Ricardo to her safe? Was that why there had been a requirement for a passcode at the Santa Luzia Cathedral too? Was the trail of the *lenços* not just a love trail, but something more? But what? Now was the time to find out.

"I believe that we may have it," Re announced, and the others looked taken aback. "Or at least I feel that I do. May I try to open it?"

Filipa glanced at him inquiringly, and Re nodded a quick assurance.

"All right, you can give it a shot. We have nothing to lose. Please follow me."

Francisco rose and led the way to a broad corridor with doors on either side. At the far end, he clattered up a carpeted short flight of stairs. They entered an oblong room with thick blue curtains drawn across the wide windows. Multiple safes lined the walls and the lawyer led them to the smallest one in a corner. He turned to Re and shrugged.

"All yours," the lawyer indicated.

The detective dropped to his knees and stared at the numbered buttons for a few seconds. Filipa watched him, a mix of nervous hope on her face. He touched the multi-metal Ganesha pendant that he wore round his neck and offered a quick mental prayer. His heart was beating rapidly, and his lips were dry. If his hunch was right… Once before, they had needed a code, and he had figured it out. Now it was time to apply it again. He rubbed his hands together and punched in '250419'. His heart beat erratically, as he turned the knob. Much to his surprise, it did not budge. Re frowned, confusion and disappointment swamping him. He had been so positive he had the code. He flashed Filipa a glance.

"What happened?" she asked, impatience lacing her tone.

"Not the right code," Re reported, briefly.

He sat back on his haunches, contemplating deeply, aware of the energy of the closed room and allowing it to seep through him. It was dense and strong, and projected a certain air of loyalty.

He had been so convinced that he had the code. Then what had gone wrong? Was there another number he ought to have seen? Perhaps on the gifts? Or in the letters? Was there some mention in the letters that he and Filipa had missed? Or was it in the *lenços*? Perhaps the day and the year the handkerchiefs had arrived? Ricardo had received each one of them on the 25th of April in different years... The code couldn't be too difficult if Ana wanted Ricardo to open the safe. Re closed his eyes and touched the safe, absorbing the feel of the cold steel. He felt that he was on the edge of discovery... *I should know the number,* the detective spoke to himself. *I should know it!* 250419... it seemed familiar.

250419... By using his logic of the date, 25 could stand for the 25th, 04 could be the month of April... so far so good... but what was 19? What numbers would complete the date?

Which date would be the most important to Ana? Birthdays? But even as his mind analysed and contemplated systematic permutations and combinations, a sudden beacon of comprehension hit him hard, and he gasped. That's it. It had to be the code! It wasn't the year the *lenços* were received by Ricardo, it was the day they had parted! 25th April 1974. The day of the Carnation Revolution. The day that was etched in Ana's life forever. The day that changed her life in permanent ways... But would it not be on the last gift they had discovered? The heart?

He turned to Filipa. "Can you hand me the fourth gift?"

She nodded and instantly delved into her backpack for it. The lawyer and Fabio watched the exchange with a great deal of curiosity.

Re held the heart tenderly, aware of the energy that instantly wound around his fingers, like magic dust. It was powerful, and he was tempted to hold the heart in his palm, but curbed it. He had no time to give way to temptation— he had to find the complete code. Instinct told him that he would discover it entwined in the heart. And he was right. As he studied the exquisite metal closely, he spotted the numbers cleverly interlaced within the centre of the heart—a distinct 7 and 4. Re inhaled deeply... he had been right. The code was 25th April 1974... the most important day in Ana's life.

Filipa stared at him. "Re?" she asked, tentatively.

The detective nodded and handed the gift back to her. "Please keep this safe. I believe I now know the correct code. Keep your fingers crossed."

He drove a tongue over his dry lips and tapped the number on the fluorescent keyboard again. 25041974. Then he turned the knob.

They all heard the click—loud and reassuring—and Re's heart soared. He had done it!

He turned the handle of the safe, and the thick metal door swung open.

"Amazing!" Francisco exclaimed. "How did you know the code?"

"Truly fantastic," Fabio agreed.

But Re's gaze was on Filipa. The look of anxiety was

instantly replaced by stark unease. Even fear? Perhaps the truth was too close at hand. Perhaps she wanted to shut the safe door and walk out of the place, never to look back. But he knew that neither of them would do that. The truth had to be flaunted in the open now, Ana had to step out of the wings and occupy front and centre stage. No matter what the secrets, no matter what the cost… it was time.

"You know what, Fabio and I are going to leave you two to explore the contents of the safe. You need your privacy, and in any case, this is confidential, right Fabio?" Francisco glanced at the younger man directly.

Re appreciated the older man's sensitivity.

"Yes, yes of course," Fabio agreed.

Re waited till the two of them quit the room.

"Filipa, do you want to do the honours?"

"No, no please, just tell me what is in it." Filipa shook her head vehemently and perched on a chair.

Re nodded. He peered into the safe, detected some folders and two pouches, and extracted the pouches. His heart began pounding again, but he kept a grip on his emotions. It was as if Ana, Joana, was about to speak straight from the dead, to them. To Filipa. Perhaps to Ricardo. He unzipped the first pouch, and his breath caught. Tiny sparkling diamonds nestled on red velvet. A single-fold note was placed beside it. *The April Captains, emergency fund in my keeping.* Re stared at it, sudden clarity flashing into his brain. The Core Group— it was the April Captains. Ricardo, Ana, Santiago, Miguel, Tomas and Agostinho… This was what the murderer really wanted! Diamonds worth millions of euros…

Re steadied his racing heart, zipped the pouch carefully, and unzipped the next one. A pair of red knitted baby socks was folded around four black and white photographs. A stunningly beautiful young Ana, and a handsome young Ricardo, arms around the waist, smiling with abandon at the camera, squinting in the sun. Re's throat caught with sudden emotion. So, this was how she looked—long wavy hair, a dimple in her right cheek, twinkling brown eyes full of life, and a vibrant energy which travelled across time and death to reach out and touch him, somewhere deep inside, in an almost nourishing manner. Re needed to see this photograph, not just to satiate his curiosity, but to connect with this woman who was a picture of perfection, but with a life far from perfect. Yet she had turned all her negatives around, and emerged a Queen in her own right, perhaps not on her own terms. How apt they looked together, Ana and Ricardo, so enamoured of each other.

Re's gaze moved to the second picture of a young Ana, another girl who looked quite like her, and a small boy between them. The boy held on to the other girl's hand. Was this Ana's sister and her son? Something about the boy was familiar. He passed the pics to Filipa. She stared at them, long and hard.

Re picked up the third photograph. It was a group of six, standing with their arms on each other's shoulders, a smile on their faces, an element of camaraderie in their pose and smiles. Re recognized them at once. All except the last one. Ricardo, Ana, Tomaz, Santiago, Miguel, and the last man had to be Agostinho. Again, he had the strange feeling of familiarity. Re's gazed narrowed as he read the inscription behind the photograph.

"Do you know this man?" Re passed the photo to Filipa.

She scrutinized it for a moment, then shook her head. "Never seen him before."

"That must be Agostinho. Read what she has written on the back."

Filipa flipped the photo and her eyes widened. "RIP Agostinho, 1973!"

"That solves one mystery. Agostinho is dead, and has been, all these years. So, one of the core group members died. We don't know how, but did it kind of disrupt their friendship?"

"At least we know now that Agostinho is not the mastermind behind this horrific carnage," Filipa concluded.

Re picked up the fourth picture, and a jolt of shock lit through him. Ana stared back at him, a picture of wild beauty—her long wavy hair blowing in the wind, the hint of a dimple in the cheek, the merry glint in her eyes, emotional maturity in her expression. Re glanced at her companion in the photo, and an involuntary gasp escaped him. Startled, he swivelled in his place to study Filipa. He saw it now—in Filipa's eyes, her stance, her dimple, her spirit...

"What is it?" Filipa asked.

Wordlessly, Re passed her the photo. Filipa stared long and hard at the picture—a young Ana, her energy subdued, yet emanating a sense of contentment. She stood beside a grave-looking Ricardo with a hint of a smile in his eyes, and he was holding a small baby in his arms.

"What... who is this?" Filipa frowned in bewilderment.

Re took his time to respond, framing his words carefully. "I believe that Ricardo and Ana had a child together. This baby girl is their love child."

Filipa sucked in her breath, her face aghast. "No! I don't believe it," she whispered. "If that's true, where is the child now?"

Re gazed at her, a blend of sympathy and concern on his face. "I think, Filipa, when Ana departed, she left not just her love behind, but a piece of her heart with Ricardo. That is why she was holding on to them and her memories, for years, with relentless hope, because they were her *family*."

"Who?" Filipa insisted.

"Ricardo and your mother. Your mother is Ana's baby."

Filipa's hand flew to her mouth, her eyes wide as the shock of revelation registered.

"My mother is... oh my goodness, this is shocking... that is why Mãe left home. Now I understand—when she discovered that she was a love child, she must have been flabbergasted, she would have felt betrayed and hurt. She must have been kept in the dark all those years, and then she must have discovered her true identity. Now it all makes sense!"

"That's exactly how it must have happened. And because your mother took the reality poorly, Ricardo hesitated to share anything with you. He must have taken special effort to make you understand the situation better. He wanted you to follow the trail of *lenços,* so that you could understand the depth of their sacrifice. And he especially wanted you to get to know and love Ana, not hate her."

"Yes, I get it now, why it was so important to him."

The detective took Filipa's hands in his, and gazed at her tenderly.

"You haven't fully got it, have you, *ma chérie?*" he said, his voice soft.

"Got what?" Filipa appeared confused.

"Ana Ribeiro is your real grandmother, Filipa. You are Joana de Cruz's granddaughter!"

Filipa stepped back, stunned as realization dawned.

"Yes, no…"

"Yes. Take a deep breath, Filipa. I know that this has come as a huge shock—over and above all the rest of it. It is natural if you take time to process it," Re cautioned.

She closed her eyes, unable to speak, and inhaled deeply for some moments.

"Just relax in the chair, while I check what's in the folder."

But Re already knew what it would be. It was an official looking document, written in Portuguese.

"You would have to read this. I think it's a will."

Filipa accepted the single sheet of thick paper and scanned through it.

"It is Joana's will. She has left de Cruz wines and her entire estate and property to Ricardo and his heirs," she said, her voice a mix of awe and fatigue.

"Which, in effect, means that your grandmother left your mother and you the entire property. And since your mother is not interested, you would be the sole heir and executor of Joana's estate," Re completed.

They stared at each other, in mute comprehension. Filipa appeared dazed, her eyes moistening, as she grappled with the sudden knowledge, trying to come to terms with it.

"Ana worked hard to create a legacy, and she left it to the man she loved, and the heirs she bore. Life has come full circle…"

Filipa nodded, tears now streaming freely down her cheeks.

Re experienced a deep sadness within him, like he had lost someone close. The image of his own lost love rose before his eyes, and the yearning seemed to multiply ten-fold in an engulfing wave, almost choking him. And then just as suddenly, it settled and seemed to merge into the yearning he had felt for Ana. Both had culminated in an unattainable fate. The loss of one seemed to overlap the loss of the other. Except that one was his life, his breath and his one love— the other was an illusion that he had pursued, grown to like, and obsess over. Life and imagination seemed to have merged, and he experienced the vastness of life. Infinity yawned before him, allowing him a glimpse into the realms of immeasurable possibilities. And comprehension dawned. Ana's story was over, but the fruits of her journey would now roll into the future through other people and means. But his own personal story was far from done. Ana had made the best of the situation—she was an inspiration. In these two days, she had unwittingly taught him what true love meant, and how it could raise a person from the lowest of depths to the greatest of heights. She had shown him not to give up. And he promised himself that he would not.

He glanced at Filipa and felt a connection to the *senhorita*. Life had dealt her too many shocks in the past 24 hours. He felt fully invested in her wellbeing, and responsible for her safety. He couldn't allow the circumstances to paralyse his own thinking. They still had work to do.

He heaved a big sigh and extended a comforting arm over Filipa's shoulder.

"And now, you are richer than you were before," he remarked, trying to infuse some lightness into the loaded moment.

"Yes, more money, but all alone in this world."

"Ah, now you are being dramatic, *ma chérie*. You have me, and more importantly, you have Fabio," he pointed out gently.

She glanced up at him and her lips twitched.

"You think so?"

"I do," he assured.

She sniffed, pushing her wavy hair back from her face.

"I wish she were alive," she murmured, brushing away the tears. "I wish I had known that she was my grandmother when I met her… I am not sure how I would have behaved… but in hindsight, I would have loved her more. Now, all that remains is a deep regret."

"I know what you mean. But Filipa, the good part is that we have reached the end of the trail of the *lenços*. And we now know what happened to Ana. We know how the love story ended. However, we haven't yet reached the end of our search. We have to take these diamonds back with us to stop further bloodshed from happening, because obviously this is what the anonymous predator is after. And we have yet to disclose the face behind this entire drama, and find out who killed your Grandpa, Joana, and Santiago."

She sucked in a quick horrified breath, "Joana too?"

Re nodded. "I don't doubt it. Same modus operandi. This murderer has to be a person associated with Joana's past— someone who knew about the April Captains, knew about Ricardo and Joana, and systematically hunted each one out, and tried to kill them. More importantly, someone who knew about the diamonds, and wanted to have them."

"Well then, let's get on with it," Filipa sniffed.

"It's three already."

"But where are we headed?"

"To Viana do Castelo."

"But that's where *I* need to go for the event." Filipa frowned. "You need to get the diamonds to Penafiel."

"You didn't get, it did you?" Re said. "The massacre is not planned for Penafiel, Filipa. It will happen at your world event, an event where Joana's symbol of peace is going to be unveiled."

"What!" Filipa uttered in shock.

"Someone wants to remove all traces of Ana, all the people she associated with, everything that she worked for, and that includes her coveted Peace Symbol. And we have to stop it. Someone has hated Ana for long. It is time to end this story of revenge. My question is, will we reach in time?"

For the first time, Filipa displayed a hint of a smile, her dimple showing, and a mischievous twinkle in her brown eyes. Re couldn't help thinking—this is how Ana must have looked.

"There are perks to having a rich ex-boyfriend. Time for Fabio to pay old debts!" Filipa announced, with a flick of her ample brown air.

Pedro threw a last look at Ricardo's study, his heart heavy. The owner of the estate was not gone for even 24 hours, and yet Pedro felt as if he had not met his best friend in days. The police would hopefully release his body soon, and Pedro knew that he would have to take charge of the arrangements for the funeral. A tough emotional ordeal ahead for him, and Filipa.

The butler sighed. It was time for him to leave for the event. In ordinary conditions, he would have either stayed back, or he would have accompanied Ricardo to the event. But in Filipa's absence, he knew that he was no more just a butler. Tiago and Stefan were already at the venue, overlooking the preparations, but he had made a promise to the *senhorita* and he planned to fulfil it. He had been entrusted with carrying the gold symbol of peace to the venue, and he would ensure its safe passage to the cathedral.

He was about to step out of the room, when the landline on Ricardo's desk rang. Frowning, Pedro picked up the receiver.

"Monteiro Estate," he spoke.

"Listen carefully and do not interrupt," a hoarse, unrecognizable voice responded. "To avoid the bloodbath, place the diamonds in a pouch you will find at the foot of the altar inside. At sharp 4:50, shut the doors, and no one will enter the cathedral till the event is over. If you disobey, you will be responsible for the bloodbath this evening and it would be the end of the Monteiro symbols of peace!"

"Hello, wait—" Pedro began, but the line was dead.

Sudden sweat broke out on Pedro's forehead. For the first time in his life, he felt flustered and weak. Ricardo gone, Filipa in danger, and the threat of bloodshed a choking reality. His fingers trembled as he dialled Re's number.

Fabio and Filipa were having a quiet conversation, and Re was awaiting the helicopter in the field behind the mayor's office, when his phone rang. Pedro's voice was anxious and tempered with fear as he narrated the threatening phone call.

"Calm down, Pedro," Re said smoothly. "We are on our way and should reach the cathedral around 4:00. We have ample time to do as we are bidden. In the meanwhile, send me the recorded call, will you?"

"OK, but I am very worried. Hope it all goes well. I shall now be driving to the cathedral, so I guess we would both reach at the same time," Pedro said.

"You are not alone, I hope."

"No, Officer Lusa sent two men to accompany me."

"Wonderful."

In a few seconds, Re's phone pinged again, and he listened to the recorded call from the enemy. *To avoid the bloodbath, place the diamonds in a pouch you will find at the foot of the altar. At sharp 4:50, shut the doors and no one will enter the cathedral till the event is over. If you disobey, you will be responsible for the bloodbath this evening and it would be the end of the Monteiro symbols of peace!*

The detective frowned. It was difficult to gauge if the voice was male or female, but despite the disguise, it sounded vaguely familiar. The tone, the manner in which the message was delivered, the words used... Re replayed it multiple times, his mind churning. One thing was indisputably certain. This person meant serious business, and they could not afford to take risks.

He quickly placed a call to Stefan—the exchange was short and urgent, but Stefan instantly grasped the mode of action to be taken. When Re ended the call, a grim smile played on his lips. It was time to reverse the game. It was time for the hunter to be hunted...

A few minutes later, Re, Filipa and Fabio took off in the latter's private helicopter. As the helicopter took flight, the detective glanced at the spectacular landscapes below. Freixo de Espada à Cinta spread in layered, sun-drenched verdant slopes and encrusted terraced plains, with the sparkling Douro gliding gracefully between the hills. In the evening glow, the small town surrounded by breath-taking scenery and vistas, was draped in kaleidoscopic shades of gold and emerald. For the second time, Re bid a reluctant goodbye to the town that had offered him much-needed peace.

Chapter
18

Officer Stefan Weiss stood in front of the cathedral, his back to the stunning coastal view, taking in the final preparations. The Basílica Santa Luzia towered majestically, fully decked in coloured tones of red, blue and yellow foot lights, against a densely clouded luminescent sky. The long flight of steps that led up to the green statue of Jesus, and the two black entrance doors on either side, were covered with red carpet. A three-foot raised platform to the left of the cathedral—which would serve as the main scene of action—had its back to the sea and the half border wall, and sported a red carpet, seven chairs and two teapoys. A bulletproof transparent shield barred the audience from moving over to the stage, and acted as protection in case of emergency. The five mayors would occupy the stage, and talk about Joana de Cruz's symbol of peace and launch it with great fanfare. For now, the mayors who had already arrived were relaxing in the tent on the opposite side of the stage. Pedro, who had been entrusted with the task of bringing the symbol from Penafiel, had just arrived. Tiago had been sent to accompany him from the foot of the hill, and the symbol was now safely in the tent with the mayors, with a special police guard on duty. Stefan saw Tiago move around briskly, a pouch strapped to his waist, looking efficient and busy, as he gave orders and got chairs aligned, while Pedro took charge of hospitality of the mayors. Officer Lusa had set up barriers at the entry point to the flight of steps below, which led up from the car parking space. People would have to go through a quick frisk before settling down on the hundreds of chairs. An action amplified since Re's phone call. The cathedral had also undergone a thorough check, despite protests from the church members, but Adriano had been supportive.

People were already beginning to troop in and were settling down in the chairs or leaning against the surrounding half-wall. An atmosphere of palpable excitement and anticipation was beginning to pervade the cathedral premises. Strategic cameras were set up to cover the event live over TV channels and social media, and two large LED screens. Hoardings talked about peace, and the need to connect with each other in harmony. *Paz em nosso coração, paz em nosso mundo.* Peace in the heart, peace in the world...

Everything seemed to be in order, yet Stefan knew, with all his experience, that the acts of perfidy and the lurkings of the evil mind could override the best of preparations and unhinge the best of security. And for that reason, he sensed tension inside him. He glanced at his watch. It was already 4:00. A car had gone to fetch Re and Filipa from the landing field. It would take him ten minutes to reach here. *Hurry Re,* he thought, *time is running short.*

The serpentine queue of the cars was lengthening on the winding road that led up to the basilica. It was a slow crawl up the hill.

Their helicopter had landed on Fabio de Sousa's private air strip and Fabio, Re and Filipa had descended and speedily climbed into the waiting car, heading directly towards the cathedral. They were almost half way up to Santa Luzia, when the long queue of cars forced them to slacken their speed.

"I forgot that traffic would be heavy today," Filipa sighed, but her tone of thrill and anticipation belied her comment. "The entire town would be here to witness this historic moment."

"Good for the event, but not so good for us. I don't want us to get stuck in this jam. It's already 4:10," Re frowned. "I am calling Stefan, he will send Lusa's squad to give us special access."

Before Filipa could utter another word, the detective alighted from the car. There was a restless energy in Re. He quickly called up Stefan and then began striding up the road. He knew he wasn't far from the cathedral, but it would be at least another ten minutes before the car even moved. The trudge uphill would do him good, he decided.

The river Lima was a gold-green as it ambled along the saffron-roofed houses and merged ahead into the blue-grey sea in a long T. The wind had picked up and Re's jacket flapped. The queue of cars snaked round the turn and vanished into another curve.

It was the next moment that, like magic, suddenly the road went empty and Re found himself on a long curving road.

Before he could wonder, the river and the trees stilled. The breeze paused. The landscape stopped breathing. A slow barrel of dark smoke descended on the road, thickening in seconds. Re watched in horror as it swirled and moved like a reptile, quickly swallowing up everything in its path. Re desperately flapped his arms to brush it aside to clear his vision. But the wall of spinning smoke grew thicker around him, tightening around his neck and cutting off his breath.

The thundering sound of engines broke into his consciousness, and Re jerked awake. The few seconds of disorientation made him falter. Two policemen on motorcycles passed him as they headed towards Filipa's car. The long line of cars hadn't moved, there was no smoke, and nothing was choking him. But Re knew what it meant. He ran his tongue over his dry lips uneasily. His starkly realistic vision had issued a final warning. The danger was nightmarishly imminent, and evil was ready to strike any minute now...

The seats were all occupied and the crowds were spilling on the sides and into the cathedral premises. An air of festivity hung thick in the multilingual chatter that pervaded the gathering. People were flaunting carnations in their hands, tucked in their front pockets, and as garlands around their necks. *This was how Carnation Day must have looked in 1974,* Re thought. It was almost like a replay of that all-important day that changed lives in innumerable ways. As the two motorcycles passed along the side of the crowds, people turned to watch curiously and waved their carnations and cheered. It was an atmosphere of happy and heady excitement as enthusiastic members of the audience bellowed the slogan *Paz em nosso coração, paz em nosso mundo*. Peace in the heart, peace in the world...

Re climbed off the two-wheeler and thanked the policeman for the lift. He waited to catch Filipa's eye as Fabio and she, too, descended. The latter turned to gaze at the audience and he saw the glint of pleasure in her eyes. She turned to glance at him, and he beckoned to her. With quick strides, she was beside him.

"What is it?" she asked. "Isn't this simply marvellous? Months of planning to make Joana's dream come true. Feels strange to think of it as Ana's dream now. In my head, she will always be my Joana. But this amazing energy, the enthusiasm... I can't believe I am here, despite everything that has happened."

"And everything that may happen," Re cut in quietly.

"What do you mean?"

Re clasped her hands in his. Her brown eyes seemed wide and anxious in a pale face, her hair windblown by the motorcycle ride. She had changed into a dark blue formal dress that she had carried in her backpack, at Francisco's office, but it was crumpled and she didn't seem to care. Her unwavering focus on the event was admirable, despite everything that she had been through. Or perhaps it was now all the more important, because she had a promise to fulfil to her grandmother?

"Filipa, I don't need to tell you that we are dealing with a dangerous criminal, a man who has killed your grandfather and grandmother, as well as Santiago. Please do not let your guard down for a second. Keep your ears and eyes open. If you spot anything unusual, anyone odd, just signal Stefan and Pedro, who will be on either side of the stage. Or simply duck and hide under the table."

For a fraction of a second, her eyes moistened, then she blinked. "I get you. But I know one thing, we have come this far, and we will see the finish line."

"We will. You will handle the stage and ensure that the show goes on. Stefan, Lusa and I will take care of the rest. I don't want you to think of what is going on elsewhere either, okay? Just focus on the event and releasing the Peace Symbol. Fabio will be here with you, right Fabio?" Re angled towards Fabio, who had followed Filipa, but was keeping a discreet distance.

"Rest assured Re—I have no intention of leaving her side for even a second. If need be, I will protect her with every ounce of my strength," Fabio declared, grim determination on his handsome face.

Re smiled. "I hope it doesn't come to that. Good luck, Filipa!"

"Good luck to you too, Re, and thank you!"

To Re's surprised, she hugged him tightly for long seconds, and he patted her fondly on her back. Then he strode up the long flight of steps towards the basilica which was a dramatic, towering entity against a cloudy gold-grey sky. Filipa and Fabio followed suit. Re caught sight of Stefan by the stage and waved to the officer, who instantly walked towards him with rapid strides.

"Did you find anything?" Re asked, without preamble.

"Nothing. We did a thorough check of the stage. No bombs, nothing anywhere."

"Good. That's one option ruled out. Are all the cathedral doors shut? And no one inside?" the detective confirmed.

"That's right," Officer Weiss nodded.

"Everyone assigned to their places?"

"Pedro by the stage, Lusa by the entrance, and Tiago by the cameras."

"Great. It is 4:45. Time for us to set this in motion."

Re opened the door on the right, and stepped into the cathedral. The chitter-chattering instantly turned into gentle murmurs, and the contrasting peace inside the church was striking. The soothing lights and the looming energetic presence of Jesus with the 16 cherubs on the blue ceiling felt surreal, like a film paused in motion. The silence was even a bit unnerving.

"I can spot the pouch," Stefan remarked.

Re strode over to the altar where on a small table, a black velvet pouch lay in full view. Exactly as the voice on the phone had mentioned. This mastermind was very much sneaking around, watching them surreptitiously, following their every action. But who was he and where was he? Re wondered, as he carefully transferred the sparkling diamonds into the pouch, pulled the strings, and replaced it on the table.

"Done," he whispered. "Keep an eye on the door. My guess is the pouch will be lifted as soon as the programme begins. I will be hiding behind, here."

"Good luck. Remember this man is dangerous," Stefan cautioned.

"I will," Re nodded, a grim expression on his face.

"Joana de Cruz was a wonderful woman. She possessed an unnatural strength to face adversities and the will to overcome whatever life forced on her. Life did not always hand her a good deal, but despite everything she went through, she emerged a woman of substance…" Filipa spoke, her voice quiet and tinged with an emotion which only she understood. "To me personally, she was a very special friend, a mentor and a guide, whose innovative ideas and dynamism shaped my thinking in positive ways. Today we have with us guests who will elaborate and talk about not just Joana and her life, but also of her revolutionary dream symbol of peace. An offering from Portugal to the rest of the world."

A cheer rang out amidst the audience as Filipa ended her short speech. Her mind was in a flurry and she felt overcome with emotion. Fabio was standing right behind her, and her gaze collided with his. A mix of compassion, love, assurance and pride shone through the intense gaze in his eyes, and a flicker of a smile appeared on his lips. In a flash, her tilted world straightened just a bit, and the burden in her heart lightened by a few milligrams. The realization stunned her. Could Fabio do that to her? Change her world from depression to excitement with the hint of a compassionate smile? For some strange reason, Ana's love song for her grandfather sprung in her mind, along with a glimmer of hope…

She handed the mike over to the moderator of the discussion and settled into her chair.

Faint sounds of cheering filtered into the cathedral through the slits and windows, and Re guessed that the programme had begun. He slipped back his spectacles and leaned against the cool stone pillar next to the altar, careful not to lean on his hurt arm. He was deeply ensconced in the shadows, and so, invisible to any intruder. Any minute now, the mastermind behind the senseless killings would show his face. Any minute now. Re inhaled deeply, mentally preparing himself for the final confrontation.

Where had the trail of *lenços* led them? he wondered idly. To Freixo de Espada à Cinta of course, and more importantly, to Ana's safe. And to the precious diamonds. But also, to Ana's will. Re's forehead creased in concentration. Ana had treasured all these in her safe for years, and formulated an elaborate plan for Ricardo to reach her and eventually the contents of her safe. And yet, he too hadn't known about them. In fact, not a soul knew about the contents of the safe. Not even the lawyer. Then how had the mastermind known about it? Known about the existence of diamonds in the first place, and then their location? Re sat up straight, fiddling with the multi-metal Ganesha pendant around his neck. Something was not right. Only two people could be in possession of this information—someone from Ricardo's core group would know that the diamonds were with Ana. Or someone closely associated with Ana, from her past...

"There are many symbols of peace already in the world—the dove, the acanthus branch and other symbols. But this symbol, as you will soon see for yourself, brings in many more elements."

As the mayor of Freixo de Espada à Cinta finished her speech on the importance of Joana's Peace Symbol, Filipa experienced a wave of pride. The words of praise and respect for Joana filled her with joy. It was Joana and her brilliant vision that they were talking about. Her grandmother? Ana or Joana? Filipa was finding it rather incredible. The woman who mentored her, and shared with her all her dreams and aspirations for a better world, was actually her grandmother? How privileged could she have been? And how great a regret it would have been for her had she never met the great love of her grandfather! And worse, if she had never known that her Avô's great love was in fact her own grandmother. More importantly, that the beautiful, stubborn and powerful love that joined them for eternity, actually flowed in her own veins too.

Her gaze cruised over the crowds which spilled on to the steps, waving their carnations with enthusiasm. They were all present here today to encourage and to welcome the new symbol of peace. To embrace a new offering to the world. Portugal's definition of co-existence and harmony. Already, some countries had applauded the effort and promised to acknowledge and incorporate the symbol in some of their official documents. Filipa couldn't be prouder of what they had achieved collectively—Joana through her vision and insistence on being different, Avô through his legacy and loyalty, and Filipa through her own blessings.

As the mayor made her concluding remarks, and the audience broke out into applause, Filipa rose for the final segment of the event. The cameras focused on her and the digital screens displayed a larger-than-life Filipa, smiling at the crowd cheering loudly, in front of her.

Re remained crouched in his position behind the wall, his ears straining for any sound. There was none… only the muted cheering of the people outside. It was surely already twenty minutes past five. The criminal should have been here by now. Re's frown deepened, as he pushed back his slipping glasses. His bandaged arm hurt, and the wound where the bullet had grazed the flesh, stung sharply.

The cathedral felt cold as a wisp of breeze hung in the air. Re was uneasy. Why hadn't the masked-voice-person arrived to pick up the diamonds yet? What was he waiting for? They had followed his instructions to the letter. The event would soon be over, as soon as Filipa presented the Peace Symbol. Re stilled, his sentence paused in mid-thought. *The symbol of peace… The end of the Monteiro symbols of peace…* symbols, as in plural, not *a* symbol…

Suddenly, the photos he had seen a short while ago rose in his mind. The faded but happy pictures, the energy of unabashed youth, of unbridled loyalties towards the country, of love that transcended adversities, time and logic, and the bonds of friendship that were tightened by shared secrets and dangers... The images merged, and past and present came together like a flash in his mind... and *he knew*... like the sudden clarity of still waters... the criss-cross journey of the last 36 hours made complete sense.

The end of the Monteiro symbols of peace... symbols, not symbol... Two symbols! The Monteiro symbols of peace were Joana's symbol of peace, but also the other one—the heiress of the Monteiro Estate. Filipa! Filipa was the second symbol, and she was in danger... the bloodbath was not going to be a bomb endangering innocent lives. It was going to be revenge!

Sweat broke out on Re's forehead. He heard the thunderous applause outside and he rose. He fumbled with his phone and sent Stefan a message. Then with the din of his anxiety roaring in his head, and with his mind snaking into multiple dark and dangerous consequences, he sprinted towards the main door and pushed it open. The exit was completely blocked by the people standing, waving, and shouting slogans. Re couldn't see a thing beyond the jam-packed bodies. He pushed with his shoulder, and pain shot through his arm. Ignoring the agony, he pushed harder, and managed to open the door and thrust his way through.

The crowd was like a sea of faces, echoing the slogan *Paz em nosso coração, paz em nosso mundo.* Peace in the heart, peace in the world...

Filipa stood on stage, her heart bursting with pride and an undefinable emotion that seemed to choke her. Her mind tapped involuntarily in rhythm with the waves of the echoes, as the crowd turned the slogan into a musical rhythm. Filipa savoured every minute of the evening, etching the shining faces and reverberating voices into her memory, tears of joy and sorrow rising in her eyes. She glanced up at the sky— there were colours of celebration in the sky too… grey clouds swimming in a saffron and peach coloured sky… *Look at this, Avô and Joana,* she called out in her mind… Here she was, on the threshold of the Almighty, in the presence of dignitaries and the Portuguese public, unveiling a symbol of love and peace. A symbol born out of an association that defied the dictates of society, time and distance, and that had risen above the ordinary. An emotion that had grown from love to something much grander than Ricardo and Joana themselves. A transition from the serving of a country of their love—Portugal—to becoming an offering to the world. Could any love be more superior and more intense than that of Ricardo and Ana? she wondered. Could any love have borne such a sweet and all-pervasive fruit? She doubted it. They had set a high bar indeed.

With a sigh, she brushed a hand over her eyes and smiled at the other mayors who nodded at her encouragingly. She turned to the mike and stared at the crowd.

"And now for the historic moment we are all waiting for. Unveiling the symbol of peace, designed by Joana de Cruz. An offering from Portugal to the rest of the world. An offering of peace and love."

It was time to bring forward the star of the evening. Filipa opened the lid of the box and there it lay, nestled in red velvet. The gold-plated symbol of peace… A simple heart formed in the letter P, but which was done so artfully as to resemble a heart, a leaf with a branch, and a P.

The mayor of Guimarães stepped forward and spoke into the mike. "The beautiful symbol of peace signifies many things, but prominently, P for peace, a beautiful heart for love and compassion, and a leaf with a tiny branch for co-existence with our environment and surroundings. And here it is…"

All the mayors gathered together and raised the symbol to the sky. The cameras enlarged it on the screen and the crowds broke into whistles and thunderous applause. Filipa beamed from the top of the stage, her face sparkling with new energy.

It was at that precise moment that Re spotted him. Standing on top of the steps, at the other door of the cathedral. He had long flowing hair, and a beard and sunglasses covered his eyes. Re would have missed him, if it hadn't been for the rolled newspaper in his hand, and the towering stance, almost a head above the other people, positioned bang opposite the stage, uncaring of the jostling public which had left its seat, and were cheering and rejoicing. It was a good disguise, but his cat-like professional cool and poise gave him away. His determined focus on his prey was bloodcurdling. He had a clear view of the stage and its inhabitants, a clean unhampered shot above the bullet-proof shield. Re's eyes darted from Stefan on the right of the stage to Pedro and

Fabio on the left, and then to the camera in the centre, where Tiago was in charge. All were too far away to hinder the attack. His heart thudding painfully, Re thrashed through the thick wall of people, plunging straight towards the man, just as he raised his arm and the gun hidden inside the roll of newspaper, and aimed straight at Filipa.

Re saw Filipa freeze as she caught sight of the hitman with the gun, a look of horror flashing across her face. The mayors and Filipa were still holding up the symbol of peace, and the clueless audience was still cheering.

"Beware, Filipa!" Re shouted, as he reached the hitman.

The next instant, everything happened simultaneously.

"Duck, Filipa!" Fabio yelled at the top of his lungs, flinging himself on Filipa and the other mayors. They all crashed to the floor unceremoniously.

At the same time, just as the hitman fired a straight shot at Filipa, Re hurled at the assailant, from behind. His arm wavered, and the bullet skewered and pierced the shield with a dull thud. For a spilt second, the world paused, gasping at what had just transpired. A dense silence licked the atmosphere. Surprise flashed across startled faces, rapidly turning to horror. The next instant, the crowd roared in terror and left their seats, and began to run helter-skelter. Re punched the hitman hard in the face and he staggered in shock. He swivelled around looking for an escape route to the back of the cathedral, but Stefan and Lusa obstructed his path. The hitman was strong and struggled, but other policeman joined them, and the scuffle lasted for a few minutes before the assailant was overpowered.

Officer Lusa hastened to the stage and spoke into the mike in Portuguese, "Calm down, everyone. This was an unfortunate incident, but the culprit has been caught and no one is hurt or harmed. Please settle down, and let us continue the programme. Please settle down, everyone. The situation is under control," he spoke smoothly and in a calm but firm voice.

Re pushed through the crowd trying to catch a glimpse of Filipa on the stage, anxiety cramping his insides.

The mayors on the stage rose, bewildered and aghast, unsure of what exactly had transpired. Filipa straightened, her hand still clutching the Peace Symbol close to her chest. Fabio helped her rise as she dusted her dress, but her eyes frantically cruised over the crowd, searching for Re. She caught sight of him finally, standing on the cathedral steps, and waved.

Re sensed the sudden pull of energy like a frantic tug. Filipa gazed at him from the top of the stage, her hair blowing with the wind, a smudge on her face. The question was writ large on her flushed face. Had they finally escaped the threatened carnage? Were they safe now? Re returned her steady gaze and nodded. Relief washed across her face and she flashed a watery smile. Then turned to talk to the concerned Fabio.

Thick grey-blue clouds in a saffron sky cast a shadow over the sea and the cathedral. Re inhaled deeply. He may have reassured Filipa, but this wasn't really over yet. Not by a long shot. He wheeled around and cut through the crowd again. He had to get inside the basilica and retrieve the pouch of diamonds. In the haste to warn Stefan and save Filipa, he had left it in the church. Would it still be there? His heart began an unexpected tattoo.

He pushed the door open and the silence inside greeted him with a chaste nonchalance. Re speeded down the red carpet, to the altar and froze. The pouch had vanished. His gaze flitted across the cathedral. Not a soul was around. He glanced under the table and did a quick search. There was no doubt. The diamonds were gone!

"Looking for something?" a voice asked from behind him.

Startled, Re spun around in surprise. He recognized the voice.

Chapter
19

Três vivas para Portugal
Três vivas pela Paz!
Três vivas para a Joana!

As the cheers rang out in chorus, Filipa waved in response. A whirr of a helicopter pierced the shouting and the cameras trained at the sky. The helicopter flew from behind the basilica and hovered for a few minutes over the stage. Then as it circulated over the milling crowds, a stream of carnations cascaded down. The big screens displayed the cheering, and the TV and FB networks carried the lively, celebratory visuals across the world.

Filipa watched, her eyes moist. Conflicting emotions of grateful joy and sadness engulfed her, as she took in the magical sight. She raised her eyes to the sky and prayed for Ricardo and Ana, for the journey and the priceless moments she had shared with them. Perhaps had they both been alive, she would have begun another happy journey with them— that was a regret she would have to live with. But for now, she had fulfilled a promise, and now she had new responsibilities to take over. Despite the heartrending losses, she knew that she could no more delay her duties. And instinctively she knew that she was ready…

The mayors shook hands with her in congratulations, and she exchanged a few polite words of gratitude. She caught sight of Pedro and Tiago talking on the side of the stage. Re and Stefan were at the door of the cathedral, deep in conversation. She turned around to look at Fabio and their eyes locked. His gaze was intense and filled with emotion. Filipa sucked in a quick breath and smiled. Her grandfather's words, from just yesterday morning, rang in her mind, *"Follow your heart always, caríssima… in the end nothing else matters."*

The sky was overcast and luminescent as the sinking sun was a tip on the horizon. A wind had picked up, strong and insistent. Re sat on the steps of the basilica, his face set in a grim frown, his mind churning with thoughts as he observed the post-programme activities with mild interest.

The big LED screens were carted away along with the chairs and the stage. But the banners of peace still trembled with the wind. The mayors had departed and the Peace Symbol would now travel with them to the capital. The last car drove down the hill, and the public had hailed their joy as they made their way down the hill. Only a few tourists hung around, gazing at the stunning sunset over a grey hazy sea.

Filipa sat on his left and Stefan on his right. Pedro, Tiago and Officer Lusa remained standing.

"At least the event was a huge success," Filipa remarked.

"Yes, despite the drama and the fact that you narrowly missed being killed," Re agreed.

"But it's not over yet," Stefan reminded quietly, and Officer Lusa nodded his head vigorously.

"But the hitman was caught," Tiago cut in.

"He was a hired man," Stefan replied.

"But the police should question him, he would reveal who hired him," Tiago suggested.

"We did question him. He said he never actually met this person. They always spoke on the phone, and the money was paid in cash after the job, at a designated spot," Officer Lusa explained.

"That brings us full circle to the beginning. Who is the mastermind behind the cold-blooded killings, and why?" Pedro concluded, exasperated.

"We kind of know why. It was to destroy Ana's existence and legacy. Beginning with Ricardo—her love—and her closest friends, who had been with her through thick and thin. It has to also be someone from Ana's past—someone who knew about their April Captains group, and that she possessed the precious diamonds."

"But we already know everyone from her past. Santiago is dead, Tomas and Miguel were almost killed, and no one knows exactly what happened to Agostinho," Filipa concluded.

"And yet, someone is still around, because a mastermind planned this revenge against Ana, almost tried to erase her bloodline, and now the diamonds have gone missing," Re said.

A tall figure stepped out of the cathedral and approached them. In the evening glow of the setting sun, he looked resplendent in his white robes and dignified demeanour. It was Adriano. He cast a quick glance over the group of people on the steps, and smiled.

"Congratulations to all. What an amazing moment in history for Portugal. We were delighted to be a part of this historic event." His baritone voice was filled with admiration.

"Thank you for all your help," Filipa nodded.

"Thank the Lord in whose presence and in whose home this event was blessed. It is all a part of the large scheme of things. Everything happens for a reason. This event too will help you find it."

His sharp eyes darted from Filipa to Re, and the latter sensed that the senior priest was not just referring to the event.

"Well, if you are done for the evening and you have no more work in the cathedral, we plan to close the doors soon," he concluded.

Adriano turned to leave, and Re rose quickly.

"Just a moment, Agostinho!" the detective called out.

Filipa gasped, and Stefan's eyes widened. Pedro inhaled a quick breath and Tiago looked shocked. Adriano turned, a hint of surprise on his face. Whiffs of strong energy laced with the faintest of apprehensions, reached out to meet Re, and he held on to it.

"What did you just call me?" A shadow fell across the old man's face.

"Agostinho," Re repeated calmly. "You are the sixth member of the Core Group of April Captains. The mysterious Agostinho whose role I could not fathom until I found the photograph in Ana, I mean, Joana's safe. All six of you, close friends and rebels, but something drove you apart. Something so strong and vicious that you vowed to take revenge all your life, did you not?"

"But… Agostinho is supposed to be dead. Joana had herself written so on the back of the photograph," Filipa intervened, appearing confused.

"And he was supposed to remain dead, until Joana and Ricardo both met him here. And discovered that Agostinho was very much alive and thriving in his new role and new life," Re said.

All heads turned in confusion towards Adriano who stood still, his hands folded, his face an illegible impassive mask.

"Agostinho?" Tiago repeated.

"You are alive? You killed Ricardo?" Pedro asked incredulously.

Adriano stared at them all, his gaze darting from one to the other, his face changing expression.

"Yes, I am Agostinho, but I wasn't the sixth in the group—I was the *first* in the group—I had *made* the group. I was the chief. I had brought them all together, except Ana. I was their leader, until one evening, in a raid by the *Estado Novo*, I got caught. And not one of them came forward to rescue me. They all scattered and went their own ways, leaving me a prisoner with the *Estado Novo*. Not a care in the world at what I went through. Tortured and wounded. They just assumed that I was dead." Adriano's voice was cold and unemotional.

A small silence followed his brief speech.

"But you weren't dead. You managed to escape and lived incognito, until Ana and Ricardo both recognized you here," Re insisted.

"No, I never met Ana and Ricardo. She was my wife's sister, and knew me well. I knew she would recognize me. So, I never appeared before her or Ricardo. But I got to know about the trail of the *lenços* and pieced two and two together. I blamed her completely for all that had happened. Ricardo weakened because of his love for her, or he would have never abandoned me. And that is when I vowed to take revenge—on all of them for leaving me to die at the hands of the enemy."

"You also knew about the diamonds, didn't you?"

"Ana was to keep them safe, but she never returned them. I was angry. My wife had died, I didn't know how to reach my son, and my life had turned upside down."

"What kind of a father are you? Did you not go looking for your son? A son who thought you were dead?" Tiago cut in.

"I looked for him and I found him, but I did not wish to cast my unlucky shadow on him," Adriano replied, staring at Tiago.

Re's eyes darted from Tiago to Adriano.

"You killed my grandfather? And Joana? And Santiago and... and..." Filipa spluttered, crimson anger on her face.

Adriano stared at her calmly. "When hate eats you up, and the thought of revenge obsesses your mind, there is little the best of people can do," he said.

"So, you hired a hitman..." Stefan prompted.

"And you wanted the diamonds," Officer Lusa added.

"And you planned to kill Filipa too, as the last heir of Ricardo and Joana's legacy. Your hate really did eat you up," Pedro commented.

"No! Stop this!" Tiago shouted.

Re's head shot towards the secretary. His face was contorted, and his eyes were bloodshot.

"Your unlucky shadow was too large, Dad, it engulfed your son completely," Tiago's voice was raised in accusation, his eyes boring into Adriano.

The others gasped and Re's lips twitched. Adriano's eyes moistened. Filipa's hand flew to her mouth in shock.

"Tiago..." Adriano hedged.

"If you had reached out to me and told me that you were alive, none of this would have happened. Before Mom died, she told me the whole story, including about the diamonds—I was furious and swore revenge. I tried to get in touch with Ana, but she had distanced herself from me. I wanted to avenge their betrayal and your death, and I planned it to the last second. I have lived with hate all my life, spied on Ana and Ricardo, and you are responsible for it, Agostinho! You are!" Tiago burst into loud sobs.

A stunned silence followed the explosion of emotion and confession. Everyone except Re and Adriano appeared shocked.

"I agree, son, I should have reached out to you, but I was worried that you wouldn't understand. You were very young when I was taken away, and you barely remembered me. I wanted to leave it that way. I also wanted to live incognito forever, afraid that the past would catch up with me. But I was wrong and selfish. I never thought about you, and what you must have gone through. I am sorry. But you don't need to take the blame for my vicious acts. I take full responsibility for them."

"No Dad, I won't let you atone for your mistakes, and for my clever scheming. I won't let you off the hook so easily, and allow you to be the bigger person here." Tiago shook his head, brushing his eyes agitatedly.

His gaze darted from Re to Stefan to Officer Lusa. "Don't believe a word he says. I killed Ana and Ricardo out of rage, and vowed to destroy anything that belonged to Ana, including her wine, her symbol of peace, and Filipa. And I don't regret any of it. I abhorred Ana since my childhood, and hated what she did to my family. I was her nephew, but she always treated me like an outsider. I am glad I did what I did."

The others stared at him, stunned. Filipa was crimson and trembling, her fists clenched. Fabio put a protective arm around her. Re and Stefan exchanged quick glances.

"Tiago—you have worked for the Monteiro family for years. We trusted you!" Filipa said.

"That was to stay as close to you as possible. I waited and spied so that I could find about the *lenços*, hoping that Ricardo would bring them out on his own. But when you set about planning the release of the symbol, I knew that I had waited far too long, and action needed to be taken."

"So, you killed Joana," Re said.

"Yes, with poison in her own glass of famous de Cruz wine. She refused to make me the heir of her estate, and said she had locked away everything in a safe, and I would never be able to get to it. That there was a code lock on it and the right person would know the passcode. I pieced two and two together. It had to be Ricardo. My mother who had never forgiven Ana and held her responsible for my Dad's death, had shared everything with me—the *lenços* Ana sent, how she moved from town to town, how she had remained unmarried in her love for Ricardo, how she used Rodrigo, how their core group had scattered and left her alone with a little son... I was filled with rage, and planned for years to get my revenge, and I knew that I had to act soon. And the right moment was just before the grand launch of the symbol. And I was right..." Tiago smirked.

Silence ensued this proud declaration. Re could feel Tiago's hurt and anger, his pent-up frustration of years, the need for revenge and the clogged wells of hatred inside him... it had turned him into a monster, cold-bloodedly killing Joana, Ricardo and Santiago, and Filipa, Miguel and Tomas too, if the hitman had succeeded. The repercussions of our acts are a sum of knots and bonds that we unknowingly create all our lives, entangling several others with consequences that endanger them.

"I am really sorry to hear all this," Adriano repeated in a low voice.

Tiago turned to him, a pleading look on his face. "Can I say a final goodbye?"

He climbed the steps quickly and embraced his father in a tight clasp. Adriano was taken aback for a moment, then spontaneously patted him on the back.

"I missed you, Dad. If only you had returned…"

Before Adriano could react, Tiago turned around and nodded at Lusa. "I am ready to go."

A policeman stepped forward with handcuffs, and clapped them on the secretary. A small smug smile played on his lips.

"Tiago, what about the diamonds," Re reminded softly. "Where are they?"

Tiago laughed, "All over the cliff, over the hillside and some in the ocean."

"No!" Filipa exclaimed, and Pedro appeared shocked.

Re stared at Tiago, a deep frown between the lines of his brows. The man looked almost wild, his eyes darting from one person to another, a smile that showed years of hatred and lack of love.

"But why?" Filipa asked, her tone angry.

"You wouldn't understand, Senhorita Monteiro. If I get nothing, you get nothing too," the secretary sneered.

Officer Lusa hastened forward and quickly dabbed and checked Tiago. The secretary raised his arms, a nasty smirk on his lips. Re realized that he was actually enjoying his own personal journey—of misplaced notions, of hatred and cruelty, and a triumph in the sense of his achievements. No remorse, no guilt. Any iota of sympathy that the detective may have felt for Tiago vanished in a whiff. Lusa glanced at Stefan and Re.

"Nothing in his pockets," he reported briefly.

"I never wanted them for myself, and I never was going to use them. I just didn't want Filipa to ever get them. Like I said, if I get nothing, you get nothing, *senhorita*."

Filipa stared at the man who had been her trusted secretary for a long time.

"You know what, Tiago, that's where you are wrong. I got everything in life. Love… lots of it from my Avô, and Joana too. The Peace Symbol now has a firm footing in history and the future. I promise you, I will take care of both their legacies. So, you could not kill either Ricardo or Joana, their love is immortal. You may have murdered their physical presence, but never their spirt!" Filipa's brown eyes flashed in the falling dusk. "And despite everything that you did… the horrendous crimes, killing my beloved Avô and Joana, stealing the diamonds and destroying them… everything… I still feel deeply sorry for you. Because you will wallow in the consequences of your acts for the rest of your life. I am positive that the country's judiciary will ensure you get the sentence that you deserve."

Fabio glanced at her, a look of immense pride and tenderness on his face. Re felt the same. Proud of this dynamic woman, who had gone through hell the last two days, but had emerged stronger and more sensitive.

As Officer Lusa led Tiago away, Filipa flopped onto the steps, silent tears streaming down her cheeks. Fabio instantly held her in his arms. Pedro wiped his moist eyes and strolled between the remaining chairs and carnations on the floor. Adriano nodded at Re and Stefan, and walked towards the cathedral. The other two followed him up the steps and into the cathedral.

Inside, the lights were dim and the saffron glow of the candles and the chandeliers seemed to descend on them like a translucent veil. Re inhaled the energy deeply and glanced at the tall statue of Jesus, dipping his head in gratitude and reverence.

Adriano closed the door and turning to Re, raised an eyebrow.

"Thank you, Adriano. What you did today was priceless," Re remarked.

"I agree," Stefan nodded.

"I felt terrible lying, but I agree that it was the only way to appeal to his malice-filled heart."

"We are lucky he didn't call out your bluff," Stefan grimaced.

"Even if he had, he would have still revealed his real identity. That he was Ana's nephew and Agostinho's son, and that would have led to more explanations. He would have eventually got caught in his own web," Re said.

"That's true."

"It was important for Tiago to feel that his father was taking the blame for his own cruel acts. His conflicting emotions—relief that his dad was alive and guilt that no matter what, his father was taking the blame for his deeds—fatherly love brought the mouse out of the hole."

Adriano sighed, "It was difficult, and if you hadn't managed to convince me, Re, I would probably never have taken this recourse. But it was lying for a good cause, so forgive me God!" Adriano glanced at the towering statue ahead of them.

"Tiago killed three people, attempted to kill three more, along with trying to destroy not just the Peace Symbol but also endangering hundreds of lives this evening. His hate had completely blinded him, and he was a dangerous maniac. He was a psychopath, set on a bloodbath, and he would have only created more dangerous evil if he had escaped today. He had to be caught, no matter how. So, your decision to pretend to be Agostinho to get Tiago to confess has saved the day, Adriano. And Portugal will be grateful to you." Re's voice was grave.

"Unfortunately, we lost the diamonds," Stefan remembered.

"That is unfortunate. Ana had held on to them all her life. She must have passed through phases of utter disillusionment and frustration, perhaps bouts of scarcity of funds, but she never once touched the diamonds. That says a lot about the strength of the woman, and her control and integrity," Re replied.

"It belonged to the core group, so Filipa would probably have had to share them with the other surviving members. Would have been of help in their old age," Stefan said.

"Er… if I may interrupt," Adriano cut in. "Is this what you want?"

There was a twinkle in the priest's eyes as he extracted a small pouch from his robe pocket. Re and Stefan stared at him.

"*Mein Gott*… The diamonds!" Stefan exclaimed.

"When Tiago embraced me, he slipped this into my pocket." Adriano shrugged.

"He wanted you to have the diamonds, because he thought you were his father," Re remarked, amazed. "All these years of hate, and he willingly gave himself up to save you, and trusted you enough to part with the diamonds."

Re took the pouch and pocketed it. *Love was a stunning emotion—it made even the worst people do life-altering things.*

"Thank you once again, Adriano. Please keep Filipa or Officer Lusa posted if Tiago gets in touch with you about anything."

Adriano nodded. Re watched him as he strode towards the altar, a tall dignified figure in white.

"I shall be leaving early morning too," Stefan said, as they exited the cathedral and stepped out in the cool evening twilight.

"I can't thank you enough for all your help, Stefan!" Re clasped his friend's hand firmly.

"Always there for you, Re, just the way you are for me… we are an unofficial team!" Stefan chuckled.

"That's true," Re returned the smile. "Say hi to Isabel from me."

"I will. Goodbye."

Re watched the tall man stride towards the group of policemen to bid his adieu. Officer Stefan Weiss—always the gentleman, always his friend.

The sun had dipped into the sea and the sky was awash with grey clouds and dull grey-peach pockets of sky. A strong wind was sweeping through the cathedral premises and it ruffled Re's ponytail. As Stefan headed towards his car, Re stood by the half-wall and stared up the basilica—a towering and imposing presence, bathed in the last few strands of lingering iridescence, a monument of incredible sacred energy. It had protected Filipa, ensured justice, and launched a new symbol of hope.

Re sensed an odd sense of peace engulfing him. The permanent tightness around his chest seemed to have eased, like the turbulent sea slowly settling into gentle waves. Ana's story had been a learning curve for him. Her story of grit, love and success was extraordinary, and it had awakened a heightened sense of respect for the lovely lady. Love was not just the fulfilment of coveted desires. It was the enduring of a spiritual journey, and the embracing of the person in the soul form. The only form that mattered. Ultimately, true love was more than just the physical. It was a journey of transcendence. And Ana had proved it…

Re turned from the monument and stared out at the dark sea. The shadow of the ocean spread from one end to the other, the waves resounding like a soothing rhythmic song in the evening. Re closed his eyes and felt the breeze and sent a personal thank you to Ana Ribeiro.

Chapter
20

The polished brown wall was adorned with the five frames. The five *lenços* neatly framed along with footnotes on the date, meaning and history. They looked exquisite in Ricardo's study, and Filipa smiled with satisfaction.

"What do you think, Re and Pedro?" she asked.

In a black dress, with her wavy hair confined to a band, she looked sober. Re was perched on the armchair, studying Filipa's effort.

"The perfect place for them, *senhorita*. Ricardo would have been happy," Pedro assured.

He was in his uniform again, and his eyes shone with deep, unspoken emotion. In his heart, he knew he was ready to protect the new heir of the Monteiro Estate.

"It's my way of showing respect and acceptance. If Avô is around somewhere, which I am positive he always will be, he will know that I love him and Joana."

"And you have given their love the societal status they deserve," Re pointed out. "I think that is a very special move on your part. You are changing Monteiro history, *ma chérie*."

Filipa smiled.

"It is brave of you, but you have done the right thing," Re added.

"Everything is ready for the funeral. Fabio is waiting for you in the outer hall. Miguel will be arriving shortly, and Tomaz is still in the hospital, but out of the ICU. There are others who are waiting to offer their condolences to you."

"I will see them all soon. Just give me a minute more, but you please go ahead," Filipa suggested.

Pedro nodded, and exited Ricardo's study.

Filipa glanced at Re, a thoughtful expression on her face.

"What do you plan to do with the diamonds?" the detective enquired.

Filipa shrugged. "They belong to the Core Group, so I will keep Ricardo and Ana's share and divide the rest between Tomaz, Miguel and Santiago's daughter."

"Good girl," Re nodded.

"Re… in case I don't get the chance to say this, I want you to know how grateful I am to you. The way you stood by me, on the trail of the *lenços*, through my doubts and inhibitions, ensuring my safety more than once… I have no words to express my gratitude, and I don't know how to thank you!"

"There are two ways to thank me," Re said, his tone serious.

"What is that?" Filipa appeared curious.

"First, if you ever feel you need me, do not hesitate to reach out. I am always here for you. And second, do not forget to invite me to the wedding."

Filipa blushed, "I will…"

The visual of wind chimes tinkling in the air rose in his mind. Wind chimes… the image that had risen in his mind when he first met her a few days ago. Re was glad that the wind chimes were back in his head.

Half an hour later, the Monteiro Cemetery witnessed a beautiful memorial service. Surrounded by trees, where the birds settled and chirped through the thick olive branches, the enclave housed four generations of Monteiros. Almost half of Penafiel seemed to have gathered in the early evening, and an air of solemn respect marked the occasion. Several people spoke about Ricardo's generosity, his sensitivity, and how he had changed their lives. Re watched from the sidelines, as one by one, people paid their respects to an iconic personality of Portugal. Re noticed that Pedro stood beside Filipa through it all, a comforting fatherly figure, and there wasn't the slightest doubt in his mind that he would take care of her till his last breath. Fabio stood on her other side, a protective arm around her waist and her gaze flickered to his, from time to time. They were made for each other. More than Filipa would ever understand, and more than she would ever allow herself to admit. The thought brought an involuntary smile to Re's lips.

After the last guest had spoken, Filipa moved forward. She held the *viola amarantina* tenderly in her hand.

"Thank you, everyone, for being here this evening for Ricardo de Monteiro, my beloved grandfather. He was a man of many wins, many hearts and many loves. Today I would like to end this memorial service by singing a song which his beloved Ana, and my real grandmother, had sung for him. I hope it will make Avô happy…"

She strummed the guitar and a hush fell on the crowd. Filipa's voice was strong and sweet, and the song seemed to fill every corner of the cemetery, the sun-dappled vineyards, the camellia bushes, the rippling waves of the pond, the dense woods and the estate. Once again, Re didn't understand the lyrics, but once again, he didn't need to. The yearning in the song and its heartrending rising melody seemed to moisten every eye and to touch every soul in the enclave. Re closed his eyes for a moment, allowing the song to seep through him, weaving a magical cocoon of peace around him.

When he opened his eyes, his attention was instantly caught by a nebulous movement behind Filipa. For a few seconds, he thought he hadn't seen right. He blinked, and it was still there—the foggy, obscure, yet radiant auras of two figures—a man and a woman like light beings, right behind Filipa. For seconds, the luminescent image wavered with the musical tenor of the guitar as Filipa's voice tapered to the end of the song, on a note of nostalgia.

Re stared, mesmerized. Savouring the incredible and enthralling beauty of the moment. The truth of all existence. Love. And the blessings of your loved ones. Filipa had it all. And Ricardo and Ana were finally together.

Acknowledgements

The discussions for this book began before the global pandemic, when the Portuguese Ambassador to India warmly welcomed the idea of writing a destination thriller in Portugal and agreed to collaborate on the novel. Then suddenly, COVID-19 gripped the world, and all plans went awry. I had almost given up on this destination thriller, but the way destiny played out its role, and the way the right people reached out to fulfill promises and collaborate, was proof that this novel was destined to be born.

I am eternally grateful to Ambassador Hon. Carlos Pereira Marques and Claudia Matias, Director, Visit Portugal, Turismo de Portugal, whose enthusiasm matched mine in every single way in writing the book and making it a success. Also, a huge thank you to Cátia Barbosa, Marketing Manager of Visit Porto and North of Portugal, who made my meticulous itinerary and ensured that I obtained enough inspiration and content to write the book.

A novel of this scale, landscaping one end of the country to the other, requires tremendous support and zeal. The journey across the North Portugal was soul-searching and enchanting, hence my heartfelt thanks to every person who ensured that my stay, travel, and research were everything I wanted them to be.

So, my warmest thanks to the following people who made writing this book a thrilling journey in itself:

- Mr. Luís Pedro Martins, President of Visit Porto and North of Portugal.

- Sofia Bacelar, official guide who showed me the nooks and corners of Porto, and Andreia Ferreira for the special visit to Livraria Lello Bookshop.

- Duarte Pinheiro and Ricardo Vieira for the detailed displays and exhibition at Rota do Românico and my visit to Centro de Interpretação do Românico.

- At Penafiel, Home by Julieta, Julieta offered me a real home away from home, and I was touched by her thoughtfulness, not to mention the lovely company of Jota the dog.

- Maria Manuel Ferreira of the beautiful Quinta da Aveleda—the inspiration behind the Estate de Monteiro in the novel.

- The Municipality and teams of Amarante (Amarante Historical Center) and Guimarães for the time they devoted to introducing me to the culture and history of their regions.

- Special thanks to Vice-President Ana Luísa Peleira of Freixo de Espada à Cinta for ensuring my comfort in the beautiful Manueline town, and the municipality for their support.

- The Municipality of Vila Verde for the memorable visits to 'Lenços de Namorados' exhibition and Espaço

Namorar Portugal, where I got to witness firsthand the making of the beautiful lenços which form the heart of the novel.

- The Municipality of Viana do Castelo and the memorable trip to Basílica Santa Luzia.

- Dr. Pedro Álvares Ribeiro for introducing me to the fascinating Casa de São Roque and Dr. António Tavares for facilitating a visit to Torre dos Clérigos.

- Pedro Cunha, who drove me from Porto to Freixo Espada à Cinta for 18 days.

Thank you to each one for the warm welcome and for showering me with love and even gifts! Although it was quite an impossible task, I have tried to incorporate as much of the North Portugal that I visited and do justice to the beauty, history, and culture of these places. I sincerely regret that I could not feature all of the lovely places due to the demands of the plot.

And finally, a huge thank you to Harpreet Singh Aurora, Deputy Director, Camões-Portuguese Cultural Centre, without whose help none of this would have been possible.

It was truly a great privilege to collaborate with Tourism of Portugal and the Embassy of Portugal, and it was certainly a distinctly unique experience.

I am grateful to Akash Shah for having faith in this book, and to the entire Jaico Publishing House team for standing by me and showing love for the book—from the edits and promotion details to the magnificent cover.

A massive thank you to my ever-supportive family who understand my crazy drives into the world of imagination, as I vanish for days on end for research and writing. Without their support, no book would have been possible.

Truly grateful to the spirit of Portugal for inviting me to experience and be a part of its energy, through the novel and long after it…

Thank you, dear readers. Book after book, you encourage me to embark on these imaginary thrilling journeys. I immensely value your role in my life as a writer.

And last but never least, I bow my head to Goddess Saraswati for making me a writer and giving me the power to share my stories. Thank you!

About the Author

Manjiri Prabhu, a distinguished figure in the literary and filmmaking realms, holds a doctorate in Communication Science. She is acclaimed internationally as an award-winning author, a prolific short-film-maker, and the esteemed curator and founder/director of two renowned international festivals: the Pune International Literary Festival and the International Festival of Spiritual India (for Humanity & Wisdom).

With a remarkable career spanning over five decades, Manjiri has directed over 200 children's TV programs, crafted more than 50 short fiction and travel films, and authored 20 captivating books. Notably, she stands as the first female mystery author from India to gain recognition beyond national borders, pioneering the realm of mystery fiction among women writers in India.

Often hailed as the 'Indian Agatha Christie', Manjiri is revered for her masterful storytelling and her ability to craft unique narratives with ingenious plots, memorable characters, and evocative language. Her recent book,

The Rampur Raza Mystery (A Sassy Library Thriller), was ceremoniously launched by the Hon. President of India, Smt. Droupadi Murmu.

Dr. Shashi Tharoor has lauded Manjiri for her ability to "Exoticize the Occident through intrepid, compelling storytelling," likening her talent to that of Dan Brown. She has been invited to esteemed international literature festivals worldwide, including The Oxford Literary Festival, Frankfurt Book Fair, and Jaipur Literature Festival.

Manjiri's literary prowess has garnered numerous accolades, including being selected as a Killer Book by the Independent Mystery Booksellers of America for her novel *The Cosmic Clues* and honoured as a 'Notable Book' in the Kiriyama Prize for *The Astral Alibi*.

Her remarkable contributions have been recognized globally, earning her prestigious awards such as the 'Global Woman Leader' by the 10th World Women Leadership Congress Awards 2023, 'Excellence in Service to Humanity' from the Rotary Club of Pune, Kalyani Nagar (2022), and 'Inspirational Women of Maharashtra—Excellence in the field of Writing'(2017). Additionally, she has been honoured with the 'Most Admired Leader of Maharashtra' by ERTC Global Herald (2017) and the Rex Karmaveer Gold Medal Award (2016) instituted by iCONGO and the UN.

Beyond her literary endeavours, Manjiri is a passionate animal welfare activist, advocating for the care and adoption of stray dogs for over 35 years.